DATE DUE

DANGEROUS WOMEN

DANGEROUS
WOMEN

HOPE ADAMS

BERKLEY

NEW YORK

BERKLEY

An imprint of Penguin Random House LLC
penguinrandomhouse.com

Copyright © 2021 by Adèle Geras
Penguin Random House supports copyright. Copyright fuels creativity, encourages diverse voices,
promotes free speech, and creates a vibrant culture. Thank you for buying an authorized edition of
this book and for complying with copyright laws by not reproducing, scanning, or distributing
any part of it in any form without permission. You are supporting writers and allowing
Penguin Random House to continue to publish books for every reader.

BERKLEY and the BERKLEY & B colophon are registered trademarks of
Penguin Random House LLC.

Library of Congress Cataloging-in-Publication Data

Names: Adams, Hope, 1944– author.
Title: Dangerous women / Hope Adams.
Description: New York : Berkley, [2021] | Includes bibliographical references.
Identifiers: LCCN 2020032010 (print) | LCCN 2020032011 (ebook) |
ISBN 9780593099575 (hardcover) | ISBN 9780593099599 (ebook)
Subjects: GSAFD: Mystery fiction. | Sea stories.
Classification: LCC PR6057.E66 D36 2021 (print) | LCC PR6057.E66 (ebook) |
DDC 823/.914—dc23
LC record available at https://lccn.loc.gov/2020032010
LC ebook record available at https://lccn.loc.gov/2020032011

Printed in the United States of America
1 3 5 7 9 10 8 6 4 2

Jacket images: sea by Paul Fleet / Shutterstock Images; sky by gyn9037 / Shutterstock Images;
ship by Infinity Images / Alamy Stock Photo; roses by Maria Taglienti-Molinari / Getty Images
Jacket design by Lisa Amoroso
Book design by Nancy Resnick

This book is dedicated to the real women
who made the Rajah Quilt.
The work of their hands abides.

This quilt worked by the Convicts of the Ship *Rajah* during their voyage to van Diemen's Land is presented as a testimony of the gratitude with which they remember their exertions for their welfare while in England and during their passage and also as a proof that they have not neglected the Ladies kind admonitions of being industrious.

> Cross-stitch inscription on the Rajah Quilt, collection of the National Gallery of Australia, Canberra

I believe I may venture to say, there never was a more abandon'd set of wretches collected in one place . . .

> Excerpt of letter from Ralph Clark, an officer on board the transportation ship *Friendship* in the First Fleet, to Australia

DANGEROUS
WOMEN

I wish I didn't know, she thought. I wish I'd never found out. I wish I could be the person I was this morning, before we sat down to our stitching.

The sea moving past the ship was almost black in the fading light. Where the Rajah *was now, in the middle of the Southern Ocean, there was only a short time between sunset and darkness. She leaned over to look more closely at the water. It rushed past the hull, curling up into small waves, which slid away to lose themselves in larger waves or long swells of water. For a long time she'd been afraid of it, walking along with her eyes fixed on the planks of the deck, seeing the ocean only when it couldn't be helped, catching sight of it from the corner of her eye. Now, after many weeks at sea, she'd grown used to it, was in awe of it and loved it, albeit warily.*

She'd fallen into the habit of going to the rail when the stitching work was finished. She liked to stand there for a few minutes, alone, trying to see what lay beyond the line of the horizon, breathing in the wide water and the high sky that seemed to go on and on till you grew dizzy staring up at it. Now the only thought in her head was what she'd learned. Every feeling in her heart was muddled, and the fear that had overcome her since she'd found out—discovered by noticing a gesture for the first time—wouldn't go away. There had been a shadow before, near the coil of rope, and she peered behind her now to see if anyone was there, looking at her. She saw nothing. But what was that noise? She held her breath, though the only sound was the familiar groaning of ropes in the rigging. Then she felt a change in the air around her, became aware of someone coming up beside her, and turned, ready to tell whoever it was to go and leave her alone.

Pain took away her words. She reached out, but as soon as it sliced into her clothes, as soon as it pierced her skin and reached her flesh, the blade was gone and whoever had held it had disappeared, too, and there was nothing left but an agony of white, shining pain, and her own hands suddenly scarlet and wet as she clutched them around herself.

The knife, the knife has killed me, she thought, and a sound filled the whole of her head and poured out of her mouth in a torrent of screaming.

1

NOW

5 July 1841
Ninety-one days at sea

A knife . . . is it true? Who's got a knife?

Hide. I must hide . . . Oh, my blessed saints, help us . . . Is there blood?
Where is it? Is it here? Someone's got a knife . . .

Who's got it now? Where is it?

They'll cut our throats . . .

The women's voices twisted into one another, rising and falling in the gathering darkness of the cabin. The lanterns had not yet been lit and the light from the small windows was fading. The women who weren't shrieking were wailing and clinging to each other, and even though no one said the words, and no one dared to ask, one question hung in the fetid air: *Is she dead?*

Those who'd been on deck when it happened sat together, trembling and white-faced, some still holding their baskets of scraps and sewing. The three women known as the Newgate Nannies shifted

3

and settled on the cabin's longest bench, gathering their garments around them, like three birds of prey folding their wings. Behind them, the sleeping berths rose up, and the dark corners of the convicts' quarters seemed gloomier than ever. The *Rajah* rolled a little in the swell, her timbers creaking with the motion of the waves.

They were now much nearer to Van Diemen's Land than to England. The sea had been as flat as a sheet of glass for the last two weeks but had grown choppy around dawn. By sunset birds had appeared, wheeling in free spirals around the masts, their black shapes standing out against the pale sky. July in these latitudes meant winter, and there was often a chill in the air.

"She was probably asking for it," said a harsh voice, sharp with spite.

"Shut your filthy mouth," said another woman, with a pockmarked face—the one who took care of the children aboard. "Say another word, you fat bitch, and I'll bash your teeth so far into your head you'll be farting them out through your arsehole."

Someone stood up as angry murmurs turned to shouts, and another hissed, "Quiet, the lot of you. They're coming."

They heard the men before they saw them. Their voices rang loud in the darkness, their feet stamping heavily on the steps of the companionway. The women stared at these strange creatures as though they were more than human: taller, stronger, calmer. The captain and the Reverend Mr. Davies, accompanied by three sailors, faced the huddled bodies of the women, like a human wall. The matron, Miss Kezia Hayter, was with them. She wore a blue knitted shawl around her shoulders, and her pale face was unsmiling. Her hair, usually so well arranged, was disheveled and her eyes were full of sadness.

As they waited for the captain to speak, some women cried; others clamped their lips together and tightened their jaws, eyes wary, daring others to blame them. There were those also who longed for matters to be as they were before, in the harmony they'd found briefly before the screams began. Before they'd seen Hattie Matthews lying there, her hair like red-gold autumn leaves scattered on the deck. Before everything was torn apart.

The Rajah moves swiftly before a sharp breeze. Her sails show pale against the night sky and black waves catch the light from lanterns on board ship, showing gold edges as they run alongside the hull.

2
THEN

Dress cotton: dark ground with pattern of small white lines resembling tacking stitches, creating the effect of snow falling in the dark

London, April 1841
KEZIA

The women in the small boat stared out to where the *Rajah* stood at anchor. Even stepping into the tiny vessel had filled them with dread of the unaccustomed rocking and the nearness of the water to where they were sitting. Now they were stiff with fear at the prospect of the coming voyage. But the *Rajah*! How did a vessel with such high wooden sides and such tall masts continue floating on the surface of the water? How would they climb up to the deck? The questions they did not dare to ask filled them with wonder and terror.

Kezia Hayter felt her own tremor of apprehension, though not at the unpredictable movement of the little boat they were in. She'd made this short journey many times in the past two weeks as they'd brought groups of women aboard the ship. No, she thought. It's not the boat. But this will be the last I see of London.

7

There was much she was eager to leave, that was true, but the expanse of the unknown now stretched in front of her. What if that which lay ahead was worse than all she was seeking to escape? What if she changed things, or even mended them? She looked up at the small white clouds dotted about the blue sky above them, pushed along by a breeze strong enough to blow their shawls into their faces.

The women around her huddled together for the short boat ride from Woolwich Dock to where the *Rajah* was moored. On the dock, life went on: hardly anyone had looked at the women, used as they were to prisoners being transported from this place. Men ran about the quay, carrying huge sacks of cargo. There were skinny children, barefoot by the riverside. Everyone seemed to be on their way somewhere, hurrying. Running and calling to one another. Kezia couldn't help but stare at the *Rajah*, floating stately and serene in the distance. What a splendid sight a ship was, she thought, and this one would be even lovelier once they'd set sail, once the sails were unfurled and blooming, like so many flowers, from every mast. The thought calmed her.

"Now, ladies, be of good cheer," said a tall, sandy-haired man, sitting near the prow of the boat. Kezia had met him during one of her earlier trips aboard. He had, in a cheerful tone and with a smile, introduced himself as "James Donovan, the surgeon superintendent on the *Rajah*, appointed by the same ladies who chose you."

Now he was smiling at the women.

"This is a very short journey. Less than half an hour, I assure you. We'll soon be aboard and you'll be settled into your quarters, leaving behind the dark and chill of London for the sunshine of the other side of the world. Think of the creatures you'll find there. Animals and birds that are both strange and beautiful. A multitude of interesting insects. Don't despair. Take Miss Hayter here as your

8

example." He indicated Kezia. "Does she seem to you in the least discomfited? Worried? No, she is as calm as a summer sea, and she'll be helping and guiding you on this voyage. You're very fortunate."

To Kezia, he whispered, "Miss Hayter, I'm sure you'll join me in my hope that this journey to the other side of the globe will be as agreeable as possible for all of us."

"Yes, sir," said Kezia. "I shall try to make it so." Now that she was boarding for the last time, she realized there could be no return from the decision she had made. She tried to imagine the weeks ahead. Would she miss her old life, her old home, even though there was much she was happy to leave? Would she be able to hide her homesickness? Or any sickness she might feel from the motion of such a large ship? She was determined to be strong for the women, who were often victims, she thought, in spite of their behavior.

Her companions were convicts from the prison at Millbank, women who'd fallen into petty crime through association with criminal men, or had been put to work as thieves by brutal husbands or fathers. Transportation was the punishment laid down by law, transportation to Van Diemen's Land on the other side of the world. Kezia was pleased to see one woman she knew by name. Joan Macdonald: a familiar face. Joan was older than most of the others, unsteadier as she sat opposite Kezia. Her hair was streaked with gray, her brow a little wrinkled, and she was picking at the fabric of her skirt. She wore spectacles and the lenses made her eyes seem larger than normal. Kezia watched as Joan stared at the planks of the small boat they were in, ignoring the landmarks they were passing.

"Joan Macdonald, I believe," said Kezia. "It's good to see you."

"Thank you, Miss," said Joan, smiling faintly.

The ship, as they approached her, towered over their own tiny craft. Masts rose up from the deck, like tall trees with thin black branches; the sails lay furled, like huge leaves ready to open. When I leave this boat, and climb the ladder to the deck, she thought, it will be the first step on a long journey. The beginning of something I cannot change.

As the women were helped aboard the *Rajah*, several sailors leaned over the rails, leering at them. They shouted obscenities, which Kezia tried to ignore, lowering her head and deliberately not catching the eye of any.

"Ooh, fancy women this trip, I see," one said, grabbing at the arm of a younger woman. "You're a pretty baggage. We'll be well cared for on this voyage, lads."

"Room in my hammock for that one," said another.

"Keep a civil tongue in your heads, men, or I'll report you to Captain Ferguson," said Mr. Donovan, standing behind them. He spoke in an icy voice, and the men swung round, their faces filled with a mixture of resentment and resignation.

Kezia marveled at how speedily the sailors dispersed and the lewd remarks ceased. On some of the boardings in the previous weeks, they'd gone on for far longer. Her voice was soft, and even if she could have spoken in Mr. Donovan's stern manner, she was sure the sailors would have paid no attention to her. Kezia knew better than to expect such men to obey a woman. Women were often overlooked or belittled, and thinking about it stirred a familiar indignation in her.

"Come, ladies," said Mr. Donovan. "Follow me, and I will take you to the lower deck. This is the companionway to your quarters." He smiled. "A companionway is the name for a staircase on board ship." He led the way to a short ladder and Kezia went down first, more comfortable and accustomed to it now than the first time she'd done it two weeks ago.

Kezia had always thought of Hell as a place of leaping fire and demons with pitchforks, but the first time she'd entered a prison, she'd changed her mind. The damp, squalid cells in Millbank Prison, where women cried out and uttered obscene words, where there was no bright color, only gray and brown and black, *that* had seemed a new kind of Hell, the opposite of everything that was pleasant and good. The sunshine, when it found a way through the high, grimy windows, had cast no more than a pale glimmer on floors filthy with dropped food, spilled slop buckets and rat droppings. What light there was illuminated tear-streaked cheeks, lank hair and eyes full of grief.

The quarters on the *Rajah* were a different kind of prison. The cabin was small enough for a person to walk from end to end in less than a minute. Only a dim light filtered in from the deck. She still could not imagine how so many women—almost two hundred—would survive in such a place for two months. At least on land, the prisoners knew that a city lay outside their walls. Even in the jail, there were corridors, more cells and a yard: an enormous building filled with bustle and noise. Once they were at sea, there would be only themselves. No visitors. Nothing but miles of water and more water, the fear of capsizing, the rocking motion of the *Rajah* and merciless storms. And all happening in a place where there were only flimsy bunks to sleep on and dirty floors below. Perhaps not quite as filthy as other prison cells she'd seen, but still. She'd worked with those who had been first to board to clean every inch.

The narrow bunks were fixed to the sides of the cabin, one above another, where the women would lie like objects arranged on shelves. Some would have to occupy mattresses near the bunks. Ten children would travel with their mothers: those who'd been given special dispensation by the court, because there was no one else to take care of them. Sending them to the other side of the world saved on places in the workhouse or the poorhouse for the parishes they were leaving.

When she'd first come aboard in late March, Kezia had stared at the wood beneath her feet and at the walls rising up around her. The floor was stained black with years of grime and filth, and slightly sticky with . . . What? Sea water? Blood? The smell was foul in her nostrils and she felt it settle around her shoulders, like a fog.

One woman had pinched her nostrils together. "Stinks here worse than a midden," she said. "And that's before we've started using the slop buckets."

"And before the ship starts rolling about on the water and most of us are spewing out our guts."

Another shrieked: "I can't! How're we meant to manage with so little light? Those aren't proper windows."

"I thought this would be better than a common jail. I thought the ship would be cleaner."

They'd sat on the wooden benches and gazed at their surroundings.

"Don't despair, ladies," said Mr. Donovan. "All will seem better when you're settled. You'll grow used to life on board, though it'll seem strange at first, no doubt."

"But there's not enough room, is there?"

Another woman had spoken up: "I thought clink was bad enough but we had proper walls, and floors in there weren't nearly as scratchy."

They'd all stood together, shifting from foot to foot, too nervous to leave the others. At last one brave soul and a few others went to examine the bunks.

"Stacked like apples in a pantry," said one. "Won't we roll off if it gets rough? I don't want to land on that filthy floor. Or get splinters in me bum."

The women who heard her laughed. Kezia had stepped forward, her heart pounding, trying to speak firmly. "We'll clean the floor and the walls before the ship sails. All of you can help make it better than it is now. We'll arrange the bedding as best we can. There will be lanterns to provide more light."

"And I will see to it," said Mr. Donovan to Kezia, but in a voice loud enough to be overheard, "that a few sailors are sent down here at once with buckets of salt water. That'll see to the worst of it."

"Thought her ladyship was one of them. Is she going to get down on her hands and knees to scrub?" said a voice, in the kind of whisper Kezia knew she was intended to hear. She had noted who the speaker was—a pretty young girl with a dimple, and a curl escaping from her cotton bonnet—and decided to pretend she hadn't heard. She'd taken a deep breath, fearful that the women wouldn't obey her, that they would be rude and crude and take no notice of her.

She had suddenly remembered her friend Mrs. Pryor's advice: "If you are firm and kind, they will respond to you. Everyone responds to kindness." Kezia took another deep breath and turned to the women: "I will do whatever I can to help you." She was privately pleased at the steadiness of her voice.

"Indeed, indeed," said Mr. Donovan. "We'll make this place more habitable. Please leave your bundles here and come up the companionway after me."

Now, two weeks on from that day, Kezia saw that the floor's dark planks were much brighter, if not exactly clean. The foul smell had almost gone, replaced by the fresher fragrance of scrubbed wood and seawater. She followed Mr. Donovan and the other women to the upper deck, where a sailor approached her. He was stocky and gray-haired, his skin weathered as brown as a piece of leather. When he smiled, his teeth showed very white in his face.

"If you please, Matron, Isaac Margrove at your service. We've settled the last of your luggage in your cabin."

"Thank you, Mr. Margrove."

"I go by Isaac, Matron."

"Isaac, then. I'm most grateful."

She followed him along the deck and stepped carefully over a low barrier to what looked like a small house set on the deck.

He opened a wooden door with a polished brass doorknob and indicated that Kezia should go in. "I'll leave you now," he said.

Kezia thanked him once more, and as he made his way back to the deck, she stepped into her quarters, which she'd visited only briefly on her first time aboard, relieved to see her possessions set neatly in a corner. She felt again a shiver of uncertainty. She thought of everything she was leaving behind and knew that, however much she trembled before the tasks that lay ahead, there was relief to be had in never having to think of certain things again.

She looked about. The place that was to be her home for the next weeks pleased her. She sat down on the narrow bunk and was aware of the peace and solitude. This little cabin, she thought, is like a nun's cell. The limited space was neat and clean, with an enamel jug standing next to a basin set into the top of the chest of drawers in which she would arrange her possessions. There was a small cupboard in which the jug could be stored when the weather was rough. The window was small and round, with leaded panes framed in wood, and Kezia could just see out of it if she stood on tiptoe.

She would have liked to stay longer but a boat was coming from London and she wanted to see the women arrive. She left her cabin and made her way to the deck. She could see someone being bundled along, ready to be placed in a boat to go back to shore. This person was stout, with matted hair, no longer young, dressed in dark, plain clothes. She was keening and wailing, clawing at her clothes. Two other women, thin and grim-faced, were holding her, gripping her arms as she writhed and shook. Prison warders, Kezia thought, accustomed to handling difficult inmates. The woman's garments were torn. She must be mad, Kezia told herself. What she was hearing could only come from someone who had lost her reason. The woman's hair was gray and hung in greasy skeins over her shoulders. Her eyes glittered with fear. The screaming went on but now Kezia could make out words, too. "Ma . . . Water . . . Take me back. Have you seen the rats?"

She had drawn level with Kezia, where she was standing on the deck, and she caught her eye. "Help me!" she cried. "Please, dearest Ma, take me home!" She'd wrenched one of her arms out of a warder's grasp and a filthy hand with bitten nails reached up and scrabbled at the air, clawing for Kezia's dress. The warders sprang to pull the woman back.

"Sorry, Miss, so sorry," one called to her, as she dragged the unfortunate creature away. "We'll take care of her, be sure of that."

The shrieks turned to sobbing, then to silence as the three women stumbled away, twisted together into a single dark, six-legged creature. Kezia stood very still, shaken by the encounter. I must recover myself before others notice, she thought. She drew her cape more closely around her shoulders and began to walk away.

As she moved further along the deck, she became aware of someone calling her name.

"Miss Hayter! Miss Kezia Hayter!"

Captain Ferguson was approaching her. Though she had visited the *Rajah* often, helping the women to clean and arrange the living quarters, she had only glimpsed the captain previously from a distance.

"Miss Hayter." He bowed, and spoke in a matter-of-fact tone: "Allow me to introduce myself. I'm Charles Ferguson, master of the *Rajah*. You are welcome."

She looked at him closely, the man who would have their safety in his hands. He was of medium height but still more than a head taller than she was. His shoulders were broad and he wore his jacket with some style. Every one of his brass buttons shone, and Kezia noticed that the linen at his neck and cuffs was very white. Captain Ferguson's blue eyes were wide, set in an open face, and his hair was on the fair side of brown. His voice, though quiet, was clear.

"Thank you, sir," she said.

He looked down at his feet and frowned. "We will meet later, madam," he said, bowed again, then turned and walked briskly away.

Kezia watched him as he vanished from sight, then moved to look over the rail and saw the dock in the distance. The line of roofs was like a silhouette cut from black paper, laid against the pale sky. Once again, she felt misgivings, and her heart was suddenly beating fast. The words of some distant members of her family came back to her.

"Van Diemen's Land? Are you quite certain, Kezia dear? It's so far away. And so hot there. Strange animals roam about, do they not?"

She smiled. The ladies who said such things were avoiding their real terrors about the trip. They weren't concerned at the distance from England, the heat, the flora and fauna. What upset them, gave them pause, was the company Kezia would be keeping. Common women. Felons.

Dearest Henrietta,
Here is my first letter to you from the ship. I'll write whenever I have the time and occasion. Then I can feel close to you, even though every day takes us further from one another. I'll send all my letters when we reach Hobart.

I'm quite comfortable in my cabin. I have my journal and some books to amuse me, and though I feel a little uncertain of what lies ahead, I'm not in the least frightened, so you can imagine me equal to anything that might face me on this voyage.

But, dear Henrietta, I will miss your presence so very much! Your smiling face, your happy voice telling me all that's happening in society. There's no one here to tease me and chide me when I'm being foolish, so I will have to manage as best I can to imagine your remarks. I hope that, as the voyage goes on, we'll settle down together and look to the future. But I'm not being transported, remember. I can return to England at any time if I find Van Diemen's Land not to my taste.

Kezia wondered how much that last thought would console her when she was in the middle of the ocean. She tried to dispel a sudden nervousness that had come over her while she was writing. She picked up her pen again to sign the letter, seeking a form of words that would convey to her sister how much she missed her and longed to see her.

From the moment she'd agreed to travel on the *Rajah*, Kezia had known she wanted to do something other than merely instruct the women under her care in the basic skills of needlework. For the first time in my life, she'd thought, I'll be able to make something . . . something out of the ordinary. What she had planned, what she was determined to make on this voyage, with the help of the convict women, she knew would improve their situation more than any simple lessons in hemming handkerchiefs.

Just then a shaft of sunlight touched the edge of the mast with gold—a good omen for the voyage? The clouds had blown away and Kezia felt a lifting of the heart.

3
THEN

Chintz piece: a densely printed pattern of blue, red, green and white flowers on a black background. Also leaves and small branches bearing blossom

April 1841
CLARA

Tonight. I've got to do it tonight. At dawn, they'll come for those women sentenced to transportation to take them to where the *Rajah* stands at anchor. I've heard the ship's name spoken, whispered in dark corners from one person to another, and I've said the word over and over to myself for two days, ever since I was pushed into this cell. I can't pray, not anymore, but I say over in my head, *Please, O God, please, take me to the* Rajah. *Take me far, far away from here.*

I don't believe in God any longer, but I'm trusting myself to get away from here. Ever since they threw me into this cell, I've kept to myself and spoken scarcely a word to any of the other women. It wasn't hard. No one was paying me any mind. They're too far gone, this lot, to care about me. The idea of a sea voyage terrifies them, and they dread a life away from what they know, far from those they love. They stand about in small groups, muttering, or picking

18

fights over nothing. Many just sit on their grubby mattresses, rip at their clothes and weep.

I'm not like them. I want to board the *Rajah* and I've planned what I must do. But I've got to act at once. It'll be daybreak soon. Some things, though, fell out right for me, coming here, and I'd already chosen my quarry.

Soon as the cell door closed behind me, I noticed her. The others left her alone, because she was feebleminded and small, too. I'm glad of her size. It'll be easier if I have to use force. I hope . . . I truly hope . . . it goes easy for both of us, but I'm ready. I'll do what I must if I have to.

Last night, in the dark, I tore my petticoat to strips. The fabric seems thin. Will these makeshift bandages be strong enough to bind her arms and legs? When I was a girl, and doing what I did in those days, I could bind limbs tighter than most. Now I'll have to truss her like a chicken, poor thing, and gag her, too. She mustn't cry out. I can't feel sorry for her. I tell myself, Be firm. Tying her up won't hurt her. She'll be drugged and know nothing.

I feel often for the bottle hidden in the pocket I'm wearing under my prison gown. I dreaded a search when they moved me here, and terror closed my throat as we approached Millbank, but the guard who brought me had his eye on the wardress, and she seemed taken with him. I thought how, over days and weeks, those two must have exchanged looks, then words and probably more than that. Most people forget their duty when lust comes over them. They forget prison rules, and I thanked my stars for that. They never found my secret hidden bottle. They never even looked for it.

I walk across the cell to where she's sitting. The other women are mostly asleep now, or if not, they're sobbing into their thin pillows and groaning. She's sitting up, staring at the space before her. I sit down beside her.

"What's your name, dear?" I say, in the voice I used to the women who came to me at their wit's end.

She tells me. I make her repeat it, pretending not to catch it the first time. I've got to be sure. Then she pulls something out of the neck of her grubby dress. It's a piece of knotted string, and hanging on it, something like a label. She holds it out to show me and there's her name, punched out in the thin metal. "We've all got labels round our necks," she says. "Scratchy devils they are, too." She loops the string over her head and tosses the label down beside her.

"And what crime are you being transported for?"

"Theft of linen goods from the market."

"You'll be on board the *Rajah* tomorrow. D'you know that? There's those who fear it, but there's nothing to fear."

She turns her eyes on me, as if seeing me for the first time. Her lank hair falls over her face. What I can see of her skin is like white cheese.

"I fear it," she says. I think those are her words, but they're hard to hear because someone is crying so loudly.

On the other side of the cell, an argument has broken out. Voices are raised. Women take sides and join in. No one's looking at us. We're far away from the din. I reach under my skirts for the bottle. I smile at her. "A little drink will help, won't it? Only don't say a word . . ." I hold out the bottle and, for the first time, it seems she's understanding my words. A light comes into her eyes.

"Aar . . . a drink." She reaches out. I know what it'll do to her. It's one of the drugs that's been useful to me for many years, and in many different circumstances. I uncork it and give it to her. Quicker than a blink, she throws her head back and swallows every last drop. The hair falls away from her face and I see she's marked by the pox. She sinks back at once onto the mattress. I call her name softly, bringing my lips close to her ear. She doesn't stir.

I don't wait. Her mouth's fallen open. I gag her, slotting the cloth between her teeth and tying it gently enough at the back of her head not to cause pain but firmly enough to shut off any cries. I'm trembling, trying to remember to breathe. I deal with her hands and her feet as quickly as I can, and pull her discarded label over my own head. When she's hobbled thus, I push her to the edge of the mattress and roll her off it into a kind of gutter that runs beside the wall. Then I push the mattress back and, as best I can, cover with her filthy blanket what can still be seen of a body. Anyone looking carefully might notice a lump by the wall but I'm hoping, more than I've ever hoped for anything, that all will be in a rush tomorrow. I cross the floor of the cell to my own mattress and lie there, putting on a show of sleep, willing the time to go by, longing for the light.

It's strange to think I'm losing my own name. *Clara Shaw* . . . I'm no longer Clara Shaw. From now on, I'll be known by the name that belongs in truth to the poor creature bundled up under a foul blanket. I mustn't think of her. I have to think of myself.

I can't sleep. Tormenting thoughts, dreadful images move behind my eyes whenever I try to close them. What if she wakes before we leave? What if the drug's lost some of its strength? Or if she has resistance to it? The cell is quiet at last, save for snoring and the sounds of nightmare. I lie staring at the lump near the wall, trying to see any movement. I'm cold. My mouth is dry. Where's the dawn? I stare at the small barred window, waiting for the sky to lighten.

By the time the men arrive to fetch us to the *Rajah*, I'm almost fainting with a mixture of fear and hope.

"Women prisoners for the *Rajah*," says one. "Line up here."

Will someone spot me as I take my place? I look at the floor. I shuffle in behind a gang of noisy women, who are fussing, crying out and calling attention to themselves.

"Silence there," says the wardress. "You'll miss your name on the register."

"No time for that," said the second man. "Count heads. That'll do."

The turnkey counts under his breath but I hear him. Eleven of us are leaving. I keep my head turned away slightly and don't lift my gaze from the floor. Now, I think. Let's leave this very second. She might stir. She might cry out . . . Even now I could be stopped.

All is done in a great hurry. No one examines us. No one asks us any questions. We're bundled out of the jail and into a cart, like livestock.

I fear the whole world can hear the thudding of my heart. On the way to the dock, I close my eyes and try to escape the sound but there it is: *Doom*, it says, with every beat. *Doom, doom.* I think of the woman I've left behind. If they find her before the *Rajah* sails, what'll she tell them? Will they believe she's who she says she is, or dismiss her babblings as a lie, uttered by a person who can't tell horses from Wednesdays? I tell myself, Don't think of her. Think of yourself. Every effort must be directed to your own survival.

We're crowded together on the benches of this cart. No one's looking at me, which I'm glad of, but, still, I let my hair fall over my face and pretend to be deeply distressed. No one speaks to me. The other women are weeping, comforting their friends or sighing. A few have covered their eyes. Some gaze at their feet. Others wring their hands. As we trundle through the streets, rattling past men and women going about their business, I half expect someone to point at me, to recognize me, to shout my real name. I slide down on the bench, staring at my feet, willing us to go faster. Oh, how I long to board the *Rajah*! There, surely, among so many, I can become a new person. I repeat the name of the woman I've tied up and hidden. It has to come to my lips naturally, instantly, whenever I'm asked to give it. At every turn of the cart's wheels, I expect someone to come running after us. Surely they'd have found her by now, and woken to the truth. But no one's following us.

"There's the *Rajah*, ladies," says the man driving the cart. "Your new home, my lovelies, and you're more than welcome to her. A fine sight, I'm sure you'll agree. You're only a short boat ride away from her now."

The *Rajah*. I gaze at her furled white sails, the high masts and the nets of rigging, and my heart leaps at her beauty. A brisk wind whips at the masts and the sky is clear blue, with white cloud streaked across it. I think we'll be kept belowdecks, for the most part. We're still prisoners. It'll be dark down there. The mattresses won't be much better than those at Millbank. I don't care. Soon the sails will unfurl and fill with the breath of the wind, and everything on the vessel will be bent on moving us away from what we've done. The *Rajah* will skim over the water, like a huge bird, carrying me with her.

When we reach our small boat, someone is already there, sitting near the bow. A lady. She's so different from the rest of us that she might be from quite another world. She's small and young, with a clear complexion and an upright carriage. Her hands are hidden by fingerless gloves made of lace, but I'd lay money they've not seen rough work. She wears a dark green dress and a maroon knitted shawl. I wonder who she might be, but only for a few moments. Then I turn all my efforts to getting into the boat without falling into the water and making a show of myself. Some of the other women are shrieking in terror, unused to the motion of the tiny vessel on the river. I'm silent. I'm happy. Soon. I'll soon be there, on the *Rajah*, sailing as far away from London as it's possible to be.

When we come aboard the *Rajah* for the first time, there's a man writing down every name. The one I give sounds strange in my mouth as I speak it aloud. I've put away my own name, removed it as if it were no more than a cheap paste brooch.

The gentleman taking our names is sitting at a table, placed on the deck. He's got a big ledger open in front of him, with an inkwell and a pen. He's noting our previous occupations and details of our crimes: burglary, forgery, stealing food. Receiving stolen goods. Picking pockets. I turn cold, then hot, and I can feel my cheeks flushing. Will I be able to speak my new name without hesitation? I say it. I say it perfectly. And my crime: theft. But what can I say for my previous occupation? My tongue feels swollen in my mouth.

"Thank you," says the man, once he's written it down. "What was your employment before you were sent to Millbank?"

The seconds that pass before I answer seem to go on forever. Many thoughts fly through my mind at once. What shall I say? I can't tell the truth. "I worked for a milliner," I answer. The lie comes to me from nowhere, and I see him write "milliner" next to my name. Why did I say that? It's true I used to enjoy trimming my bonnets, in the days when my life was different, but from that to being a milliner is a long step. Never mind, I tell myself. No one'll care what I tell him. Lying won't matter.

"Thank you," the man says again, and then, "Next, please."

I hurry to catch up with the woman who was in front of me in the queue and follow her. I want nothing more than to go below and hide in the dark. Someone catches my arm as I pass and pulls me to him, grabbing my breast and squeezing it hard. I pull away roughly, and a man's voice says, "No need to be so fancy with me, dearie. I'd wager a sovereign you were on the town, and it's a long way to Van Diemen's Land."

A sailor, boss-eyed and ugly. Men will try whatever they can. They're men. Their cocks must be stirring at the prospect of so many women, never mind that the unfortunate creatures are dirty and poor, pockmarked and shabby. Once I see he doesn't recognize me but is only trying his luck, I face him directly, leaning into his ugly face, so close that I can smell his disgusting breath. I speak softly, but my eyes never leave his face.

"One finger on me and I'll report you to the captain. After I've kicked your tiny balls to a porridge. And stabbed you in the neck with my scissors."

He scuttles away like the cockroach he is. He won't trouble me again. If I know anything, I know men. He'll be telling himself only that he picked the wrong woman and soon he'll try again with someone more obliging.

I'm trembling, even though no one saw our exchange. I wasn't disturbed at being accosted by a man. This had been happening to me since I was a young girl, but I feared discovery. I want more than anything not to be noticed, not to be singled out. To mingle so seamlessly with the rest that I am as good as invisible on this voyage. Our group is the last to board and for now I'm safe in the belly of the *Rajah*.

It won't be long before we sail. I can't let my guard down. I fear that someone will know me for who I really am. I long for the light and the air but will spend as much time as I can in the stifling darkness. The convict women who are my companions for the journey are thieves and swindlers, most of them, and I'll pretend to be one, too, though I've stolen no more in my life than a woman's name, and the crime of which I'm convicted is far worse: the worst of all crimes.

I try not to think of what I've done. What I'm judged to be, as well as what I might become, depends upon whether I'm discovered. If anyone were to find me out, I'll no longer be a petty criminal sailing toward a new life in Van Diemen's Land but a woman with blood on her hands, who'll be brought back to England to hang by the neck until dead on a prison gallows.

Word among the women is that we'll be casting off soon, maybe even tomorrow. If anyone finds me out before then . . . The breath leaves my body when I think about it. They must not. Being aboard this ship is a chance for me to leave behind the person I was. Many women have come to me, seeking me out since that first time, long ago, when I thought I was coming to the rescue of a single person.

Before I was thrown into Millbank, I used to take babies from mothers who couldn't care for them. Some would find homes with women who longed for a child. Others . . . well, I tried to lessen their pain and quiet them as gently as I could. There were some who'd call me dreadful names. But to those who sought my help, I was a comfort, an angel, a savior. No one, except those who have lived it, can understand the desperate state of some women after the birth of a child. I asked no questions. I did my best with each one.

Almost as soon as I've found my berth Miss Hayter comes up to me. I'm sitting on my mattress when she stands beside it and says my name. I stand up at once, almost as though this new name is the one I'd had since birth. Since childhood, I've learned everything quickly and a new identity won't trouble me. Reading and writing, I got the measure of them quick enough. My father saw to that and I thank him for it. "If you can read and write, you're set for life," he told me. "They can't hoodwink you with funny marks on paper, can they? Can't pull a fast one . . ." I wasn't very old before I realized that I could profit from speaking well, too, in my old lines of work. Among these women, my speech will be rougher than usual to fit in with the rest. I may find it hard to remember the name I was born with, I'll be so much in my new character.

"Please excuse me," she says. "May I ask if you've ever done any sewing?" She smiles. "I see you are set down as a milliner. Have you ever tried patchwork?"

"Yes," I answer.

Miss Hayter takes a notebook out of a small bag hanging from her wrist and writes my name, with a tiny pencil, in a column of others. Patchwork . . . I know how to cover holes with squares of fabric to make a garment last longer. Perhaps that'll be enough.

"You may join our group," she says, smiling. "I'd like to gather some of the women to take part in a joint endeavor. To make something that will be the work of all of us. I'm sure you'll be useful to the company."

She's shorter than me by almost a head. Her face, though not pretty, is pleasant enough and her eyes are clear and brown. Also, she has an air of calm about her. She walks the deck as though she were strolling through a park or taking the air at the seaside. Perhaps this was why the Ladies' Committee chose her to be matron on the *Rajah*. Would the women listen to her? Pay attention to her orders? A kind smile isn't going to serve her too well with some of the rougher, cruder women here.

I stand a little to one side and look at the women around me. I wonder at their lives, their crimes. I know that not a single one has killed a fellow human being. If they had, they wouldn't be here, but cold and dead with a rope round their neck.

Sleeping's hard. I see her, the one I'd left behind, tied up in Millbank. Something about her is me. Someone with my mind and her body is mounting wooden stairs that lead to the gallows. I wake up as the noose is pulled tight around my neck, gasping for air.

I hoped to escape from my terror in dreams but she haunts

me. Would she have the wit to protest her innocence, to tell them what had happened? There would be no tin ticket round her neck with her name on it . . . perhaps I'd condemned her to death. Surely she would speak. Perhaps because she was feebleminded, some jailer would recognize her.

The gallows dream is one nightmare, but there's another. I see babies sleeping. I hear them crying, and every one is gazing at me out of huge eyes. There are so many of us shut in down here, and I imagine all the women breathing at once and the pale ribbons of their breath weaving into the dark hollows of the space above our heads.

I look around me at the others lying in the dark. I feel cold suddenly. *What if one of them knew her?* Crossed her path long ago. Whenever I speak her name, I won't know who among my companions might once have met her. Even the silent and dim-witted may have friends. I'm not safe. I can't count myself free.

Marion begins to shriek. "I can't," she's saying. "I can't stay in the dark. Out! Take me out! I have to go out! On deck—someone, take me out. Please, I beg you all."

"Shut your mouth," someone says.

Another mutters, "Woken us all up, haven't you? Selfish bitch, that's what you are. Don't care about the rest of us trying to sleep in this dump."

"Middle of the bleeding night, innit?" says another. But two women lying next to her, whose faces I can't make out in the dim light, are helping her. I can hear what they're saying.

"Don't listen to those cows, Marion. And close your eyes. You'll feel better then. It'll be daylight soon and you'll be able to go out. I'll take you myself. As soon as it's light. They won't let us out at this hour. They'd bring us back as soon as we were out on the deck."

Joan has come over to see what's going on. "Hush, Marion dear," she says. "Hold my hand. Close your eyes and hold my hand. Think of the sky. Think of how big and blue it is. Go to sleep now."

In the end, Marion falls asleep, soothed and comforted, but I'm wide awake. I've never been afraid of small spaces, or of confinement, though it terrifies many, but with the smell of unwashed women's bodies, the snoring and the heavy breathing, the cries and murmurs coming out of so many mouths, it's hard to find rest.

I hope that my life will change. I wish for Clara Shaw to be put away forever. I wish for myself a new life with a new name, far away from England. If anyone were to discover who I really am, I would be forced to protect myself. In such a circumstance, I'd have no choice. I would be—I would have to be—prepared to act.

4

NOW

✦

5 July 1841
Ninety-one days at sea

The captain began to speak, the deep timbre of his voice filling the dank, cramped space of the convict quarters. "For those of you who weren't up on deck," he said, "I'm very sorry to have to tell you that your companion, Hattie Matthews, has been attacked and badly wounded." He paused and looked around, over the heads of the nearest women so that his gaze fell on them all.

"She going to die?" a woman called from the darkness of a far corner. She must have counted on staying hidden, must have thought she stood a good chance of going unnamed. She was wrong. Captain Ferguson was a thorough man.

"Come forward into the light if you wish to ask a question. And tell me your name."

"Maud Ashton," said the woman, pushing past her companions.

She stared at her feet, and it was clear that she wished the dark would swallow her again.

"Miss Matthews is gravely ill," the captain went on, "and we don't know whether she will live. Mr. Donovan, our surgeon, is with her now. I will ask my crew if anyone saw anything as the sun set and I will interrogate them most thoroughly, you may be sure. Meanwhile, every soul on this ship must hope very fervently that she *does* live, or someone on the *Rajah* is a murderer."

The Reverend Mr. Davies stepped forward. "You are, all of you, convicted felons, but this ship has been taking you to a new life, where you might have hoped to begin again. If one of you is found to be guilty of this assault, then your future in Van Diemen's Land will not be what you hoped for. No, indeed." He glared at the assembled company and his rich pulpit voice made those nearest to him flinch and cower away.

"We're not stabbers," someone at the back shouted. "You got no right to say that! We ain't done nothing."

Those around her began shouting, too. "You've got no right . . ."

"We'd never . . ."

"There's nothing to say we done anything . . ."

The three sailors strode into the crowd, pushing past the women to reach the ones who'd been shouting at the back.

"Shut your face," one cried. "Sit down and keep quiet if you know what's good for you."

"Listen to the captain," said another. "Where's your manners, you scabby baggage?"

The women retreated, and gradually the noise subsided. The sailors returned to stand behind the captain. Miss Hayter frowned and pressed her lips together, as though she were biting back a reprimand at the sailor's language and tone.

Whispering passed through the crowd as attention turned again to Maud Ashton. Mr. Davies stared sharply at her, as her mouth fell open and her eyes widened.

"I never! I couldn't. Not murder! Oh, God, not that. Not knives. I don't know nothing about no knives," she howled.

"Sit down, woman!" Mr. Davies thundered.

The captain stepped forward and spoke more calmly. "Please return to your place," he said, quietly but clearly. "No one is accusing you. But I will discover the truth, and when I do, there will be consequences. You will each be questioned and anyone who is found to be lying, or concealing something, will be confined until we dock at Hobart, then handed over to the authorities there. They will be prevented from seeking employment, and you all know that if Miss Matthews dies, a gallows awaits her murderer when we land."

Joan turned to Phyllis, another from the sewing circle, and muttered under her breath, "We're all in danger now. Who's to say that the guilty person won't knife someone else? We don't even know why they had a knife. Or where that knife is. How can we sleep quiet in our bunks with a mad person about?"

"If you've not done nothing," said Phyllis, "then you've not got nothing to worry about."

"We all have, if this is some addled lunatic," said Joan. "No telling what'll happen. And what if they don't believe us? We've been sentenced once and made to come on this ship, and now they want to pass more judgments on us. What if they put someone in a cell and they're innocent? How can they find who's really to blame?"

The captain spoke again. "Now, I must repeat that I hope most sincerely you will all be as helpful as you can. Mr. Donovan, Mr. Davies and I, with Miss Hayter, who knows you a great deal better than we do, will get to the bottom of this terrible event. I am setting up an inquiry. Anyone who has even the smallest piece of information should divulge it when questioned. I *will* find out the truth, and the person responsible will be punished appropriately. The *Rajah* will not come into port with secrets festering and perhaps a murderer on board. Do you understand?"

Murmurs came from every side. Then Agnes Dwyer put up her hand.

"Yes, Dwyer," said Captain Ferguson. "You have something to say?"

Even the captain knew the names of the Newgate Nannies. No one had asked why Dwyer and Selwood went mostly by their surnames, though Tabitha Brown was called Tabitha.

"Most of us were down here," she said. "Miss Hayter's lot had just finished their stitching. We were wanting to eat our scraps of supper. We're only up on deck for a short while in the morning and again in the afternoon. Once the sun's gone down, we're all here. You want to find out who was up on deck and save yourselves a deal of trouble. Those as weren't on deck couldn't have done it, could they? Stands to reason."

The women shuffled uncomfortably as she spoke. Some were whispering behind their hands to their neighbors; one spat at another who'd said something to her that no one else could hear.

"How much longer do we have to listen to this?" a woman in the front dared to say, and a sailor went up to her and marched her to the back of the quarters.

"Quiet, all of you!" Mr. Davies bellowed, and silence fell again.

"How many of you *were* on deck?" Captain Ferguson asked. "Put up your hands, please. Those who are honest enough to confess won't look kindly on anyone claiming to have been on the lower deck when this dreadful thing happened. I beg you, don't lie."

Kezia Hayter stepped forward and looked around her before she spoke. Sarah Goodbourne and Emily Paxton had their eyes cast down to the floor. Emily's pox scars showed livid in the lantern light. Phyllis was hand in hand with Ann, looking nervously around her. Phyllis was a motherly person and found it easy to fall into caring for anyone she was with. Now it was Ann who had her protection. Ann was willing to hide in Phyllis's shadow. Marion trembled and tears stood in her eyes. Miss Hayter was unsmiling, and her voice was quiet but clear. As she spoke, her hands were clutching the ends of her shawl so tightly that her knuckles showed white. "We, my needlewomen and I," she said, "were on deck toward sunset. All eighteen of them, and myself, of course. I told everyone we'd be stopping soon and most of them went below. A few of us remained." Her voice shook a little as she turned to the captain and the others. "I cannot believe," she went on, "that one of my company was responsible for something so"—her hand went to her throat—"so very dreadful."

Joan, Marion, Sarah, Ann, Phyllis and Emily put up their hands. Then Emily pointed at Tabitha Brown and almost spat, "You were there, too, Tabitha. You know you were." She stared at Tabitha, who made a face and muttered a curse before she said, "I was just going to tell the gentleman. Think you're so clever. I was just getting ready to speak, you silly bitch." Tabitha showed her crooked teeth in a grin, as if nothing had happened.

"Enough!" the captain said, raising his voice above the hubbub. "Is that everyone?"

When no one spoke, the captain said, "Very well then. Seven of you. Can you vouch for one another? Was there no one else you saw, maybe one of the sailors, on the deck at sunset? Stand up, please."

They did so, and everyone stared at them. "Wouldn't you know it?" someone called. "It's those stitching ones, innit? They've been thinking they're a cut above the rest of us since London and now look at 'em. Not so fine and fancy now. Talk about pride coming before a fall!"

Joan spoke: "The sailors on the watch were there, but no one else. At any rate, I don't remember anyone else. I wasn't really looking to see who was there and who wasn't. Miss Hayter'd just left us. She took the patchwork with her, wrapped up, same as always. It was very quiet . . ." She stared at her feet, as if looking down might help her bring something else to mind. "Hattie said something about how beautiful the evening was, then walked toward the rail. We turned back to our own pockets, to make sure we'd taken everything we'd brought up on deck. We were getting ready to go below . . . Then I think we went sternwards, about to come down here."

"Very well," said the captain. "We have seven women. You've come forward voluntarily, for which I commend you. The rest of you were down in these quarters so couldn't have stabbed Miss Matthews. Beginning tomorrow, our inquiry will speak to each one of you, to try to establish who"—he stared at each woman in turn—"might have done such a thing. It is very hard to believe that any of you would have acted in this way. We'll get to the bottom of this sorry affair."

He said no more, but the women gazed at him, their eyes fearful and their mouths hanging open.

"Spare yourselves the trouble, why don't you?" someone called. "Ask Hattie. She'll tell you who stuck a blade in her, sure enough, without you having to go through this ragbag of nonsense."

At that moment, there was a noise of rapid steps coming down the companionway.

Mr. Donovan, known to the entire ship as a pleasant, cheerful man, always ready with a greeting, was sweating in spite of the chill, his mouth set in a grim line. He spoke as though all his energy had been exhausted.

"Captain, if I might answer?" The captain nodded. "I've been at Hattie's side till now and I must return to her directly. Her little boy, Bertie, is with her. I've asked Hattie who her attacker was. Several times. But she cannot reply. She's without consciousness much of the time, but perhaps when she returns to herself . . . I would urge you all to be vigilant. Bertie will be brought down shortly. Good night."

The captain interrupted the uneasy silence that had fallen. "Mr. Davies, will you lead us in a prayer?"

The women bowed their heads as the clergyman began to speak: "Lighten our darkness, we beseech thee, O Lord; and by thy great mercy defend us from all perils and dangers of this night; for the love of thy only Son, our Savior, Jesus Christ. Amen."

The men and Miss Hayter went back up the companionway, leaving the women alone. All around, they began to talk, their voices rising and falling in the near darkness. *Will the captain sort it out? . . .*

Poor Hattie. Oh, she must be in agony. I know what knives can do . . .

Some rough ones on here . . .

Is there a knife hidden? Is it still here?

We won't be straight till it's sorted. Captain'll sort it.

In the end, the voices faded away and noise became silence, like the flame of a candle guttering into darkness. Someone knew something. There was a woman, perhaps more than one, who might have said something, who might have produced a fragment of truth that would show the way, but fear held her back, every enlightening word stuck in her throat, like a bit of gristle that would choke her if she spoke.

Around the ship, the black waters rolled and stretched to a black horizon. Down in the convict quarters, wakeful women muttered in their bunks, and the heads of the sleepers were filled with dreams of blood.

5
THEN

Cotton patch: wide bands of olive-green alternating with narrow bands of blue. The olive bands overprinted with bright sprays of red, white and blue flowers. The blue stripes marked with white vertical lines and red spots

April 1841
HATTIE

"You take your dirty thieving paws off my son's food, you little bitch." Hattie was shouting loudly enough for the women nearby to stop what they were doing and stare at her, but she didn't give a damn what they thought. If her son was being done out of his dinner, no matter how revolting, of hard ship's biscuits with greasy gravy thrown over them, by a skinny, pasty-faced thief, she wouldn't stand by. "You're a nasty bit of work, taking the grub out of a child's mouth."

Her left hand was now clamped round the thief's wrist and squeezing. She leaned in close to the girl's face and stared into a pair of eyes wide with terror. "You get along, and keep as far away from me and mine as you can in this hellhole. D'you understand? Or do I have to squeeze your skinny little wrist even harder? I can, you know. Could break it if I wanted to."

"No, please stop." The girl was shaking her head and pulling to try to free her wrist. "I'm going. I promise I won't do it again. Let me go. Please."

Hattie gave one last squeeze, because she could, and let go. "Piss off, then." The girl rubbed her wrist and scuttled off. Hattie smiled. Won't be seeing her again, she thought. Or if I do, she'll make herself scarce. She went to sit beside Bertie, making sure he was eating his food. Vile or not, it was all there was and he needed to get it down him in order to stay healthy on this voyage.

Everyone down here, she knew, had been divided into smaller groups, called "messes," of about a dozen women. One of the Committee Ladies had explained, even before they left Millbank, that they would live aboard ship in smaller groups, sharing food, and keeping their particular berths, and the area around them, as clean as was possible. The bunks were narrow and hard, as hard as prison beds, but what she'd learned of the others in her own mess didn't dismay her. She remembered some of their names and would soon know the rest.

There was Susan, who looked old, with her white hair and sad face, sitting mute beside the bundle of her possessions. And Phyllis, who would be a fusspot, Hattie knew, from the way she arranged her things around her, then looked about for something else to organize. Good luck to her, Hattie thought. Let her be the cook and the one responsible for whatever she felt the need to clean up and tidy. Izzy Croft was there, too, still sitting very close to her friend, Becky Finch, who was small and plump, with mud-brown eyes and hair to match. Hattie couldn't understand what either woman saw in the other but had long ago given up wondering what drew people together. She'd been locked up with those two and remembered them in corners with their heads together, giggling. Prison gossip said they were as good as married. Well, she thought, it's not my business what they do.

Hattie knew herself well and her companions, after hearing her lose her temper, would also know her a little better. She'd have to be more careful, she could see, because she was determined to be taken for a cheerful, charming young woman on this ship. She'd grown used to putting on a show, but some of her innermost thoughts would have alarmed many who saw only her pretty face and gentle smile. Before Kitty was taken away, the world had seemed to Hattie a kind place. She'd been kind, too. Since then, she'd learned that you had to do what you could to make life better for yourself. Some things she'd done had been far from kind, but she'd only done them to improve their situation, hers and Bertie's, and for no other reason. What would be good for Hattie and Bertie was now always at the front of her mind. Sometimes getting what she wanted came at a cost, and kind Hattie vanished behind a woman who wouldn't flinch at what she might need to do. And in defense of Bertie, there was nothing she wouldn't do.

Many of the women Hattie had spoken to on the *Rajah* were sad. They longed for the family they'd left behind, for their lives in England: all that remained to them was the shame of a sentence that had banished them to the other side of the world. Hattie didn't share their dismay. On the contrary, if she couldn't be free, she was eager to see a new place. Van Diemen's Land, she'd been told, was hot and sunny for much of the time and, best of all, a territory where someone determined to make a new life could do wondrous things. She imagined Bertie running along a beach, playing in the waves and coming home to her in a house that would be plain but clean.

Hattie was good at daydreaming and she was aware that this gift made her unusual among her acquaintances. Most people, she knew, couldn't see further than the very next day. They think they love their children, she told herself, but it's not like my love for

Bertie. My love's as different from theirs as diamonds are from paste. From the moment of his birth, every one of Hattie's desires had been bound up with Bertie: his future, his education, his welfare. She vowed to herself that she'd use every ounce of her energy to make Bertie's life good and comfortable. The idea of her son suffering in any way plunged her into the deepest anguish, and often during his early childhood she would stand beside his cradle as he slept, gazing at his little face, offering up silent prayers that God might take special care of him.

"Isn't he a bonny boy?" came a voice.

The woman who'd spoken was skinny, with some fair hair sticking out from under the scarf bound round her head. Thin lips, watery gray eyes, her skin somewhat marked by pox. She wasn't much to look at, but her voice was low and sweet, and Bertie was peering up at her. She bent down to him and said, smiling, "He'll be well looked after, be sure of that," she said. "My name's Emily—Emily Paxton." She leaned down to talk to Bertie. "I've been asked to teach the children, so I'll be giving you your lessons. What's your name?"

"Bertie," said the child, turning to see if his mother was noticing this attention from a stranger. "Albert, really, but I'm called Bertie."

"Well, Bertie, remember that you can always come to me for a game and a song. And there are other children here on the *Rajah*, you know. We'll learn together, and enjoy ourselves while doing it."

"Do you have children of your own?" Hattie asked, then regretted it. Perhaps Emily had left them in England and would not like to be reminded of them. She had been lucky, being allowed to bring Bertie with her to the *Rajah*. Not everyone could. If you had relations in court, they'd hand the child to the family, but Hattie had had no one with her in front of the judge, and she'd been as sweet and obliging as she could be so he'd agreed that her child could accompany her to the other side of the world. If he hadn't, Hattie knew she'd have killed both of them, rather than endure separation. Bertie would never have been able to live without his mother. It would be good to have help with him, good to know that he would be taught his letters, and this woman seemed pleasant enough. Hattie could see her hesitating now, as if unwilling to answer Hattie's question.

"I had a son, but he died."

"Oh, Lord, there's a thing. I shouldn't have asked. How hard, how sad for you." Hattie took Emily's hand and squeezed it.

Emily pointed to the pox scars that marred her cheeks. "This got him. Two years ago. Wish it had taken me instead." She looked hard at Hattie. "Can you imagine what that's like? Your child gone?"

Hattie's eyes widened. She put out a hand and grasped Emily's shoulder. "Oh, no, I can't. I really cannot . . ."

That was a lie. Hattie could imagine such a situation far too well. There had been nights in his life, while her son was sick or small or teething and crying, when Hattie had conjured up picture after picture in her mind of Bertie's corpse laid out in a coffin. She'd imagined his funeral a thousand times and had many times considered carefully what she would feel in such circumstances. There, her imagination failed her entirely. A black abyss opened in her mind and she saw, and felt, nothing but icy darkness. Now, because Emily had reminded her of it, it was as though something was grasping her heart, deep within her body, and she felt faint and sick. She had to close her eyes till the sensation of horror left her. This was an effort, but at last she smiled at Emily. "I'm so very sorry, Emily."

"I try not to think of him too much. I've not said his name to anyone. Not on this ship. When the smallpox came, we both fell ill and God took him. Don't tell the others. Please . . ."

"I promise I won't say a word to anyone."

"I'll whisper his name if you promise not to tell."

"I won't say it to anyone," Hattie said. "I promise."

Emily leaned forward and whispered a name into Hattie's ear.

"That's lovely," Hattie whispered back.

She wanted to say something more, offer a bit of comfort, but couldn't find words. What could you say when a small child lay dead? If Bertie was struck down by a horrible illness . . . Hattie couldn't think of such a thing without tears coming to her eyes. She reached out to embrace Emily, and Emily let herself be held, but pulled away after a few moments. She said, "Thank you, Hattie. No one's been this kind to me, not for years. No one asks. Thank you." She smiled.

Hattie was about to say something when the matron came up to them.

"Good day to you," she said.

"Say good day to the kind lady, Bertie," said Hattie, pushing her son forward a little with one hand and using the other to straighten his threadbare coat.

"Good day, Miss," said the child, smiling. "My name's Albert, but Ma calls me Bertie."

"Not *Miss*, Bertie," said his mother quickly. "Miss Hayter, or Matron. This is the lady who's in charge of all of us."

"The captain's in charge," said Bertie.

Hattie felt mortified. "That's rude. The captain's in charge of sailing the ship, but Matron's in charge of *us*. I told you so, don't you remember?"

"The captain *is* in charge, Bertie. You're quite right," said Miss Hayter. "My work is to help your mama and the other women in every way. And I'm sure you'll help me, won't you? How old are you?"

"I'm six, Miss," said Bertie proudly, standing straight and saluting. "I'm big enough to help you."

Miss Hayter laughed and Hattie felt both proud and embarrassed. She said, "He's used to speaking out, Miss. I've tried to make him mind me, but he can be cheeky. He means no harm."

"Of course he doesn't," said Miss Hayter. "He's a delightful child and a great credit to you." She paused. "I see from the register that you worked as a children's nurse and also in a laundry. Did you sew in either of those employments?"

"Yes, Miss Hayter."

Hattie could have added, though she didn't, that the crime of which she'd been convicted had also often involved using her needle.

"Then you'll be of great use to me in my work on this voyage. I'll speak very soon to you and the others I've chosen about my plans. Tell me your name and I will write it down."

"Harriet Matthews, Miss Hayter. I'm called Hattie, though."

"Thank you, Hattie."

Hattie looked on as the matron wrote her name in a little notebook, which she took out of a bag that hung from her wrist.

Emily whispered to Hattie, "She's only twenty-three, they say."

"That's young to be in charge of all of us," Phyllis added. She'd come up to see what was going on.

"I was looking after four bairns by the time I was seventeen," another woman said.

"Your bairns wasn't rough as a metal file, though, was they? Not like us." Women standing nearby laughed, and Hattie turned to Miss Hayter again.

She was a small woman, and she did look very young. Some light brown curls had escaped from the bun at the back of her head and lay now on her neck. Her smile was kind, and when she looked at you, she seemed to be considering you carefully. She wore a dark red gown, with a small shawl in knitted lace around her shoulders. Her voice was light and clear, and her words, though spoken quietly, carried authority. She spoke like the genteel ladies Hattie had overheard in fancy shops. Some of the rougher women would be rude or unkind to her, but Hattie felt sure that Matron would answer everyone with good sense and civility.

As Miss Hayter left them, Hattie made up her mind to be on Matron's side, whatever she was proposing. All her life, she'd prided herself on her ability to see where her best advantage lay and she understood that, on this voyage, it would lie with being as close to Miss Hayter as possible. Bertie settled on a bench and Hattie sat down beside him and sighed.

Now Matron was about to address them all, and Hattie looked at her, and at the others listening eagerly to what she had to say.

"I am Miss Kezia Hayter," she began, and then she waited till the mumbling and fidgeting stopped.

"You have, every one of you, been given a chance. It will seem to you now as if you're leaving behind your home, and your loved ones, and all that you've known." Hattie could see that Miss Hayter was struggling to sound confident. She had fixed her eyes on something at the back of the crowd and her voice faltered a little. "You'll be traveling very far from England, some of you for many years. What lies ahead of you on this voyage may make you fearful. You may regard this sentence of transportation as a grievous penance, but consider this, too. The *Rajah* is also a vessel to take you away from your past lives, the tribulations and trials you may have suffered, whether from your own fault or because of your circumstances. It's my task to help you, and I've undertaken this task in the full knowledge that it is God's work I'm doing."

Hattie hadn't seen any evidence of Him helping much, but Miss Hayter was almost smiling, so she must believe it.

"I will do my best to teach you skills that may be useful to you in Van Diemen's Land. The days will pass more quickly if you are occupied, and I intend to teach you what little I have learned of sewing and the making of patchwork. We'll sing a favorite hymn of mine at the end of each day's work. 'Teach Me, My God and King.' Some of you will perhaps know it already, but you'll learn it from me if you don't."

Some women were shuffling their feet, and Miss Hayter spoke more quickly, noticing their impatience.

"The children will be instructed in their letters," she said, pushing both her cuffs further up her arms, "and schooled every day. If any others wish to improve their education while on this ship, there are some here who've assisted teachers in the classroom, and they will be able to help those women learn to read and write. God always rejoices in welcoming repentant sinners and that is what I fervently hope you'll be." Miss Hayter was smiling now, perhaps happy that the end of her speech was nearly upon her. "The time at sea is a chance for you to improve your lives and you should see it in that light. Work will make the days pass more speedily, and even though there's much sadness in leaving behind what you've known and loved . . ."

That was no more than the truth, thought Hattie. Several women looked grim, as though they'd lost a pound and found a penny. Some were sniffing into their sleeves. Many eyes were red.

". . . there's also a chance to change everything about your life that you would wish to change. Good night to you all."

While she was speaking, Hattie noticed, the women listened, but as soon as she left, the quarrels began.

"Bossy little madam," said one woman. "What right's she got to tell us what we're going to do and not do? What if I don't want to learn nothing? Don't need to learn a bleeding hymn, that's for certain sure."

"She never said she'd make us," someone else said.

Hattie didn't know these two.

"What's it to you if she wants to help us? You look as if you could do with help, stupid cow. Anything anyone did for you'd be a huge improvement, if you ask me."

The first woman launched herself into the air and fell on the other. She snatched the scarf off the second woman's head and pulled her hair. Her adversary gave as good as she got: she kicked out at the first, then grabbed her skirt and tugged so hard that it ripped apart at the waistband. The women looking on broke up into two groups, egging on their favorite. From their shouts, Hattie gathered that the first was called Tilly and the second Grace.

"Go on, Tilly, you show her. Scratch her eyes out! Go for her! Hair! Yes! Pull it, Tilly, go on."

"Gracie! Let 'er 'ave it. Nails! Use your nails, Gracie."

The shouting continued. Hattie made sure to be nowhere near the crowds that had gathered when a sailor came down the companionway. Sent to restore order, he went up to the women as they were wrestling on the deck. Picking up the bucket of seawater that stood near one of the bunks nearby, he threw the contents over Tilly and Grace as though they were two fighting dogs.

"Had enough now? Going to settle down? Or fancy a bit more, do you?"

The man who spoke was enormous, with a bushy black beard growing to halfway down his chest. He lifted a very damp Tilly off the floor and shook her. "You'll have me to deal with if you make any more trouble here. Get it? Jack's my name. Go and get dry, you stupid creature."

Meanwhile, Grace was struggling to get up, hoping to avoid being hauled to her feet by Jack. She almost did it, but he took hold of her arms anyway and crossed them in front of her body, pulling her toward him till her face was almost crushed against his beard.

"This here's a good ship," he said. "A quiet ship. Peaceful. Understand? Any misbegotten whore'll have me to deal with if they cause trouble, and you wouldn't want to find out what I'd do to you, either. Promise you that."

Then he was gone, up the companionway steps as quickly as he'd come down them, and Hattie marveled at the effect of his visit. Tilly and Grace melted away to hide among gaggles of their own supporters, and everyone fell to discussing what had happened, adding their own embellishments to the story.

A short time later, someone carrying a lantern came into the convict quarters, and as the women recognized the captain, a silence fell and every eye turned to the man who stood among them. He looked a little strict to Hattie, and stood quite straight with his hands clasped behind his back.

"Good evening, ladies," he said. "My name is Charles Ferguson and I am the person who will guide this ship to its harbor, God willing. I've not been its master very long, but I am certain of one thing: voyages on which people work amicably together are much pleasanter for everyone than those on which they are constantly squabbling and shouting. Jack tells me that some of you have been fighting, and I will say this. Matters will go hard for anyone who makes trouble for others. You're not used to being at sea and there'll be things that will seem strange to you, perhaps frightening, too, but all's bearable if you're among friends. I'd advise you to be pleasant to your companions, but if you can't manage pleasant, then polite will do." He glanced about him, rather uncomfortably. Was he expecting them to laugh at his little joke? Hattie wondered. When no one said anything, he turned to leave.

"Good night to you," he said. "Miss Hayter, your matron, also stands ready to help you."

"Cheery soul, in't he?" said Dwyer.

Selwood added, "Proper ray of sunshine."

"Doesn't matter, does it?" Hattie said. "All he's got to do is steer the ship in the right direction."

That first night on board, Hattie lay in her bunk, just below Bertie. She listened to the other women's muffled sobs, unable to fall asleep, unaccustomed to such darkness and the strange smells. But although she was uncomfortable, she also felt as though here was an opportunity to change her life a little. There'd been several times during her life when she'd charmed her way to more attention and more payment than another woman might have achieved. Wasn't there a saying about catching more flies with honey than with vinegar? Hattie was good at spreading honey with her words and looks whenever there was a chance of reward. And here was a chance to climb up, take advantage of what a new country might have to offer someone who was quick and bright, if not well educated. Her mother had taught her to read and write a little and that had always been enough. She'd been praised and petted by every man who had ever crossed her path. Children adored her, and had been important in providing her with most of the money she'd ever made.

Stealing clothes from children was not, Hattie persuaded herself, the worst of crimes. She'd worked the streets around the shops and markets and they came to her willingly, lured away easily from their nurses, who were often busy with their purchases. She held out to them the prospect of petting a kitten if they followed her. Bertie had played his part. She'd explained it to him carefully.

"If you smile nicely at the little ones," she'd told him, "they'll come with us to our room, and we'll just take their lovely clothes from them, then send them home to their mamas and papas."

"But why'd we need their clothes? Won't they be cold?" Bertie frowned.

"Not for long," Hattie said. "Their parents will search for them and find them quickly. Then they'll get new clothes, and won't that be a fine thing? Maybe they'll meet a constable who'll take them home directly. They'll be quite safe . . . and you may have a twisted sugar cane if you help me."

"But we haven't got a kitten," Bertie reminded her.

"Never mind that, Bertie. You go to sleep now."

When the children left her small dwelling, a room in a house full of tiny rooms, they always ran and ran, startled by the sudden change that had come over Hattie. She'd make her face stiff, stop smiling and force the children to stand in front of her and not move while she removed their outer garments. Her voice changed, too. Not a single boy or girl had dared to defy her. Hattie made Bertie stand outside the door when she was changed in this manner. She hadn't wanted him to see his mama being cruel. She herself knew she would very likely never have to carry out any of the threats she made. *I'll cut all your hair off and leave you bald, you whining wretch. I'll beat you. I'll pinch you till you cry if you don't stand still—and look what sharp nails I have!*

It was only to put food in Bertie's mouth that she'd treated other children so. She'd never have sunk to crime if the two of them weren't in danger of starving to death. That was all in the past, Hattie thought now. In Van Diemen's Land she would be kind all the time.

6
NOW

✤

6 July 1841
Ninety-two days at sea
KEZIA

Bertie was sitting on a bench, his knees drawn up to his chest, his head resting on them. Kezia knelt beside him, unsure how to comfort him. She was saddened more than she knew how to express by what had happened to Hattie, but also filled with a deep unease. The boy had been crying, and his shoulders were still shaking. Emily was sitting next to him, stroking his hair.

"Emily," Kezia said, "I'm so grateful to you for looking after Bertie. You're very good with him. So kind . . ."

"Poor little mite. We're all doing our best to take care of him."

"I must talk to him, Emily. May I take him from you for a while?"

"Yes, Miss," Emily replied. "Go with Miss Hayter, Bertie."

He stood up, and it seemed to Kezia that all his boyish energy had drained away as surely as his mother's blood. "Bertie, we're going to visit your mother now, but you must be brave. You won't be able to speak to her because she's sleeping. She has to sleep if she is to recover. Do you understand?"

Bertie nodded, but said nothing. The silence as they made their way toward the hospital was like a heavy weight they were carrying together and Kezia spoke only to break it. She talked of Mr. Donovan's cleverness, of how well his mother was being tended. She pointed out a seabird that had briefly perched on the rigging, and asked Bertie if he was enjoying his lessons. He nodded in answer to everything but still didn't speak. After a calm night, the weather was turning, and the *Rajah* was creaking as she moved, rising and falling on the heavy swell, her sails filled with the strengthening wind.

Kezia found herself dreading what she would see when she reached Hattie's side. Would she be speaking? Please let her be better. Please let there be calm weather again. She squeezed Bertie's hand as much to give herself courage as to comfort him.

After he'd let Kezia and Bertie in, Mr. Donovan went to sit on a chair beside a table on which his instruments and potions were laid out. Hattie lay in a narrow berth. Her eyes were closed and her red hair had been neatly plaited. Joan, who had been chosen to help Mr. Donovan if anyone fell sick, must have done that, Kezia thought.

Bertie hung back, clinging to Kezia, frightened at the sight of his mama lying so still and so pale. Then he ran to her and flung himself on her body, crying out, "Ma! Ma! Wake up, Ma! It's me, Bertie! Please, Ma!"

He buried his head in the sheet that covered Hattie, with his arms up around her neck and his face on her breast. She didn't move in response.

Mr. Donovan came to him and began to whisper in his ear and slowly, very slowly, Bertie let go of his mother and sat up.

"Bertie, she can't speak to you," Mr. Donovan said. "Her sleep is not like your sleep. She can't wake up. She is deep, deep in her own sleep, which we hope will make her better. You sit next to her, Bertie, and hold her hand."

"Can she feel me?" Bertie asked plaintively. "Does she know I'm here?"

"We don't know, Bertie," Mr. Donovan said. "But if she does, it will comfort her."

Bertie sat on the bunk, trembling. Kezia put her arm around him, feeling his bones through the fabric of his shirt. He should have been eating good food: milk, eggs, cakes and meat puddings, not dry ship's biscuits and gravy. Kezia remembered what she'd been like when she was six. Papa had died when she was Bertie's age. He lay in his bed, and Kezia couldn't understand why he wasn't speaking. Why was he so silent and pale? Her papa, who'd always responded to her every question, who'd smiled at her with love each time he spoke to her, who was never too busy to read with her, or look at her drawings . . .

"He's dead, Kezia," Henrietta had told her. "He isn't going to speak again. Not ever."

Kezia had begun to scream then and would not stop. Mama had taken her out of the room and put her alone in the bedroom she shared with Henrietta and locked the door. She had felt his absence, like a wound, for a long time after that day. She felt the loss of him still.

And now Bertie would perhaps know that grief. As she took his hand, Kezia felt more sorrowful than she had for many years. It was almost time for the first of the meetings with the women who'd been on deck yesterday. "We should go back now," she said. "To your mama's friends. They'll take care of you."

Bertie went with her, dragging his feet, glancing back at Hattie. "Can we come again?"

"Someone will bring you here every day," said Kezia. "I promise. You'll visit your mama every single day."

Kezia came into the captain's cabin a little before the first sitting of the inquiry. There was something she needed to say to him before the others arrived. The captain had decided that the seven women identified as the ones nearest to the scene of the attack would be questioned here, in his private room. The place was as different from their own living quarters, as near to a physical manifestation of the law's majesty, as it was possible to arrange on board ship. The table had been polished. As ever, the brass was gleaming. Kezia knew that one young sailor, no more than a boy, really, was occupied every day with the polishing of the *Rajah*'s brass fittings. On land, a woman servant did this kind of work. Perhaps when this young man married, he would prove useful to his wife, but Kezia doubted it. The captain's logbook was open and the ink and pen laid ready for the Reverend Mr. Davies.

"What I would dearly like to know," Charles said, "is what anyone would have against Hattie Matthews."

"There's something I must tell you at once," Kezia said quickly. "I should have told you earlier and I'm sorry I didn't."

At that moment, there was a knock at the cabin door. Mr. Donovan and Mr. Davies came into the room.

"Miss Hayter," said Mr. Donovan, "you look pale. I hope seeing Hattie has not distressed you too much."

"It was indeed a distressing sight," Kezia answered, wondering how Mr. Donovan could be cheerful even in circumstances as serious as these. "And I'm worried about Bertie, of course. But I'm sure I'll be much relieved when we find out more of what happened. The women are uneasy, and I'm also concerned."

"How is Hattie?" Mr. Davies asked Mr. Donovan.

"She drifts in and out of consciousness. I'll visit her from time to time during these deliberations, but I have Joan Macdonald sitting beside her. I trust her to fetch me if I'm needed."

"Indeed," Kezia murmured. "If only Hattie could tell us who attacked her, there would be no need for this."

Mr. Davies sat down and smoothed the page of the logbook in front of him. He was the person deemed most accustomed to writing and had been asked to note down what was important at each meeting. Kezia thought he took it for granted, behaving as though the logbook was his, and as if he was quite used to noting proceedings in every kind of meeting. Mr. Donovan went to stand near the window, looking out at the sea through the small panes of leaded glass.

Charles said, "Miss Hayter, I am glad you're here to draw out the confidences of the women."

"*We* are perfectly capable of doing that," Mr. Davies muttered.

"But a friendly face will reassure them," Kezia said firmly. "Otherwise they may be quite overwhelmed by their surroundings and unable to speak. They would then be of no use to you in your proceedings."

Now Charles smiled at her. "We'll try to discover where the knife came from, of course," he answered, "but you mustn't forget that these women are criminals. A judgment and a sentence have been passed on every one of them. They are convicts being transported for every sort of misdemeanor."

"Not one of them is a killer or the kind of woman who would

carry a knife about her person." Kezia stood near her place at the table, trying to calm the rising anger she felt. "They all have scissors, it's true, but, Mr. Donovan, you said a knife had made the wounds, not something as small as a pair of sewing scissors."

"I did, and I stand by that," said Mr. Donovan, turning away from the window to answer her.

Kezia went on, "And as for being criminals, you know very well that they're guilty of petty offenses, and being transported because there's hope for their rehabilitation. There's a difference between stealing clothes from a market stall that you need to sell in order to feed your children and plunging a blade into a young woman's . . ." Kezia hesitated, more intent on controlling her own feelings than explaining to the others what she was sure they already knew. It would do her women no good if she were to lose her temper, but she felt seconds away from shouting at the men.

"Whoever did such a thing," Charles said quickly, and Kezia sensed from his tone that he was trying to soothe her and bring her back to the task before them, "was clearly desperate."

Kezia sighed. "There are nearly two hundred women on this ship, Captain. I can't know all of them as well as I'd like to, of course, but I thought I could speak for my women. We . . . they have been so diligently at work on our joint endeavor that they've become a group of like-minded persons bent on one good end." She put up a hand to tuck in a strand of hair that had escaped from one of the pins that held it. "I thought, also, that ties of friendship and, yes, even love were binding them together. Was I wrong? Might it not have been one of the crew, after all? Have you spoken to them? If it turns out that one of my women is the culprit, there must have been much of which I wasn't aware and that hurts me more than I can say. I should have done better, worked harder at understanding what ailed them."

"I'm sure you are not at fault," said the captain. "But it would be useful to know about them before we see them. I did not take down their names."

Kezia said, "Their names are Joan Macdonald, Emily Paxton, Marion Williams, Sarah Goodbourne, Ann Skipton, Phyllis Armstrong, Tabitha Brown . . . What can I tell you about each one? Some I know better than others. Marion Williams, who will come here first this morning, suffers with her health a little."

The captain nodded and Kezia went on: "She hates to be confined, feels as though she cannot breathe in small spaces, has bad dreams and imagines that every sort of illness is either afflicting her or about to descend on her." Kezia wondered what else she could say that would convince the men. Did they understand anything of weakness? Of terror? Of pain? "She's fearful and timid, and would no more pick up a knife to harm Hattie than fly to the moon."

"You must not say such things, Miss Hayter," Mr. Davies said. "We, who are listening to evidence, cannot decide who is innocent and who is guilty before we know the truth of what's gone on."

How dare you tell me what I must and must not say? Kezia thought, but she forced herself to bite back her answer and instead walked to her place, saying nothing till she was sitting down.

"I think I may be allowed," she said gently, facing Mr. Davies, "an opinion about the character of my women." She smiled as sweetly as she could. "I can't believe—I still can't believe—that any of them could possibly have done such a thing. Marion isn't very clever, though she's kind. I've seen that with my own eyes. I've seen her helping her neighbors. She has no enemies that I've seen. I know she likes Hattie—she told me herself, somewhat ruefully, that she wished she had half of Hattie's optimism about the future."

Kezia went on speaking forcefully, determined that none of the men should interrupt her. "Phyllis maintains order among the women. Sarah's quiet but there is intelligence in her eyes when she dares to raise them. Ann is quick with a sharp response but can be hard to read. She's not someone I could vouch for as firmly as the others . . . but I'm sure there's no violent impulse in her. If Joan is responsible, I will never believe good of anyone ever again. I'm convinced she's innocent of the crime for which she's being transported. Mr. Donovan has nothing but good things to say of her work in the hospital."

"She's an excellent helper." Mr. Donovan nodded in agreement.

Kezia continued, more quickly and urgently now. "Emily Paxton teaches the children well and they love her. Surely children wouldn't love someone who could use a knife on another woman. Don't they perceive innocence and guilt with more accuracy than their elders? Tabitha, if I'm honest, I *can* imagine her having some familiarity with a knife. She's one of the Newgate Nannies. But if it is her, then why?"

"That is what we must find out," Charles said. "We are speaking first, you say, to Marion Williams."

Mr. Davies dipped his pen. "Is that Marion with an *a* or with an *o*?" he asked.

"I think an *o*," said Kezia, "but you must ask her when she arrives." She thought it typical of the clergyman to be more concerned with spelling at such a moment than with the character of the woman he was about to see.

Charles appeared at her right shoulder. "May I have a word with you, Miss Hayter?" he murmured. To the others, he said, "I must confer with Miss Hayter privately, if you'll excuse us."

Kezia rose from her place and followed him to the other side of the room, where a pair of comfortably upholstered chairs were drawn up near the window.

"Let us sit down for a moment," he said. "I want to ask you

something." He looked over to where Mr. Donovan and Mr. Davies were deep in conversation. "You were about to answer my question about who might have had a grudge against Hattie Matthews."

Kezia put a hand over her mouth, as if, even now, she could still prevent this secret from being spoken. "I'm sorry," she said, "that I didn't speak of this before. It was wrong of me. I should have told you, but I promised to say nothing. There *was* a threat against Hattie, not very long after we left London."

Kezia was about to say more, but the door opened and Marion Williams came into the room.

7

THEN

Cotton triangle: indigo print with lines of widely spaced yellow chevrons. In between the chevrons, a pattern of yellow flowers and leaves

April 1841
CLARA

We've set sail at last. All of us came up from the lower decks and stood at the rail, even though it was windy and chilly and the sky was threatening rain. A stiff breeze was blowing from the east, and it made us shiver, clutching our shawls more closely around us. We watched first London, then the mouth of the river, then the whole of England growing smaller and smaller and finally disappearing. Many women have already found friends. Well, they've been confined below for many days, some of them. Several came from further away than London—Edinburgh, Ireland, Wales—but London is my home, and no matter what happened there, I'll still miss it.

I remember my dream from the night before, and comfort myself that it was only my mind playing tricks to trouble me. I'd had no bad dreams while I was busy in my own life, going about my work. But since my time in prison, they come to me often. I see small babies, some wrapped in swaddling blankets, others naked, many crying, and I try to pick up each one but they slip away from me and are lost in a kind of mist. The sound of their wailing stays in my head long after I've woken up. I'll say nothing about my past life on this ship. No one needs to know my history. Being transported to the other side of the world means what's done can be forgotten. Except at night, and I'll bear that.

I find myself mesmerized by the swell and roll of the waves. Far below us, the dark sea moves like a living creature.

As everything we knew vanishes over the horizon, I feel weak. Then I become aware of someone next to me and turn to see a woman weeping. It's Joan Macdonald. She's making no sound, but she's taken off her spectacles and put them away. Tears have begun to fall from her eyes, unchecked. I wish I had a handkerchief I could offer her. She's trembling, too, and pressing her lips together, as though keeping back a terrible cry of anguish. I've no desire to draw attention to myself, but her evident unhappiness shakes me a little.

A sailor, who's been standing nearby, comes up to us and holds a handkerchief out to her. "Isaac Margrove, if you please," he says. "At your service. It's a clean handkerchief. Be my pleasure if you made use of it."

Joan looks at him, startled. He takes her hand and closes it around the fabric. "A gift, madam," he says. "And you're welcome." He smiles at Joan and she makes a noble effort to smile back but fails.

"I thank you kindly, Mr. Margrove."

"I go by Isaac," he says, and turns to walk away. He's a good-looking man of about fifty, with iron-gray hair and a straight back.

Joan wipes her eyes and her nose, and puts the handkerchief away. Her sorrow seems different from that of the other women. It comes, I think, from somewhere so deep within her that my heart would have to be made of ice to be unmoved by it. I say, "Will you tell me what's the matter?"

I half expect her to say nothing, but she turns and looks at me out of faded brown eyes. She points toward England, visible on the horizon.

"I can't bear it," she says then. "There they all are, and I'm here . . . How will I live without seeing them?"

"Seeing who?" I ask, even though I can guess the answer. It's surely the same for everyone. The ones who have children will yearn for them. The ones who have living parents will fear their deaths, their sicknesses and being unable to help them. Maybe a few are like me: glad to be rid of what they've left behind. More than one spouse, I'm sure, is relieved to be rid of a cruel or bullying husband. But Joan Macdonald is unlike the others. She doesn't seem eager to tell me of her losses, putting out a hand to steady herself against the rail. But our conversation must have calmed her a little, for she's stopped crying. She makes some effort to compose herself, wiping her eyes again on Isaac's handkerchief, then putting it into a pocket of her apron. She takes out her spectacles again and puts them on. She collects herself and says, "My Lydia gave birth two months ago. That's one child I won't see growing up. And the others . . . all of them. My two daughters and four grandchildren. I shan't see them again. And what of my place, my house? The garden . . ." She shakes her head, as if to dislodge images too sad to think about. "It's not much, where I live, only a couple of rooms, but daffodils. Will there be daffodils in Van Diemen's Land?"

"I don't know," I say, "but there will be other flowers. Native to the place . . ."

I know nothing about what does and doesn't grow on the other side of the world but I speak as though I know it well, without even a hint of vagueness or hesitation. Then I add, "And you'll come back to England at the end of your sentence. How long is your term of transportation?"

"Fifteen years," she answers. I wait to hear details of her crime, but she says only, "I'm innocent. I didn't do what they say I did." She speaks without passion, as though she's passing on a piece of ordinary information, but she sounds more determined and energetic than she did before. I smile. I know, even though I've not spent long with convicts, that most of them claim they're innocent. Fifteen years is a long sentence and this woman seems frail. She must have been far stronger in her youth, but now she's like a flower that's been crushed underfoot.

"That's that, then," she says. "Nothing but the water all round us for weeks on end. Those children will need care."

She points to where one of the boys has clambered onto a box on the deck. Two others, a dark-haired boy and a younger girl, are squealing and laughing.

"'Ere, watch what you're doing," shouts one of the women standing nearby. "You nearly had her eye out then."

"Didn't," says the boy, sticking his tongue out at the woman, who rushes at him and slaps him across the back of his legs. He's wailing and crying now and his mother, a fat, slow woman, rolls along to his rescue. I haven't seen her before.

"Get off him. Not your business to go slapping people about for no reason." Slapping anyone looks as if it might be too much effort for her. To her son, she says, "You! Stop it! Before I box your ears off."

"What's happening here, ladies?"

And here he is. The captain. His words cast a spell of stillness and silence over them. No one answers his question so he goes on. "The children were playing, I think. No great harm done." He ignores the mother and addresses the boy himself. "I'm the captain of this ship, you know."

The boy nods, overawed, and rubs at his sore leg.

"When my men misbehave, d'you know what I do?"

"No, sir."

"I promise you, you don't want to find out . . . and I'll not look kindly on passengers who misbehave, either. Am I being clear?"

"Yes, sir. Only I didn't. I didn't misbehave. We was playing. It were an accident."

The captain says, "Very well. We'll say no more . . . but no mis-behavior. I have your word, young man?"

"Yes, sir," says the boy, and goes to hide himself in his mother's skirts.

"Very good," the captain says. "Good day to you." He moves off quickly, clearly eager to be away from the women, who are all star-ing after him as he strides away.

I turn to Joan. "I don't think the captain's used to having women and children aboard the *Rajah*."

"He'll have to get used to it, then. We've all got to make do with what we've got. I'm not used to nursing, but I've said I'll do it to help Mr. Donovan."

"We won't be able to see it for much longer," I say. "The land, I mean."

Joan and I stare over the rail at the sea all around us. The sun's come out and it glitters in the unexpected light, as if someone's scattered diamonds over its surface.

8
THEN

Cotton piece: dark ground scattered thickly with very small dots in pale green and widely spaced stylized sprays of leaves, also green

April 1841
KEZIA

In all my life, Kezia thought, I've not seen so many women together in one spot. Almost two hundred of them, standing in a crowd that seemed to have been robbed of color. What she saw before her was a sea of brown and dun and black and gray, with not a glimpse of red or yellow or heartening green to relieve the gloom. Kezia's eyes rose from the mass and she stared at the iron-gray sky, and the white crests of foam on the dark waves breaking around the hull. The movement of the ship still terrified many of the women. Kezia noticed it in the way they walked on deck, putting out their hands to steady themselves on anything that seemed to be solid and fixed, as though they expected at any moment to be thrown off their feet. The weather had not been rough but, still, the *Rajah* was like a living creature, ceaselessly moving and rolling and pitching.

"A penny for your thoughts, Miss Hayter," Mr. Donovan said,

sounding as ever both cheerful and friendly. The captain, Mr. Donovan, Mr. Davies and Kezia were standing together on the forecastle of the *Rajah*. Kezia hadn't wanted to confess that she was nervous about addressing so many people at once, so she replied, "I was thinking how deep the sea must be. How much water there is in this world." Which was a lie at that particular moment but which, she comforted herself, was the truth in a more general way.

Now they were singing and prayers soon followed but for once Kezia's attention was not fully fixed on attending to them and their meaning. She was distracted by the sky. In London, there were often low clouds to cover it. There were shops and churches and grand houses to distract the eye, but here it was easy to become lost in an immensity of gray. The *Rajah*, too, took her attention from what she should have been thinking about: the graceful curve of the swelling canvas sails, the men who sailed her gathered behind the women, listening to Mr. Davies as he said the Lord's Prayer and then began to preach.

When the short sermon was over, the captain stepped forward and said, "I thank Mr. Davies most sincerely for leading our prayers this morning. We are all, I have no doubt, uplifted and improved from listening to him. We count ourselves very fortunate to have him aboard the *Rajah*." He then turned to Kezia, who was standing a little further away, and smiled. "And now Miss Hayter has asked to be allowed to address you. Miss Hayter . . ."

He held out a hand in her direction as if to guide her, and Kezia went to stand next to him. Would her voice carry, with the breeze that was blowing? Would they hear her? She must make a special effort to be audible and remembered long-ago elocution lessons from a Miss Matilda Brown: "Speak not from your throat, Kezia dear, but from your deepest lungs and stomach." She and Henrietta used to giggle at the very thought of Miss Brown having lungs and a stomach.

Now, though, she took a deep breath, trying to remember other advice she'd been given. *Keep your head up. Remember to breathe. Fix on one person quite close to you and address your remarks to them.*

"Good morning, everyone," she began. She'd thought long and hard about how she should address the convicts. "Ladies" sounded wrong to her. She had also considered "friends," meaning the word as a tribute of sorts to Mrs. Fry and her Quaker beliefs. In the end, she settled on "everyone" as being both accurate and plain.

"I wish to speak to you about something I want to do on this voyage. I may have mentioned it to some of you already. The Ladies' Committee, who are active in our prisons, have seen to it that you have each been given materials to keep you occupied while we sail to Van Diemen's Land. I know that some of you are hoping to make items to be sold when we reach our destination. Others will want to knit and sew to make things for their own use."

Kezia pushed away a lock of hair that had fallen onto her forehead. "My task on this ship," she went on, "is to help you in whatever you decide to do. But there is something else, something I've been planning for some time, and I hope you will enjoy helping me with it. A coverlet made from patchwork. I've designed and made a central panel and, after speaking to a few of you, I've chosen those I'd like to help me in this task." Kezia took a piece of paper out of the small bag that hung from her wrist and unfolded it.

"I've written down some names," she said, glancing up at the crowd in front of her. "Please come forward and gather here if yours is read out." She pointed at a space on the deck, just below where she was standing.

As Kezia read from the list, she was aware of sailors going about their work: some on the rigging, some in groups on the deck, half listening to her but talking among themselves. They were keeping their voices low. The convict women stood still for the most part, but there were fidgets and gigglers. Kezia knew that everyone's good behavior would last as long as the captain and his senior officers were beside her. She sensed the women she was naming weaving their way to the front of the crowd. "Joan Macdonald, Hattie Matthews, Emily Paxton, Susan Downer, Phyllis Armstrong, Lottie Marshall, Isabel Croft, Beth Jones, Dora O'Hare, Louisa Taylor, Ruth Elmerside, Elsie Chambers, Alice Hardiman, Tabitha Brown, Rose Manners, Sarah Goodbourne, Ann Skipton, Marion Williams."

She turned to the captain, who stepped forward rather hesitantly. He seemed at first overwhelmed at hearing so many women's names read aloud, but he pulled his shoulders back and addressed them in a voice well used to speaking in the face of a howling gale. "Thank you, Miss Hayter. We wish you well with your efforts and it will be . . . interesting to see what you achieve. You may now return to your quarters, except those Miss Hayter wishes to see. Thank you all."

The gray, brown and black sea of bodies broke up into smaller groups as the women made their way from the deck. Some were laughing now that their enforced silence had ended. A few had their arms around one another and were singing together. *Oh, give us your hand, you sailor bold.* A few men clustered round the women, pinching them and trying to steal a kiss, till an officer approached and packed them off to their duties.

"Oh, shame on you, sir," said one woman. "Only having a bit of a laugh."

"Go below," said the officer, "or you'll be on report to the captain."

"Give us a kiss, duckie," said another.

The officer shooed her toward the lower deck, pushing her with his hands. "Get down there now," he said. "Time to go back to your quarters."

The small band waiting for Kezia looked at her with a light in their eyes that came, she knew, from being selected for this work. Everyone thrives when they are praised and approved of, she thought, and especially when that approval comes with some kind of preferment. Kezia noticed that now the noisy women had gone, the others she'd not chosen had begun to shuffle away. She would try to speak to them, not neglect them in favor of her company.

"Lord love you, Matron." Tabitha Brown cackled. "Never in me life been picked out to help anyone. Feel like quite a lady. Sewing, you say? Well, I'll have a go. Don't mind doing that a bit. Always ready to help, me. Ask anyone."

"Ssh!" someone said, and the small gathering fell silent.

Kezia smiled at them. "Good morning to you. I'm very pleased to see you here and my hope is that you'll regard what we're about to embark on as something that will not only improve your sewing skills but will also be a pleasurable occupation during this long voyage."

They looked at her with puzzled frowns and pursed lips. She took a deep breath and pressed on.

"There is a verse in the Bible, from St. Paul's Epistle to the Ephesians, which says: *Let the thief no longer steal, but rather let him labor, doing honest work with his own hands, so that he may have something to share with anyone in need.* That is what you will be doing: making something with your own hands." Kezia turned her head a little so that her gaze fell on the women to her left. "Those of you I've chosen have done some needlework before, and some of you have made patchwork. I know that you have had to work in ways that are demeaning to you in order to feed yourselves, and I know you'd like a chance to improve your behavior. The fault has often not been yours but driven by necessity. What you learn here will help to bring you an honest income. I know that you want to sell what you make, and you'll have time for that, too, but this is something I want us to make together, as a gift for the Ladies' Committee."

"Never heard of 'em!" someone said. "Who says they deserve a gift? I can think of several beaks and warders I'd like to send something to, but you'd only find it floating about in a pisspot."

A few of the women snorted with laughter. Kezia steeled herself against the coarse remark and replied as calmly as she could, addressing everyone in a level voice: "You'll find as you get to know me better that I don't dignify foul talk with an answer. You seek to shock me but I'm not shocked. Let's continue as though you never spoke." She smiled benignly at Rose Manners, who, she thought, had been the one to make the remark. Perhaps she was always foulmouthed. Kezia hoped that no one could detect the discomfort she still felt at such crude language. She was determined to be attentive to Rose's speech when they were together, but she also knew she must become accustomed to such expressions and not flinch when she heard them spoken.

She continued: "I know each of you a little and will know you all well, soon enough, but for today, please raise your hand as I say your name. Thank you." She began to read from the paper she was holding, like a teacher taking the register. The women answered, "Here, Matron," as each was mentioned.

Kezia sighed. Her hope was that the women would find a piece of work growing under their hands, and marvel that their own efforts were making it beautiful. And when they saw the possibility of beauty, what other discoveries might they make? What other changes to their situation might they seek?

Kezia had thrown herself into the preparation. First, she had made a series of small watercolors in which she imagined the finished article, though she knew this would change. She painted birds, colored bright scarlet and lapis lazuli, or emerald and gold. She copied flowers from nature and from printed sources. She drew garlands of leaves and tipped the edges of the petals with the palest green. Kezia had hidden these pictures among the pages of St. John's Gospel. Then she had searched every shop that sold chintzes, looking for suitable designs to match those she'd imagined. She had cut out flowers and birds and sewn them with tiny herringbone stitches onto a backing of plain calico in the style known as *broderie perse*. The work had obsessed her and she'd spent many hours on it, stitching and stitching far into the night, imagining it as the central panel of something bigger that the women would make alongside each other on the voyage. She'd composed some words of dedication to be embroidered on the central panel. Over the last few days she'd summoned these images to her mind whenever she felt overwhelmed by all that lay before them.

These had also been the sentiments of the Ladies' Committee. They had come with her to distribute to each of the nearly two hundred transported women the bundles that contained everything deemed necessary for the voyage. As well as aprons and caps, needles and threads of various colors, there was knitting wool, though not in large quantities. There were spectacles, a comb, scissors, a thimble and, in each bundle, two pounds of assorted fabric, mostly roll ends and oddments from the cotton merchants of Manchester. Kezia had her own bag of materials, including a short length of chintz in a heart-lifting shade of pale yellow, patterned with tiny roses, which dearest Mrs. Pryor had presented to her as a particular gift. "Because it is such a pretty color," she'd said. "Like pale winter sunlight." She had silks, some pieces of cotton dyed in Turkey red and other bits she'd begun collecting as soon as she knew she would be traveling on the *Rajah*.

Kezia believed passionately that transportation was a means to improve these women's lives. Far away from the circumstances that had led them into wickedness and crime, they might, she thought, become new women leading new lives. If they could sew, if they could sell what they had made on the voyage, they would recover some self-respect, leave behind their previous habits and change permanently for the better.

Kezia took the notebook out of the velvet purse she kept it in and looked at the list of names she'd written there, the women she'd chosen. She sighed. If these are the chosen ones, she thought, everyone else is unchosen. Left behind. Would they feel themselves to be of less worth? Would they make life difficult for women they might regard as having been specially favored? I'll have time, especially once my women are used to the work, to oversee other projects. My women . . . Kezia blushed at her vanity and chided herself. They are not my women. I cannot think of them in such terms. They're simply the ones I consider will be best to make what I have planned and dreamed of.

She turned her attention to the fabric they would be using. Every day, she thought, we'll have to cut as much as we need. It wouldn't be sensible to have small squares and triangles of material fluttering about, getting lost and dirty before they could be used. Each square would be four inches or so, with enough material around it to fold over for seams.

❖

That night, Kezia sat down to write to Mrs. Pryor.

> *My dear Elizabeth,*
> *You would have been proud of me today. I spoke out*
> *fearlessly in front of many people: all the ship's company and*
> *the convict women, too.*

Kezia put down her pen and read what she'd just written. It was almost true, though "fearlessly" was an outright lie. Her heart had been hammering against her ribs as she'd spoken, and throughout she'd been conscious that Captain Ferguson was watching her. She'd been aware of his gaze, felt it like a warm touch on her shoulder.

Kezia picked up her pen again:

> *I have chosen several women to help me work on the*
> *project we've spoken of so often. I hope I can help them*
> *improve their situation.*

Making sure they aren't constantly bickering and tormenting one another will take most of my time, she thought. She would be alone among women who had led hard lives. They had been coarsened and hurt by many things that had happened to them. They will be unhappy, she told herself, but I will be both fair and firm.

Should I write about my own feelings? Kezia had been grateful to be sent to Van Diemen's Land; perhaps Elizabeth and Mrs. Fry had noticed how unhappy she was.

For months before coming aboard, Kezia and her mother had quarreled constantly. Her mother had been eager for Kezia to marry a man she did not love in the least, and it was possible Elizabeth had guessed.

She would never have bowed to her mother's wishes, but how difficult it would have been for Kezia to face London society, to be thought an ungrateful daughter, and a failure at the very ordinary business of making a good marriage. I'll be glad, she thought, to be far away from England and happy with any progress we make on the stitching.

9
NOW

✥

6 July 1841
Ninety-two days at sea
KEZIA

Marion was flanked by two sailors, and Kezia wondered how the sight of the burly men appearing in the convict quarters to march her to the captain's cabin had affected her. Marion was nervous at the best of times.

Kezia went to take her seat next to Mr. Davies and wished she had brought her folding fan with her. The cabin was stuffy and perspiration was visible on every brow. They were lucky. At least, Kezia thought, it is warm here. Down in the convict quarters, it was often chilly, now that the *Rajah* was nearing her destination. Marion looked pale, and to Kezia, it seemed as if someone had smudged charcoal beneath her eyes. The woman stared at the thin rug spread over the planks of the cabin floor, meeting no one's gaze.

"Thank you," Charles said to the sailors, as they moved a chair and set it in front of the table.

"Good morning," Mr. Davies said, looking at Marion, then at the log in front of him. "Please will you give us your name, age and the crime for which you are sentenced?"

"One moment please," said Charles, and leaned over to whisper in the clergyman's ear. Mr. Davies nodded and looked at Marion again. He frowned and pulled at his cuffs to show his displeasure.

"Well, I disagree with him but the captain has said that your name alone will be enough. Other details we have already, of course, in the register that was completed when you came aboard the *Rajah*. That had slipped my mind. So. Your name, please."

"Marion Williams," she said.

"Marion with an *o* or with an *a*?"

"An *o*, sir," Marion whispered.

"Please sit down, Marion," said Charles.

She was hesitating, so Kezia nodded at her encouragingly and, at last, she was seated in front of the four of them. We must look frightening to her, Kezia thought. As though we are judges on a bench and she is in front of us to prove her innocence. Not one of the women aboard the *Rajah* would have good memories of men on benches, sitting in judgment.

"There's no need to be frightened, Marion," said the captain. "We're only here to discover who wanted to harm Hattie. I would like you to tell me what happened on deck yesterday. Let me begin by asking where you were when you heard Hattie cry out."

Marion squeezed her eyes closed, as if to shut out the horror of the memory. "I was on deck, on my way below, when I heard her scream, like a pig having its throat cut."

"So you were facing away from where Hattie fell?"

Marion nodded.

"And when you heard the scream?" Mr. Davies looked up from his writing.

"I ran to her. We all did. To where she was. She was lying there. She'd stopped screaming. We tried, all of us did."

"Tried?" the captain asked.

"To help her. Help Hattie. We lifted her up a bit, tried to see where she was hurt. Someone wanted to unfasten her clothes, but there was so much blood. We got it all over us . . ." Marion's voice faded to nothing. She sniffed and wiped a sleeve across her nose. Kezia saw that she was biting her lip and trying to calm herself, but she recovered and began to speak more freely, as though she was seeing the whole scene before her eyes while she spoke.

"Covered in blood, we were. Didn't know what to do. Poor Hattie wanted Bertie. That was what she wanted. Someone asked her who'd done that to her but what she wanted was little Bertie. We were shouting at Emily, 'Go and fetch Bertie. She wants Bertie.'" Marion paused and stared in the direction of the window. "But when he came, that was later and Hattie'd gone. First Miss Hayter came, then Mr. Donovan, and some men to take her away to the hospital. Poor Bertie! It was dreadful to hear his cries."

Marion's voice shook and she twisted her hands together in her lap. Kezia saw that she was doing everything in her power to control herself. She took a deep breath.

"Why did you all choose Emily in particular to fetch Bertie?" Kezia asked.

Mr. Davies turned to Kezia, frowning. "Surely," he said, "that's a question of no consequence whatever. A very trivial question, if I may say so. In the circumstances. Perhaps it would be better to leave the questioning of witnesses to the captain."

Kezia struggled to find a response that would avoid rudeness while making clear to him that she had every intention of asking any question she saw fit.

But then Charles spoke: "Miss Hayter's question is not trivial in the least. She may ask whatever she wishes. She, more than any of us, knows these women and we need her assistance if we're to arrive at the truth in this affair."

"Very well, then," said Mr. Davies, and asked the question again, as though it were his own.

"I'm not rightly sure, Miss," she said. "Emily and Hattie were close, right enough. Everyone knew that. I'd say Emily was Hattie's best friend."

"Is there anything else you'd like to say, Marion?" the captain asked her. "Do you know where someone might have found a knife?"

Marion shook her head vehemently. "No. I don't know nothing about knives. Not me. Hate them, more than anything. Never saw any knife, never."

"Very well," said Mr. Donovan. He exchanged a glance with the captain, who nodded, and added, "You may go now, Marion. I think we're agreed."

"Yes, Marion. You are excused," Mr. Davies put in. Kezia could see his irritation as Marion scuttled out of the room, as though fiends were at her back.

"We've learned nothing new," he muttered.

Kezia waited to hear what the others would say, but Charles took her by surprise. "Miss Hayter has something she would like to show us, I believe."

Kezia saw Mr. Davies opening his mouth like a fish, no doubt to make some objection, but he closed it again and turned to her. "Indeed," he said, "and what might that be?"

"There had been a threat against Hattie."

"What sort of threat?" Mr. Donovan asked, leaning forward over the table with a sudden new interest.

"I have it here." Kezia willed her hands to stop shaking as she took a small notebook from the pocket of her dress, opened it and laid it flat on the table. Then she lifted a piece of cloth from between the pages and held it up for the men to see.

"What is it?" Mr. Davies asked.

"A square from our patchwork," Kezia told him. "We use them complete, or cut them in half to form triangles . . ."

"I see that it's a square," said Mr. Davies, "but I fail to see how such a thing might be interpreted as a threat."

Kezia heard the laughter in his voice. "You must look at it more carefully, sir," she said. "Read what's embroidered on the fabric. Turn it over."

Mr. Davies took the little square of pale blue flower-printed cotton from her and peered at it: *Speak & you die.*

He shook his head and passed it to the captain, who looked carefully at it, then handed it to Mr. Donovan.

For a few moments, there was silence.

"Where did you find this?" Charles asked.

"It was left on Hattie's pillow several weeks ago. She came to me. She was quite distressed and I regret saying nothing about it before." Kezia bowed her head. "Perhaps if I'd spoken earlier . . . but I gave Hattie my word that I'd say nothing. She was so frightened . . . but I thought it was perhaps a trick played by an unkind woman. I didn't think it was of great importance. I decided it was probably someone making mischief." Kezia's voice faltered.

"Regrets are of no use to us," said Charles. "We shall find out who embroidered this patch, in the course of our investigations, because that's of the utmost importance. Whoever is responsible for it *must* be the same person who attacked Hattie."

The others nodded, but Kezia was less sure. She could not have explained it to anyone, or even to herself, but she felt that such an answer was far too simple.

10
NOW

✤

7 July 1841
Ninety-three days at sea

There was hardly any wind. This was the best kind of weather for those women who spent hours of the day stitching on deck. Today a mood at odds with the pale sunshine had settled over them. Without their matron, who had not yet joined them, the women were quieter, still shocked by what had happened to Hattie, less inclined to bicker. They seemed more peaceful and better disposed toward one another, hiding their fear for Hattie and for themselves. Everyone had been looking over their shoulder since the stabbing, for who could tell what would happen next? There were no cross words. Everyone was working on the outer border of the patchwork, and the carefully ordered arrangement of flowers and plants, stripes, dots and many colors lay spread over their knees, like a meadow made of different fabrics.

"Once, when I was a girl . . ." said Phyllis, peering into the pocket she, like all the needlewomen, wore pinned to her waist. She took out a small pair of scissors and snipped at the loose end left hanging as she came to the end of the thread in her needle. She paused, her hands on her knees, before choosing the next square, then continued. ". . . my ma sent me to fetch ale, to see if my father was in the alehouse and bring him home if I could. That weren't easy. He was stuck to that stool and I didn't want him back anyhow. Free with his fists, when he'd had a few." Others nodded.

Phyllis went on: "He came with me all right, that night, but not before some poxy bastard'd made a remark. Felt my tits as I handed over the bottle. Da didn't say a word and I wanted to kick him—hard. Kicking was the worst thing I could think of doing, then. I wanted my father punished more than the other fellow. Why'd he do nothing to protect me? I stared down at the plate lying on the counter. Someone'd left a piece of pie with a fork sticking up out of it. My head was full of black fog, like, and I picked up the fork and stuck it as hard as I could into that bastard's hand."

"Should've gone for his balls," said Tabitha, knowingly.

"Couldn't reach 'em," Phyllis answered.

"Was there blood?" Sarah asked. Everyone looked up, their hands stilled, needles poised.

Phyllis smiled. "Jugfuls. I was strong and young and crosser than a wet cat. I stabbed him as hard as I could and must've got a vein or some such because blood poured out of him, all over his hand, which he pulled away, quicker than quick."

"Then what happened?" Ann leaned forward. "What did your pa do?"

"He dragged me out of there by my hair. Kicked me all the way home and sent me to bed with no supper. Ma brought me up a bread crust spread with a bit of dripping once he'd passed out. God, he stank. I could smell him from where my bed was: beer and piss and sweat. How Ma slept next to that, I'll never know. I left home soon after. Ma didn't stop me . . . She'd have left if she could, but my sisters were only little. Once I was in service, and went back to see them, Da was dead. Story was he'd had a seizure, but I don't know. I'd have poisoned him if he'd been my husband. Maybe she did and maybe she didn't. Never asked. But I've often thought, what if there'd been a knife sticking out of that pie? What would've happened then?"

Phyllis turned to thread her needle, and the others bent their heads to their work. Alice muttered, "Dear Lord, preserve us from all harm." No one took the slightest notice, for she was given to voicing prayers from time to time, almost under her breath. A slight breeze had sprung up, lifting the edges of the coverlet, as the sunlight caught the steel of a dozen needles and sent glitters of light into the air.

Smooth sailing. The Rajah moves lightly: wood and rope and metal borne by the weight of water. Her sounds are a creaking and a sighing of the wind in the canvas of the sails. She's looking west, to where the sun dips below the line of the horizon. The land is falling out of sight behind her and she's lost all memory of it. The horizon calls to her. Reach me, it says. Find me.

11

THEN

Cotton piece: white ground with alternate mustard and white bands. Mustard bands with black motif; white bands with turquoise and yellow flowers

April 1841

KEZIA

Kezia made her way along the deck to the captain's cabin, feeling rather proud of herself for overcoming the slight nausea that had afflicted her earlier in the day. She was also hungry, and hoped that the smells wafting from the galley would be translated into tasty food. I must have found my sea legs, she thought, if I can look forward to my dinner.

The captain's cabin was small but managed to combine a study with a dining room in all respects like such a room on land. The chairs were upholstered in dark green leather. The table gleamed in the light of a lantern suspended above it. Someone had polished it so hard that Kezia could see the pale outline of her face reflected in the wood.

"My dear Miss Hayter," said the Reverend Mr. Davies. "It is a great pleasure to meet you properly at last. I regret that I have not talked with you before now. My dear friends Mrs. Fry and Mrs. Pryor have spoken to me of your accomplishments."

"Thank you, sir," said Kezia. "I'm very glad to be of service."

He was a tall, thin, sallow man, with a piercing gaze and a nose that was rather too long. His mouth was pinched and small and gave his face a discontented appearance, but perhaps he was still grieving for his wife, who had died recently.

"I am told," he said, peering down at Kezia, "that you have plans to occupy some of the women with needlework. I believe you began on the work today. Are you quite sure this is appropriate? It seems to me that a sewing circle is the very opposite of a punishment, and we must not forget that these women are being punished."

Kezia tried to find polite words in which to express her thoughts, though she felt anger rising within her. She managed to govern herself enough to say quietly, "The loss of their freedom and the impossibility of seeing those they love for many years is the punishment, sir. There is no need to add to it with other things. You will agree with me, I feel sure, for do you not serve a God who is, above all, merciful?"

Mr. Donovan was suddenly beside her and must have overheard the conversation. "She has you there, sir, to be sure." He laughed. Then he turned to Kezia and added, "I believe you've asked permission from the captain for the women to take exercise on deck."

"On deck?" Mr. Davies could hardly contain himself. "Surely that would be—"

"Very sensible," Mr. Donovan said. "We don't want a ship full of ailing women, falling sick and even dying."

"Surely no one will die for lack of exercise, sir," Mr. Davies protested.

"Well, we'll never know because the captain has said they are to breathe fresh air and walk about every day. Within certain limits, to be sure."

Mr. Donovan went to speak to another of the officers and Mr. Davies turned to Kezia again, this time asking about her work in the London prisons. "I have preached at Millbank on occasion," Mr. Davies continued.

"Indeed, I heard you," said Kezia. The clergyman looked gratified at this news. He began to discuss sermons in general and his own in particular. Kezia wondered how long he'd go on talking about himself, if he were left uninterrupted. He might go on for the whole evening, she thought. How could she stop him? She was grateful when Captain Ferguson appeared and put a hand on his elbow.

While she'd been brushing her hair before dinner, Kezia had wondered what it would be like to speak to the captain in a social way. Would he be any less formal and reserved than he'd shown himself thus far? She had hoped they might have a more cordial exchange, but he spoke only to Mr. Davies and she felt somewhat disappointed.

"Come, my dear fellow," he said, "let us sit down. Take a glass of sherry, sir. And you, too, Miss Hayter."

Kezia declined the sherry but let herself be guided to a seat next to Mr. Donovan. The captain was on her other side. If he did not make conversation, Mr. Donovan was certain to do so. He would be an entertaining neighbor, she knew. She was so relieved not to be sitting next to Mr. Davies that she almost confessed this aloud.

Three young sailors came in, carrying china plates laden with roast mutton, potatoes, peas and gravy, which they set before each diner.

Mr. Donovan was asking questions almost as soon as the mutton was in front of them.

"Will the nautical life suit you, Miss Hayter? Have you ever been away from England before? How will your family fare without you, do you think?"

Kezia had seen Mr. Donovan in the company of the women belowdecks and knew he was the sort of person to be interested in everyone. Because he was so amiable, those who spoke to him were friendly in response.

"I shall miss my brothers and my sister, of course," she said. "But they have one another, and I shall write to them."

"How many were you? Are you the eldest?" Mr. Donovan went on.

"There's no stopping my dear friend James," said Captain Ferguson, turning toward Kezia and almost smiling. "He'll continue until he's extracted every ounce of information he requires. And he is the most inquisitive of men, I assure you."

"I have no objection." Kezia turned to the captain. "I'm resolved to answer every one of his questions about me and then he will have none left for the rest of the voyage."

"She has you there, James." Captain Ferguson laughed, and Kezia noticed how his laughter transformed his features. Is he handsome? she asked herself, as she cut into a potato.

Mr. Donovan said: "To be sure, I'll be listening eagerly to any words that come from Miss Hayter."

Kezia swallowed her mouthful, put down her knife and fork on the plate and smiled at Mr. Donovan and the rest of the company, who had stopped talking among themselves and seemed ready to listen to her. It came to her suddenly that her presence on the ship was most unusual for these men. They'd never considered such a strange thing as a matron before.

"My father died when I was six, sir," she said. "My sister, Henrietta, is four years older than I am, and I have three younger brothers: Robert, George and John. My cousin, George Hayter, is a painter in the court of our queen."

"Indeed," said Captain Ferguson. "Mrs. Fry told us so. The creator of the fine portrait of our monarch painted shortly after the Coronation. We are honored to have such a well-connected person on board the *Rajah*."

"And your mother?" Mr. Donovan's curiosity had not been sated. "Will she not miss you?"

"That I doubt, sir," said Kezia, raising her eyebrows in surprise at his directness. "She and I are . . . Well, she has much to occupy her without worrying about me." She asked then for the salt, though the meal had been salted enough, simply to distract the man. She had no intention of explaining to anyone the intricacies of her dealings with her mother. I know my own feelings for her, she thought. God probably does, too, and is tearing out His beard in despair at the distance between us. None of this, she was sure, was anyone else's business. She ate the rest of her dinner in silence, smiling pleasantly when anyone glanced in her direction.

"I believe," said Mr. Donovan, turning to her suddenly, "that Molly Forbes ran right up to you before you embarked. I'm sorry for that. I hope you weren't too frightened. She was a poor creature, and it was my duty to put her ashore. I don't think she would have harmed you. More noise than malice, I think."

"I wasn't in the least frightened, sir," Kezia said untruthfully. She had made up her mind to show as little fear as possible on the voyage. These men would be too quick to call it a woman's weakness. "I was concerned only for her welfare."

"Most commendable, Miss Hayter," said Mr. Donovan. "That does you great credit. I, too, find it hard to refuse anyone a chance at a better life, but it's my duty to take only those women in passable health on such a long journey. A wayward passenger unbalances the whole company. My work and yours, and the comfort of the transported women, were in my mind—how best to achieve harmony on this ship. I've had to send only a few ashore this time, for they were too severely deranged to benefit from transportation."

"Though perhaps the insane would profit from being far away from their more rational fellows," said Mr. Davies. "I believe that the asylums in England are very crowded."

At that moment, the three serving sailors arrived to clear away the plates. Once they had left, Kezia excused herself from the company.

"I will accompany you, Miss Hayter," said Captain Ferguson. He stood up and waited for her to join him at the cabin door. She had not expected his attention and found herself blushing. What would they say to one another as they walked along to her cabin? He picked up a small lantern, which was standing on a sideboard, to light their way.

"I bid you good night, gentlemen," said Kezia, turning to address the men still gathered around the table. A chorus of "Good night" followed them out of the cabin.

As they walked along, Isaac Margrove ran up to them. "Captain, sir," he said, "you're wanted on the quarterdeck, I fear."

Captain Ferguson turned to Kezia. "Isaac will go with you to your cabin. Good night, Miss Hayter. My apologies . . ." He moved from foot to foot, not sure what to say. "I hope you've enjoyed . . . I've enjoyed this evening. It's been . . . very pleasant. But I'm needed. So sorry, Miss Hayter. Good night."

"Good night to you, sir."

He was almost out of sight before Kezia realized she hadn't thanked him, and felt irritated with herself. He will probably not even have noticed, she thought, which irritated her even more.

Isaac was not tongue-tied in her presence. "It's a pleasure to see you again, Matron. I hope you're well settled."

"Thank you, Isaac, yes," Kezia said. "I'm feeling quite at home."

"It's good to have a matron on board. We're mightily proud to have such a thing on the *Rajah*. Not had one before. Not ever on any ship I've sailed on."

They had reached the cabin and Isaac placed the lantern carefully on the chest of drawers. "Good night to you, Matron," he said. "And give a care to the lantern. Fire's the worst of all hazards on board ship, I'm sure you know."

"Thank you. I'll take great care. Will you be safe making your way in the dark?"

He laughed. "Bless you, Matron, I know every single timber of the *Rajah*, every one. I could walk the decks and holds and even climb the rigging with my eyes shut! Don't trouble your head for me."

"I'm glad to hear it." Kezia smiled at him. "I'm most grateful for your assistance, Isaac."

Kezia had never before changed her clothes in such a confined space. Every movement in her little cabin took much longer than she expected, but at last she was in her nightgown with her pink shawl wrapped around her shoulders. She considered her dress, neatly laid over the back of a small chair. She'd pushed her shoes under it, her stockings rolled up and tucked into them, and now she wondered how the convict women, lying very close to one another belowdecks, would manage to keep their belongings tidy and, more than that, clean. Each group would have to organize washing clothes and themselves, or the voyage would be of some discomfort to every nose on the ship. Kezia determined to raise the matter with someone . . . perhaps Mr. Donovan, who was, after all, a doctor and would not be shocked by having to think about ladies' garments, washed or otherwise.

She took out her Bible and read, as was her custom, the passage prescribed for the day. Then she knelt beside the bunk and prayed, as she did every night, aware of the side-to-side motion of the *Rajah*, the enormous depth of water under the ship. Ever since she was a small child, Kezia had imagined a list of those she prayed for as if it were a register written on paper, and as she mentioned each name, she imagined herself crossing it off with a stroke of her pen. Now she added the women in her charge to those she must pray for. First came Papa, then her brothers and sister, her friends, especially dearest Mrs. Pryor, the women she had met during the course of her work for the Ladies' Committee and, last, Mama.

When had she realized that her mother had no particular fondness for her? As a very small child, Kezia had been aware that Mama's smile seemed to appear more readily when her gaze fell on Henrietta or the boys. For a long time, she had thought the fault was hers: *Kezia, you are disobedient. Kezia, you are willful. Kezia, take your head out of that book. Kezia, go to sleep at once. I'm heartily sick of this story of nightmares.*

A litany of complaints against her seemed to have issued from her mother's lips for as long as she could remember. Once, when she was about twelve and Henrietta sixteen, she'd asked her sister directly.

"Do you think Mama likes me, Henrietta?"

They'd been in the parlor, sitting on either side of the fire, sewing. Neither the devil nor anyone else would have found idle hands in the Hayter household.

Henrietta looked astonished. "Like you? Why, you silly goose, of course she does. She loves you. Every mother loves her children, does she not? Why d'you ask such a foolish question?"

"I don't know," Kezia answered. "I daresay I *am* being foolish, but . . ."

"But what?" Henrietta put down her handiwork and stared at Kezia, as if her sister had grown a second head.

It was hard to put into words, but Kezia tried. "She never holds me. She hasn't kissed me for—for a very long time."

"You're talking nonsense, Kezia. She always kisses us good night."

Was it worth arguing? Kezia wondered helplessly. Did Henrietta really not notice the ritual at bedtime? After saying good night to the boys, their mother came into their room, sat on Henrietta's bed, talked of one thing and another, stood up, then leaned over and kissed Henrietta affectionately. She patted the end of Kezia's bed as she passed it on her way out of the room, saying as she went, "Good night, Kezia, my dear."

My mother's love, Kezia thought, *is like a lantern.* She imagined it passing briefly over her head from time to time and leaving her behind in the dark, moving on to shine its light over others. She would turn to the wall and stare at it, every single night, willing herself to see nothing beyond its rough surface. Even during the summer, she felt cold in her bed.

Kezia sighed. Henrietta hadn't been attending, that was clear, and, really, why should she? The rhythm of the house flowed on and on, and only Kezia was keeping count of both rebuffs and kisses.

"She doesn't talk to me, as she does to you and the boys," Kezia went on. "Have you not noticed?"

"You are being more than fanciful, Kezia. I fear you're being petty."

Kezia thought, I'm not being petty at all, and stabbed her needle with renewed energy into the cotton of the pillowcase she was embroidering. Nevertheless, it was true. Her mother hardly ever found anything to discuss with her younger daughter. She gave instructions, which Kezia obeyed to the best of her ability, but she never chatted. Kezia and her mama never laughed at anything together; they did not exchange interesting gossip, or discuss important matters, such as what the younger daughter might reasonably do with her own life.

Kezia tried to turn back to her prayers. *I must be anxious tonight, Lord,* she thought. *Forgive me, I will be more attentive now.* Once she began to think too carefully about her mother, it was hard to forgive her entirely. She sighed. "And, Lord," she whispered aloud, "look kindly on Captain Ferguson and the crew of this ship that they may take us safely to our destination. Also, the women who are seeking to make a new life on the other side of the world. Send them courage and determination, and let them be drawn into the comfort of your love."

She stood up and went to turn down the lantern. The flame guttered and died. The only brightness came now from the lanterns on deck. She listened to the timbers creaking and felt the weight of the ship, and wondered how it was that this great collection of men and women, in a gigantic wooden chest of sorts, didn't sink immediately to the bottom of the sea, how they were borne up by the mass of water under their vessel.

Early the next morning, Kezia stood on deck and gazed out at the ocean, noticing that the horizon was no more than a vaguely drawn line in the distance. The waves, quite lively and white-crested in the strong wind, were chasing one another till they broke against the sides of the *Rajah*.

"You have found your sea legs more speedily than most, madam. Good morning to you." Captain Ferguson was standing beside her at the rail.

"Good morning, Captain. Yes, I found it surprising at first to be moving up and down and from side to side so much, but I'm grown used to it now. And I find I'm too occupied to concern myself much with the motion of the ship."

"That's the very means by which we train the youngest of our crew. They come on board new, homesick and sometimes frightened, though they'd never show it, and we set them to tasks at once—send them up the rigging, give them boxes of supplies to haul about, have them running up and down so fast that any seasickness is soon forgotten. They are too exhausted to be ill, I assure you. There's always work to be done on a ship, of course. And I see you've already started yours." He indicated the groups of women walking in twos and threes along the deck.

Kezia nodded, pleased that her plan for the women's welfare, her request that they should have exercise every day, had met with the approval of both the captain and Mr. Donovan. "I think it's important to walk about in the fresh air as much as possible. Perhaps"— she smiled at the captain—"when we sail into calmer waters and warmer temperatures, the women might be allowed to sit outside on deck to work. To do their stitching?"

"We'll see . . . we'll see. Perhaps you and I may also walk together from time to time."

The word "why" nearly escaped from her lips but Kezia said simply, "Of course."

Kezia glanced at his profile without moving her head. Captain Ferguson had seemed to her a little formal in his manner, and somewhat tongue-tied in her presence. Could he really be interested in her business? Why had he suggested that they walk together?

"Then let us start as we mean to go on," he said, and held out his arm. She was surprised and a little nervous as she took it. We might

95

be promenading along the seafront at Brighton, she thought, as they began to walk along the deck together.

"Tell me a little about your work, Miss Hayter," he said. "You have made a list of women who might help you in a project you've devised. You told me so at dinner last night."

"I have," said Kezia. "What I did not say last night was that this project has been in my mind for some time."

"Indeed," said the captain. "When did you first think of it?"

Kezia looked first up at the sails and then at her feet. "Before anything else," she said, "I must speak of Mrs. Pryor. She is like a mother to me in many ways. She's an important member of the Ladies' Committee, but I've known her since I first began to work at Newgate."

How to explain to the captain the joy she'd felt when Elizabeth Pryor had begun to pay attention to her? When she had recognized in Mrs. Pryor a kindred spirit? Someone who understood her better by far than her own mother. A woman who could see that more might be done with a needle and silk than simply making samplers or embroideries. Mrs. Pryor understood that there was art in the placing of this fabric next to that, in the disposition of colors near or far from one another.

"She and I both agree with Mrs. Fry," she said, "that a shared piece of work has great value. All work you do for yourself is good, but when you work together to make something for another, or for others, why, then, the mind of many is bent on the same outcome and this forms . . ." Kezia stopped, not knowing how to convey precisely what she believed. Fortunately, the captain interrupted her.

"A bond between strangers. A common aim. Of course, also a chance for friendships to flourish."

Kezia smiled. "Those are my sentiments exactly." She said nothing of her desire to educate the women, to lead them to better things. Neither did she mention her intention of beginning or ending each session with a verse from a hymn. Perhaps by the time they reached Van Diemen's Land the women would be accustomed to asking for a blessing on their work.

Kezia knew, from her work with prisoners at Millbank, that certain confessions would come her way as they sewed together, from women eager to unburden themselves. The stitching seemed to allow them to speak without looking directly at anyone else, and she'd observed that once a woman had spoken, it was easy for others to follow her example. Here on the *Rajah* they would do so more than ever. There were fewer people to overhear them telling of their hopes, fears and sorrows.

"I'll do my best to help every one of my needlewomen," she said at last.

"I'm sure you will, Miss Hayter. I must leave you for the moment, I'm afraid, but we'll walk and talk again."

He bowed briefly in Kezia's direction and moved toward the stern. She had been wondering what to say in answer to his remark and was relieved he hadn't stayed to hear her. She was looking forward to their next meeting but it would have been excessively familiar to say so.

Aboard the Rajah, 6 April 1841

Dearest Sister,

I am a seasoned sailor after only one night at sea! I wish that were true, but it is not. I find it strange beyond anything to have no firm surface beneath my feet. Even in calm weather, I'm aware of constant movement. A sheet of water stretches from where I am to the horizon on every side and it makes me fearful, I can't deny it. Everything that ties

97

*us to the land is gone. No buildings, no trees, no other
people, just miles and miles of shining water reaching, it
would seem, to infinity. Captain Ferguson is very adept at
settling his crew and all of us. If I had to find a word to
describe him, it would be "reassuring." I walked with him
on deck today, and while I was in his company, I could have
imagined myself taking a turn round Richmond Park. I felt
no more qualms about our ship being alone on the ocean . . .*

Kezia put aside her pen. It was true that she felt the ship was safe
under Captain Ferguson's command. She'd thought of him as rather
shy, his shyness expressed as stiff politeness, but today he'd been
more . . . she sought the right word . . . *ordinary.* She was looking
forward to their next conversation. She picked up her pen again,
resolved to paint a picture for her sister of the convict quarters and
the women in her charge.

12
THEN

Cotton patch: narrow stripes in mustard yellow, white, black and turquoise, with each stripe printed with lines of flowers in contrasting colors

April 1841
HATTIE

Miss Hayter had come down to speak to them again. She'd instructed them about washing, cooking and sleeping, and was now coming to the end of her speech.

"Captain Ferguson is a good man and I'll ask him to allow you to have some exercise and fresh air. We'll do as much of our sewing on deck as we can because we'll need light." She looked at the space around her as though she was seeing it for the first time. "It's very dark down here. We're now on the high seas, and I ask you to pray with me for a good voyage and safe harbor in Van Diemen's Land."

The women closed their eyes and bent their heads, as Miss Hayter went on: "Oh, Lord, hear the fervent prayers of your daughters gathered here, about to embark upon a long voyage at sea. Bless our labors, and keep us in good health and spirits that we may have the strength to do your work." She searched in her bag, found her Bible and opened it. She covered her mouth with her hand and cleared her throat. Someone sniggered and there was ssshing and giggling from others. Miss Hayter raised her voice a little and said: "I'll end with a psalm:

> *They that go down to the sea in ships, that do business in*
> *great waters;*
> *These see the works of the Lord, and his wonders in the deep.*

I hope to God, thought Hattie, that we don't see too many wonders. Whales or sea monsters or giant birds.

> *For he commandeth, and raiseth the stormy wind, which*
> *lifteth up the waves thereof.*
> *They mount up to the heaven, they go down again to the*
> *depths: their soul is melted because of trouble.*

Hattie prayed sincerely for no storms. What might happen to the *Rajah* if there were storms? Would Bertie be frightened? She had never been in a storm at sea but perhaps she, too, would be terrified.

> *He maketh the storm a calm, so that the waves thereof are*
> *still.*

That sounded more hopeful . . . a calm after the storm. Pray to God for that, Hattie thought, and glanced at Miss Hayter, who had lifted her face from the book and was looking at them all now, with her head held up. That must mean she knows it by heart, Hattie decided. Must have said these words a thousand times.

Then are they glad because they be quiet; so he bringeth them
unto their desired haven.
Oh, that men would praise the Lord for his goodness, and
for his wonderful works to the children of men!

Hattie gazed at the listening women. Many of them looked poorer and more unfortunate than she did. More dejected. Most were thieves like her. They'd stolen to feed their children, and she had stolen the clothes off children's backs. They were petty criminals, but there were others who'd been born to crime: cheats and the children of thieves. I was respectable once, she told herself.

Before she'd fallen pregnant with Bertie, she'd been a maid in a good house full of rich people, who were her masters, and she'd spent her days attending to the clothes of the women. She had mended small tears with such fine stitches that you'd never have guessed at the damage. She hemmed and tacked, pinned and unpinned, and all the while she was well treated by the family she worked for, the Whitings.

She was especially well treated by the men, if you could call being pawed and touched and grabbed from behind "well treated." Hattie had nothing but scorn for Mr. John Whiting, the father of the house, and his two sons, Christopher and Jeremiah, but she knew that yielding to their desires was necessary. Out on the street, she thought, that's where I would have been if I hadn't, with not a penny piece to show for my work. And in truth, some of their attentions had not been unpleasant. She'd liked young Jeremiah well enough, and even though she was dismissed when her pregnancy became visible, she could not, ever, bemoan the fact that Bertie was here beside her. If she had not borne her son . . . well, that was a thought Hattie never followed to its logical end. Even though what she'd planned had not come to pass as she expected, even though his birth had led directly to her present plight, Bertie was the best thing that had ever happened to her.

She thought of him as consolation for an older loss that still weighed heavy on her heart if it came into her thoughts. When it did, Hattie had grown used to fixing her mind on happier things, for otherwise her days would be spent in longing and misery. And that, she often told herself, would do neither herself nor Bertie any good.

She gazed across the wooden planks of the floor to where small groups of women were talking, arranging themselves to be near their friends. The ones who'd come from the same prison had ready-formed alliances and cliques. The Newgate Nannies, for instance, had already settled themselves comfortably in a dark corner. They were older than many of the women, and dab hands at spotting a chance to make a penny. Margery Selwood, known as Selwood, had a wicked tongue in her head, and the others parroted her every word. Agnes Dwyer, called Dwyer, was heavy and had one eye that looked at you askance and a tattoo on her arm: five dots arranged in a pattern that told of a past as a prostitute. She was the most feared of the three, and there were few who would dare to cross her. Tabitha Brown was the weakest—she had followed the other two. Spying was her chief talent. She listened. She moved among the prisoners without causing alarm and was thus able to overhear much that benefited the other two. The three, who did not mind their reputation but rather encouraged and reveled in it, were quick to point out to younger prisoners the advantages of keeping in their favor. They gossiped ceaselessly. When she was in Newgate, Hattie had seen how they traded in secrets, took advantage of the weaker warders and lorded it over the other prisoners in a variety of ways. She had made a point of being obliging to them at all times. She'd been in Newgate just a few days when she'd caught Tabitha's eye.

"You've fallen a long way, and no mistake," Tabitha said, peering at Hattie and picking up a strand of her hair. She rubbed it between her fingers and grinned. "That's treasure, that is," she whispered, leaning closer. "Pure gold."

Hattie tried not to flinch at Tabitha's foul breath. She knew better than to walk away, so she smiled. Tabitha went on, "You could get them guards to do whatever you wanted . . . maybe even open the cell door."

"Leave her alone, Tabitha," said Dwyer, and Hattie was grateful. The danger had passed before Tabitha could force her to do anything dangerous. Even now, on the *Rajah*, she was a little grateful for Dwyer's assistance, but she wondered whether Matron's faith and fervor were a match for the Newgate Nannies.

After Miss Hayter left, Hattie found herself next to someone she'd barely noticed before. This woman was tall and slender, and wore a scarf over her hair. She decided to speak and sighed theatrically. "I daresay," Hattie began, "that I've slept in worse places in my life, but I can't think of many. What a hole this is! How'll we keep it clean? I fear for my boy's health."

The woman nodded. "Yes," she said. "It's not the cleanest place I've ever seen."

Hattie smiled. "My name's Hattie Matthews. What's yours?"

"Sarah Goodbourne."

"Pleased to meet you, I'm sure," said Hattie, and held out her hand. After a moment of hesitation, Sarah shook it.

"My bunk is over there," Sarah added, and pointed to a mattress near the entrance to the living quarters. "I wish you a good night."

"Good night," Hattie said, determined to be friendly to everyone. And I'll look after Bertie, she said to herself, and try to be as happy as I can.

She turned to where Bertie was sitting on his thin mattress, his legs dangling. "You're a good boy, aren't you, Bertie? But you must lie down now . . . It's time to go to sleep."

After she'd settled her son and pulled the scratchy blanket over his shoulders, Hattie climbed into her own bunk. Around her, the other women were settling for the night. The ship's timbers, even while she was still at anchor, creaked and groaned.

In spite of her cheerful demeanor in the daylight hours, it was at night that Hattie started to remember things. Bad memories came to her, as they did, she supposed, to many of her companions. There were those who groaned aloud or muttered in their sleep while others found it hard to fall into slumber. Hattie tried to push away those thoughts with pleasant ones. Still, shadows from the past, conversations she'd rather not have remembered, danced through her head.

A house had ruined everything. Hattie knew (and no word from any doctor would shake her belief) that the sorrow of losing little Kitty, the youngest of Hattie's siblings, had killed her mother. One day they'd visited someone at that house, and from that time, Ma had wasted away, until she was nothing more than a bag of bones with the light gone from her eyes. The terrible house still came to Hattie in nightmares.

I won't think of it, Hattie told herself. I'll forget it. She stared at the wooden planks above her head and turned her thoughts to the ship, the voyage and what she might gain from it. What would Van Diemen's Land be like? Sunny and hot, she thought. Bright and new. Familiar dreams of that far country soothed her. The *Rajah* was moving and Hattie was trying to grow used to the constant motion of the waves beneath the ship. She glanced across the gloomy space. The lantern that hung from a beam threw a little light on the tiers of bodies covered with dark blankets. Hattie rose from her own bunk and stood up to kiss Bertie and said, "Nighttime, my angel. Off you go to sleep now."

"When will we see the big sea, Ma?" Bertie sighed, as his eyes closed.

"Tomorrow," said Hattie. "I promise." He'd not been satisfied with the dark brown water that lapped around the hull: his mother had promised him blue water and waves. She returned to her own thin mattress and rested her head on the flat pillow, staring through the gloom at the knots and whorls in the timber above her head.

13

NOW

✦

7 July 1841
Ninety-three days at sea
KEZIA

Kezia woke early. Her nights were filled with dreams that dis-appeared with the morning but left a shadow in her mind. She worried constantly about Hattie, and it was hard to reassure the women that they were safe, when she herself was filled with mis-givings.

Once she was dressed, she took up her embroidery and tried to concentrate on it. She had fallen into the habit as the days became cooler, and it was a time she used to enjoy. The light was better in the early morning and it was almost comfortable to sit on her bunk and take up her silks. The tiny black neatly worked words were done. It was only a few days ago that she'd embroidered "June 1841" on the fabric. Now, as she added a few stitches to the border, her first thoughts were of Hattie and she could not sit calmly. There was a woman on this ship, a woman who, in all likelihood, might be driven to harm someone else. She could even, Kezia thought, as a new chill of foreboding came over her, seek to harm me. She put her work carefully away. Part of her wanted never to leave her own safe berth. She felt less uneasy when she was alone, and this distressed her.

Since the inquiry into the crime had begun, Kezia found herself quaking inwardly at any strange sound. The familiar creak of the rigging, the noises of the crew, the shouts and bangings common to life at sea had the power to shock her, to make her glance behind her more than she used to. I am fearful of someone else, she thought. Perhaps it had been one of the sailors, after all. How thorough had their questioning been? She could not help suspecting, though, that whoever had knifed poor Hattie was among the women in the convict quarters. Whenever she went down to see them, Kezia found herself looking carefully about her. We will discover who it is, she told herself, trying to find the courage she encouraged in others, but until we do, they're all frightened and so am I. The only person who isn't nervous is the one who stabbed Hattie. If only, Kezia thought, I could find a woman who *isn't* looking over her shoulder.

She sighed. She would have to leave her cabin. As she made her way to the hospital, Kezia was grateful that the *Rajah* had such an excellent surgeon superintendent. Thus far, the health of the women on the voyage had been good and he'd had nothing more complicated to deal with than sore eyes and constipation. Now, though, Hattie's condition was taking up much of his time. He never left her side, apart from his attendance at the inquiry, but he always left Joan in charge when he was absent, with strict orders to call him from the proceedings if there was any change in Hattie's condition.

In the hospital, Joan was sitting beside Hattie's bed and Mr. Donovan was at his log.

"Good morning to you, Miss Hayter," he said, smiling. "Did you pass a peaceful night?"

"Not very peaceful, I'm afraid," Kezia answered. "I am as concerned for Hattie as you must be."

Mr. Donovan nodded. "There is no change," he said, then stood up and came closer to Kezia. "Joan has been sitting devotedly beside poor Hattie's bed all night, but I'm afraid she's showing no signs of improvement."

Kezia moved to stand beside Joan.

"She's like a ghost, Miss," Joan said, and her voice was full of weariness. "I lean forward sometimes, just to make sure she's still with us, God help her. Her breath is so faint . . ." She sniffed and wiped her eyes with a corner of her apron. "Mr. Donovan's a marvel. Always smiling, always talking to Hattie as if she's in her right mind. Don't know why he does that, when she can't hear him or answer."

Mr. Donovan said, "Because we don't know if she can hear us. That's what I've told you all along, Joan, and it's true. Some part of her may hear everything. That's why I talk to her. And why I tell you to sing to her, Joan."

"And I have, Miss. I've sung every song I know. The ones I sang to my babies . . . That was the worst thing of all. There I am, singing Hattie songs I've not sung in many years and I'm blubbing as good as any baby as I do it. Wiping my eyes and blubbing."

"That meant I had two women to look after, Miss Hayter—Hattie and Joan."

Kezia could tell that Mr. Donovan was trying to be hearty and cheerful, to change the mood around Hattie's bed, but Joan was still as pale as ever and Hattie did not move. She took Joan's hand and said, "Let us go out on deck. The sun is shining a little and work will distract you from your sorrow."

Joan stood up and leaned over to kiss Hattie's brow. "Poor thing," she murmured. "Poor young thing."

Kezia waited till Joan was almost out of the hospital, then bent to whisper in Hattie's ear, "God will have care of you. If you can hear this, Hattie, be comforted. We are working to find who did this to you, my dear." Turning to Mr. Donovan, she said, "Thank you, sir, for your kindness. And for your good heart in these matters."

"It doesn't help anyone to be gloomy, I've found . . . Good day to you, Miss Hayter."

No one was smiling when Kezia and Joan sat down and began to thread their needles. The women were unusually silent. They had their heads bowed to their work. No one asked to borrow scissors. No one squealed when they pricked themselves. They stitched doggedly, their shawls gathered about them against the chill of the morning. Perhaps it was their solemnity that made Kezia say what she did. She remembered what Mr. Donovan had just said and perhaps she, too, had a duty to lift everyone's spirits. An air of gloom and anxiety had dominated their sessions since Hattie's stabbing.

"I met the Queen once," she said.

"You never! Queen Victoria?"

Tabitha was the first but others soon added their cries of disbelief. "You didn't. How could you? You're joking with us, Miss." A chorus of voices, and laughter to go with the words. They didn't believe her, that was clear.

Well, Kezia thought, it's stopped them thinking about Hattie, if nothing else. She went on sewing as she said, "It's true. I met her in Buckingham Palace."

"You've been in it?" That was Rose. "Must've been in your dreams, Miss. That's when you've been in there!"

"No." Kezia looked at her. "In my real life. Three years ago."

"Go on, then, Miss, tell us about it," said Izzy. "We could do with a good story. A fairy tale." She cackled.

Rose patted her arm. "Put a cork in it, Izzy. She won't tell us if you don't listen."

"My cousin," said Kezia, "is George Hayter. Have you heard his name?" No one spoke, so she went on. "He's a court painter. He was asked to paint the Queen, and I was living in his household at that time. He asked me to go with him. To help him. Of course, I was very curious to see Buckingham Palace."

"What's it like, Miss?" Ann wanted to know.

"The ceilings are extremely high. The corridors are very long and have red carpets and much gilding everywhere. And so many lights! Splendid lights. Crystal chandeliers."

"Must be armies of servants dusting them all," said Joan. "I wouldn't like it. Living in a palace like that."

"Lucky, then," said Tabitha, "that it won't ever happen to you."

"Go on, Miss," said Emily. "What happened when you got there?"

"Well, Cousin George set up his easel and I helped him choose the paints he needed. When the Queen came in, I was astonished to see how small she is. She's shorter than I am, and we're almost the same age. She's very pretty and she wore such a lovely white dress. Satin trimmed with gold lace. She was also wearing a crown, but when she went to sit on the throne, Cousin George told her she might take it off because he wouldn't be painting that part of the picture today, so she removed it and said, 'I'm very grateful, sir. It's rather heavy, I fear.'" The women were staring at her with their mouths open, wanting more. She sighed and said, "I'm afraid that those were almost the only words I heard the Queen speak. I watched her sitting there as my cousin painted, wondering what she was thinking about, because she has many affairs of state to occupy her. Then, when it was over, she thanked him and left the room."

"That's wonderful, Miss. Imagine!" said Emily. "Such a famous lady and you've seen her. In Buckingham Palace, too. You must think of that day so often. I would, if I'd met the Queen."

"I do think of it. But what I remember most was the painting. Watching my cousin making such a perfect likeness of the Queen from colored paste laid on a palette was like seeing magic happening." Kezia did not add that it had made her want to create something beautiful herself, much less that she was engaged now in doing precisely that. No one would have believed her. The women, she noticed, were whispering now.

"What are you saying, Ann?" she asked.

"I only said how good it was to forget about it. It's hard to put it out of your head, Miss. There's someone here who's ready to kill."

The wind sighing through the ship's masts was the only sound to be heard. A cloud crossing the sun made sudden shadows fall on the women, darkening the morning.

"Well," said Kezia, "let us sing a hymn to put such thoughts out of our minds."

They sang, but Kezia knew they were not attending to the words and were singing less heartily than on other days. Every mind was somewhere else.

Kezia saw Charles walking toward her as she made her way back to her cabin. How strange it is, she thought, that when he appears, I am cheered and comforted. She felt as though a weight had been lifted from her. They'd started taking walks along the deck together

111

on one of the early days of the voyage, and she looked forward with pleasure to those occasions.

"I've come to meet you," Charles said. "Being master of this ship takes up almost none of my time and leaves me with many hours to wonder how I can contrive a meeting."

Kezia smiled at his jest. He took her hand and tucked it into the crook of his elbow. Kezia curled her fingers into the fabric of his jacket. How comforting it was to be walking thus, so close to someone, so . . . She cast about for words to express her feelings. She felt warmed by Charles's concern and attention. His care for her.

"You've been a long time at the stitching today," he said.

"Yes," Kezia answered. "They're all restless and frightened. The mood among the women is . . . Well, they're anxious, as I am."

"There's no need for that. You may be sure that I'll protect you against anything."

"I'm grateful, Charles, but you don't know—none of us knows— whether we may all be in danger. The women are finding it hard to sleep. They're so fearful."

"Of course they are," Charles said. "I'm worried, too, but also quite sure that we'll discover the culprit soon. The idea of a possible murderer on the ship is appalling."

They walked the deck in silence for a few minutes and stopped at the rail. She shivered. "Surely we must go down for the interrogations now," she said.

"Proceedings," he corrected her. "That's what Mr. Davies calls what we're doing. He referred yesterday at dinner to 'tomorrow's proceedings.'"

"He has good penmanship," she said. "'The proceedings' will look well on paper at least. It's fortunate that his opinions will not be recorded there."

"But you're worried, I can see."

"I'm feeling . . . Well, I know that my concern is selfish and trivial in the circumstances . . . All our efforts are turned to finding the truth of Hattie's attack and that makes it hard for—" Kezia stopped abruptly.

"Hard for what?"

"I almost dare not say," she answered, "but we have—*they* have—worked so hard on the patchwork coverlet, and I'm very anxious, now, that we may not finish it in time. I am torn between worry for Hattie, and watching the women in case one gives away anything that might lead us to an answer. And then, every moment when I'm not with you and the others is taken up with stitching. It would be the saddest thing if the coverlet were not finished. When I return to my cabin at night, many thoughts fly around my mind and make it hard to sleep." She did not say that thinking of him gave her respite, but it was true.

"You may be excused from the proceedings, if you wish, you know," he said gently.

"No, no!" she said. "I must be there to help the three of you speak to my women." Kezia wondered whether she should tell him how she feared what Mr. Davies might say to them if she were not there to stand up for them. She was well aware of his views, and if she was not there, how much more unforgiving would he be? She decided to keep silent for now, but said instead, "I fear for the women in my absence. Of how they might be coerced in some way. I must be there."

They stood close together by the rail, each staring down into the water as it slipped past the *Rajah*'s hull. Kezia was aware of Charles's presence beside her: she felt a current flowing between them. Above, the sky was bleached almost white and there were only a few clouds to be seen. The sea, its great weight and depth (to which Kezia had never quite grown accustomed), moved below them slowly and heavily, and it came to her that the *Rajah* was like an insect perched on the back of an enormous, constantly turning creature that lived and breathed as they did.

"We should go below," Charles said.

Kezia moved away with a sigh. "Tabitha Brown is not like Marion Williams," she said. "She may be capable of violence, I fear. I caught her, one day, pulling another woman's hair for no good reason that I could see. I led her away from where the others were sitting, and after a while she calmed down, but she *does* have a temper and I'd wager she'd know where to lay her hands on a knife."

"There are knives in the galley. My men have knives. They need them for their work. And if one of the women has been—how shall I put it?—a little too friendly with a sailor, why, it's the work of a moment for her to slip a knife into her clothes."

Kezia stopped walking. "Do you suspect such a thing? Are you sure your men are to be trusted? My women have been told repeatedly not to consort with the crew."

Charles said, "I've no doubt you've given your instructions, and so have I, but if I know anything about my men and the direction of men and women's natural impulses, I'd wager that a certain amount of . . . *friendship* has gone on. My men know what's allowed and what's not, but I'd be foolish to expect complete obedience from every one of them."

Where? she wanted to say. When? Every moment of the women's time was accounted for. They were cleaning the living quarters or washing clothes and themselves in inadequate buckets and barrels of seawater. They were preparing what meals there were. They were eating them. They were sewing, most working alone, but her women were stitching together the patchwork coverlet for many hours of the day. They chattered among themselves, they fell into arguments—which sometimes became fights, with hair pulled, scratching and spitting—they felt ill, they walked the decks at the time set aside for exercise. When was there a chance to meet sailors and do whatever they did with them? It would be the women blamed if they were caught.

They walked together in silence along the deck. The wind blew strands of her hair into Kezia's eyes, and she tried to forget the anger and anxiety she felt by staring toward the horizon, which often calmed her. Clouds lay low in the sky, and Kezia pulled more closely around her shoulders the shawl she was wearing against the chilly wind.

14
NOW

✦

7 July 1841
Ninety-three days at sea

The Newgate Nannies were tramping the deck.

"What's the point, I'd like to know? Can't go anywhere you want to go, and there's nothing to look at that you haven't seen before, so I say it again, what's the blasted point? I've trod these sodding decks for miles and miles and weeks and weeks, and what good's it done me? That's what I'd like someone to tell me." Dwyer threw a baleful glance at her two companions, who were marching along the deck beside her during the exercise period.

"It's her, innit?" said Selwood. "Matron. Says we need to move or we'd all freeze into a sitting posture forever, down on the lower deck. I like breathing air. Don't you like breathing the air, Dwyer?"

Dwyer glanced at her out of the crooked eye that was turned in her direction . . . You could never tell with Dwyer if she meant her gaze to fall on you or on something else entirely, but Selwood and

Tabitha were both used to her. "Nowt wrong with air as such," Dwyer grunted, her words almost blown away by the stiffish breeze. "But you can't half get too much of it. Look at it. Can't trust the weather, can you? Calm this morning and blowing a gale now. I'd call that a gale, I would."

"That's not a gale," said Tabitha. "That's nothing like a gale."

"Well, hark at Mistress Sailor who suddenly knows about such things as gales and ships and the sea. Her, who's never been near water in her life . . . a stranger to the contents of her washbasin, she is. Nearest you've come to water, Missy, is when you've been pissing in a corner!" Tabitha didn't bother answering. Dwyer had been flinging insults at her ever since Tabitha had met her, seven years ago, when she'd been serving her first sentence. Dwyer only made an effort to insult those who had been her cronies for a long time: they understood one another. Dwyer added: "Weather's the least thing I'm thinking about. I like being out here, away from holes and corners where stabbers might be hiding . . . Didn't get a wink of sleep all night, fretting."

Selwood changed the subject. "What's up in Matron's gang, then, Tabitha?"

Dwyer stood for a moment at the rail of the ship and looked down at where the caps of the waves were tipped with white foam.

Tabitha said, "Nothing's come to me that you don't know. They're a wishy-washy lot, mostly, but now they're worrying about the questions and answers going on with the captain and them. Not got any closer to finding who stabbed Hattie. That much I do know. Phyllis is a bossy baggage, who thinks she knows better than anyone else. Alice never says nowt, but mutters prayers from time to time, and she's handy enough with the singing. That hymn! It goes round in my head in my sleep, that does." Tabitha put her hands together and piped up in a surprisingly high voice:

All may of thee partake.
Nothing can be so mean
Which with his tincture (for Thy sake)
Will not grow bright and clean.

"You're blistering our lugholes with that squawking, Tab," said Dwyer. "What's it mean anyway? What's a tincture? Tell us what one is—go on."

"That means"—Tabitha frowned—"that it don't matter how low and horrible you are, if God puts His mark on you—tincture means something like color—you'll stop being horrible and low and get bright and clean, like it says."

Dwyer's laughter bubbled up from her stomach. "Not worked yet, though, has it?" she asked. "Not on you, it hasn't. You're not bright and clean that I can see. Is she, Selwood?"

"She's not," said Selwood, joining in the general mirth. "Even her loving mother couldn't call her that. But never mind about hymns. Tell us what's going on with the others."

"Ruth's a tough lass," said Tabitha. "Lottie's the best of us with her needle, though Joan's good. Bit spiteful, a couple of them, and mean, and some of them stupider than a chair leg, like fat Susan Downer, but no one's a stabber, I reckon. Izzy and Rose are all lovey-dovey. Sarah Goodbourne's about as interesting as a plank. Emily's soppy over Hattie. She's good with the teaching, though, and Bertie's always hanging around her. She doesn't send him away, not that I've seen. Doesn't want to fall out with Hattie, I daresay. Louisa's a bit slow to catch on, but no one is *dangerous*."

"If no one's dangerous, then why's the deck still dark from where Hattie's blood soaked it? Tell me that!" Dwyer nodded to make her point more forcefully. "Someone wanted Hattie dead. Why?"

"She knew something about someone, that's why. That's the only thing I can think of. A secret."

"She was a real chatterbox, that Hattie," said Selwood. "She didn't know no one from before. Not that anyone told me. Not that I'd seen."

"How about a man?" Dwyer ventured. "Wherever there's trouble, there's usually a man at the bottom of it."

"Hattie wasn't putting it about," said Tabitha. "Too busy with her boy. And chatting to all of us, sewing."

"She might just be better at hiding it than some. Know that young sailor, William? Have you seen him? I've had my eye on that Emily for a bit, but others don't seem to have taken notice. Come across them more than once, hidden away in corners. Having more than just a quick peck on the cheek, I reckon. She's all over him."

"I'd be all over him, too, given the chance. He's as tasty as a plum, that one."

"Two plums!" said Tabitha, and giggled. "Love to suck those two plums myself. You wouldn't have to ask me twice!"

Dwyer and Selwood clutched their sides, laughing. "Not sure," Dwyer said, "what Matron would think of women who . . . let's say *consorted*, as we're being fancy, with members of the crew. Not sure what the captain would think about a sailor of his who put himself in places he'd no business to be."

Tabitha and Selwood nodded.

"Meanwhile, we're stuck here trudging this blasted deck. Don't give her much of a chance, that Hattie," said Dwyer.

A sailor approached them as they reached the companionway. "Tabitha Brown? Is there a Tabitha Brown here?"

"Me," said Tabitha. "I'm Tabitha Brown."

"You're wanted in the captain's cabin. I'm to take you there now."

Tabitha smirked at the others. "There you are. I'm summoned."

"Keep a watch on your flapping lips," said Selwood. "Least said, soonest mended, don't they say?"

Tabitha and the sailor began to walk away.

"I've had enough of this exercising," Dwyer said. "Time to go down to our lovely drawing room on the lower deck and see if the butler will bring us a cup of tea."

15
THEN

Cotton piece: pale blue ground, scattered with scarlet and blue flowers

April 1841
HATTIE

Hattie could tell that Miss Hayter hadn't expected so much difficulty when she suggested that some of them come together to work on something. I could've told her, Hattie thought. Trying to get people to do something at the same time, trying to get them to listen to what you were saying, let alone do what you want them to do when you want them to do it, was hard, unless you used some kind of force, and Miss Hayter wouldn't do that. Now she was frowning with the effort of trying to explain to a whole lot of useless convicts what she wanted them to do. I'd not have stood for it, Hattie told herself. I'd have threatened them with something. They'd buckle down soon enough after that, but now they were like cats in a sack.

First, some women didn't want to sit next to certain others. Ruth Elmerside was muttering, "I'm not sitting by that Phyllis. Never stops talking. Worn my ears out already."

Phyllis slapped Ruth across the face. "Shut your trap, you lying hussy. Don't you dare—" She was about to hit Ruth again when Miss Hayter raised her voice. It was the first time Hattie had heard her do so. It wasn't exactly shouting but she stood up and said, "Silence, all of you," in a louder voice than she'd ever used before, and Hattie felt more hopeful, but soon others piped up, moaning and complaining: *She's taken my scissors . . .*

They're not your bloody scissors . . .

Why d'we have to do this anyway? . . .

Why d'we need to sit together? . . .

I can't bear her . . .

She's smelly . . .

Can't thread this sodding needle, can I?

Blasted ship keeps moving around too much . . .

Hattie turned to the woman next to her, Joan Macdonald, and sniffed. "Some of the rest of them make my head ache, but you're all right. I've noticed that."

Joan said nothing, but Hattie thought she nodded. She'd taken a pair of spectacles out of her pocket, and was holding her work close to her face, making a great effort to produce small, even stitches, in spite of the motion of the ship—it could make you lose your rhythm and jab your needle into the fabric in entirely the wrong place—and the moans of her companions. Miss Hayter was now occupied with Marion Williams, who was a funny one: terrified of being in the convict quarters and running up to the deck any chance she got. Sailors would bring her down and she'd start moaning again. Poor creature. She wasn't right in the head, that was sure. No one liked being in the dark and the stink, but most had got used to it because they had to. Marion was different. Miss Hayter was speaking gently to her.

"Look at this, Marion," she said. "See this blue cotton? What does it remind you of? The sky . . . If you look at the piece you're sewing, and try not to see the place you're in, you'll have blue sky all round you. The blue will be in your head. Then see this one, white with red flowers. Count the flowers, Marion. See *them*. Fix your eyes on them. Sew the piece with the red flowers as neatly as you can round this piece of paper, and do the same with the blue piece. Then you can sew flowers and sky together and that will make things easier, won't it? You'll have a small garden in your lap."

Marion picked up the cloth. She stared at it, entranced, as if she'd never seen such a thing before. Then she took her needle and, after some help from Miss Hayter and several failed attempts, threaded it with trembling fingers. Her eyes, which often darted everywhere, full of terror, bent over the work in her hands and Hattie watched her grow calmer as she sewed. Every so often, she'd look up and her face would become panic-stricken again, but then Miss Hayter whispered in her ear and gave her another bit of fabric to look at, which soothed her and made things a little better.

Hattie noticed that the women working on the patchwork had split into small groups, mostly according to age. The young ones, Rose, Izzy and Beth, chattered away together and weren't paying much attention to their work. Rose had become particularly friendly with Izzy. Becky, who'd been Izzy's best friend at the beginning of the voyage but wasn't in Matron's company, looked sullen all the time. Hattie thought she was being pushed out of Izzy's affections in favor of Rose. They had their heads so close together that they looked like a two-headed creature.

Whenever they sat working on deck in the open air, any passing sailor caused a flutter of giggles and a frown from Miss Hayter. Ann was silent. Lottie never said much either, but everyone admired her sewing, and Miss Hayter often held up her work to the rest of them as an example. Alice was devout and fervent when prayers were said and sometimes muttered a prayer of her own, as if it were a comforting song. From time to time, a woman would throw her work to the deck and stand up. Today it was Izzy, who had detached herself from Rose for once. She was a skinny creature with long fair hair that she wore in a plait under her scarf.

"I've had enough," she pronounced to those who were sitting near her. "Blast this patchwork. I want to lie down. My bunk's not much more than a board, but I'll take that above bending over some stuff and pricking my fingers till they bleed. My back's killing me. Worse than forced labor, it is, honest." She flung down her work and began to walk toward the stern of the ship.

Hattie looked up from her sewing and noticed that everyone was sitting quite still, watching to see what would happen.

Miss Hayter caught up with Izzy and they stood together by the ship's rail, their heads close.

"What're they saying?" Phyllis asked. "Anyone hear anything?"

"Silly madam. Can't you see how far away they are? No one can't hear nothing." That was Susan, clearly irritated by being unable to take part in the drama that was going on out of earshot.

"She's threatening Izzy," said Rose. "I can tell by the way Izzy's mouth is trembling."

"Not much she can threaten her with, though, is there?" said Tabitha. "She's not going to push her overboard or tie her to the mast, is she?"

There was no need to answer. Izzy and Miss Hayter were walking along the deck toward them. Hattie picked up the two patches she was sewing together and everyone else, she saw, was concentrating on what they were doing. Izzy sat down, picked up the work she'd dropped and began once more to stitch. Rose moved to sit even closer than she was before.

Miss Hayter sat on Izzy's other side and gazed at the women.

"Please, everyone, look at me. If any of you," she said mildly, "would rather not be working on this coverlet, tell me now and I will find someone to take your place. You're the best needlewomen from among those being transported, but I'd rather teach someone who's never picked up a piece of fabric than work with a person who prefers not to be one of us."

A silence fell as she turned her gaze on each woman in turn. Each said nothing and dropped her eyes to her lap. Hattie could hear the wind sighing through the rigging, the ship's timbers creaking as the *Rajah* rolled from side to side, but not a word was spoken.

"Very well, then," Miss Hayter said. "The subject is closed. We'll say no more about it."

Hattie wondered what the matron could have said to Izzy to make her so ready to take her place among them. That, as a maker of the coverlet, she would be given a good character when they arrived at their destination? That if anyone chose to leave the group, their lack of loyalty would be punished? Perhaps she had reminded Izzy that, as the voyage progressed, those making the coverlet would have more time on the upper deck than others. Any of those might have persuaded Izzy. Whatever the reason, whatever she'd said, Izzy had stayed in the group. Perhaps it had been pointed out to her that they, the eighteen chosen ones, were regarded with envy by more than a hundred other women. *You're privileged*, Miss Hayter might have said. *You're lucky.*

16
NOW

✤

7 July 1841
Ninety-three days at sea
KEZIA

"Speak up, Tabitha Brown," said Charles. "We can't catch what you're saying if you speak directly to the floor."

Tabitha Brown smiled and Kezia regretted she'd been given the opportunity to do so. "Tab's gnashers," Dwyer called them: long brown tombstones in a very bad state of repair, like a cemetery that no one had cared for in years. Brown teeth for Tabitha Brown, Kezia thought, and she chided herself for such a frivolous notion on such a serious occasion.

Tabitha was more used to benches full of judges and magistrates than Marion Williams was. Her attitude struck Kezia as brazen. She sat on the prepared chair a little restlessly, scratching her armpit and staring quite openly at the splendors of the cabin: the polished wood, the gleaming brass and the soft leather of the well-upholstered chairs.

"This is a proper fancy place and no mistake," she said, to no one in particular. "Captain's cabin, eh? You don't stint yourself, I see."

"Impudent creature!" Mr. Davies spluttered. "Keep a civil tongue in your head or we'll have you taken back to your berth."

Charles intervened. "Let us proceed now, please. Miss Brown will not be taken back to the convict quarters till she's told us what she knows of the attack on Hattie Matthews."

"Miss Brown, eh?" Tabitha rocked with laughter. "No one's ever called me that before, I can tell you. Thank you, sir, you're a proper gent, not like—"

"Tabitha!" Kezia said, her voice uncharacteristically raised. "Sit quietly, please, and let us go on."

As Tabitha answered the men's questions, Kezia wondered whether the seven women they would be interrogating had spoken of the matter among themselves. I'll ask, she thought, when it's my turn to question her.

"So, tell us again. What did you hear Hattie say? Her exact words, please, Tabitha," said Charles.

"Well, she wasn't herself, see? First, she said, 'Bertie,' then she said, 'Not Freddie.' And she was pointing at Emily to go and get him. Emily'd started walking away but Hattie pointed at her. She was pointing toward the lower deck, really."

"Are you sure?" Kezia asked. "Why didn't you say something sooner? That's a strange thing to say. Who is Freddie?"

"Haven't an idea who Freddie is. Only know she said it, plain as I'm sitting here." Tabitha leaned forward and directed her remark to Kezia in a confiding manner. "That's what I thought, Miss. Not the kind of thing you'd say."

"Did Hattie say anything else?" James Donovan asked. "Before I arrived?"

"She passed out, sir. Very quick after asking for little Bertie. Broke my heart to see it, I can tell you. Emily fetched him in the end, but she took her time over it, I can tell you. Hattie'd been taken off to the hospital by the time he got there. Terrible, it was. Poor little chap."

Tabitha put on the saddest expression of which she was capable, which was, Kezia could see, somewhat of a challenge for her. Her face was more comfortable with either of two expressions: vacant or sneering. But even someone as dull as Tabitha must have realized that neither face was suitable for the present occasion and was trying to arrange her features into an aspect that might be deemed more sympathetic.

"Can you tell us anything of the talk among you belowdeck about this matter? Your companions, I mean." Charles spoke quietly but he looked Tabitha straight in the eye. She lowered her gaze.

She sniffed. "We talk about it, it's true, but no one has any idea about why. They say all sorts, some of them, but they don't know nothing."

"What sorts of things do they say?" Charles was persistent.

"You know . . ." Tabitha made a sound halfway between a laugh and a bark of contempt. "She's made someone jealous, taken her sweetheart, that kind of thing, or else she was blackmailing someone. Knew something someone didn't want telling."

"What sort of thing might that be?" Mr. Davies said.

"If we knew that," Tabitha said, with some justice, Kezia thought later, "we wouldn't be sitting here asking questions, would we?"

"You must speak more respectfully," Kezia interrupted her, fearful of Mr. Davies's reaction, but surprisingly, he merely nodded.

"You're quite right, Miss Brown. We would not. So it behooves us to discover what that might be. Thank you. You may return to your quarters. You've been very helpful."

Tabitha stood up, beaming, and bobbed a curtsy in his direction. "Thank you kindly, sir."

When she'd closed the door behind her, Charles said, "I must say I think Tabitha Brown is right. Hattie knew something. We haven't given sufficient weight to the words embroidered on that patch of material you showed me. Someone who goes to that trouble surely means what they say, don't they? We should try to solve that puzzle in order to find our motive."

"I feel we have lost so much time. If I'd taken it more seriously, we might have prevented the stabbing," Kezia said. "I feel greatly at fault. I simply asked Hattie if she knew of anyone who might have something against her, and she searched her memory, then said no. I believed her. I still do. I don't think she was lying."

"But just imagine for a moment," said Mr. Donovan, "that Hattie was indeed truthful and had no idea why she should keep silent. It does not follow that there wasn't something that *someone else* wanted to be kept hidden."

"We're wasting time," said Mr. Davies. "We have seven witnesses to the crime. This is a very grave crime but it shouldn't be beyond the wit of the four of us to discover what actually happened. Only one of those on deck could have stabbed Hattie. It is our duty to find out which of these convicts is lying."

As Kezia went to join her women under the awning, she wondered again, as she had wondered often before, might someone other than one of their suspected women have knifed Hattie and run away? Before the others who rushed to her side were even aware of it? Should she mention this possibility? There were so many places to hide on the *Rajah* that she found herself walking about the vessel nervously, aware of unusual noises and glancing behind her often, especially after dark. Anyone could be hidden behind a barrel, a crate or a coil of rope.

17
THEN

Cotton piece: Turkey red printed with a regular pattern of large dark squares, containing either six small rectangles or a smaller square

April 1841
CLARA

I suppose you could say we're rubbing along now, getting used to one another. When Miss Hayter gathered us together there were seventeen of us: too many to sit crammed into a circle, especially in the space around our berths. Emily left us for a short while every day to teach the children, but she sat with us for much of the time. There were days when this or that person took to her bunk because she was seasick or on her monthlies. Joan sometimes joins us late, I've noticed, and yesterday Miss Hayter asked her what she'd been doing, but Joan only said she was sorry and offered no explanation. We all knew she had duties in the hospital, helping Mr. Donovan, but there were days when she seemed to me to be flustered and a little pink in the face, even though she soon recovered. Most of the time, there's about fourteen of us working on the stitching.

"When we reach warmer latitudes," Miss Hayter told us, "and

when the work has grown a little, we can sit together, but for now, it's easier if you do your sewing in smaller groups."

So we've pushed some benches into a rough circle, near the place where the daylight spills into the quarters from the door that leads to the companionway. I feel the sunlight, when there is sunlight, on my back and that's pleasant. The first few days on board were hard. The very motion of the ship was frightening to most of us, as though we were sailing on a living creature, with a mind of its own, not on an assembly of wood, canvas and metal. Even though the weather wasn't really rough, there was the constant thick and horrible smell of vomit on the lower deck as some of the women emptied the contents of their stomachs and moaned fit to wake anyone who'd managed to fall asleep. It was hard to keep the place clean. No sooner had someone thrown up than the rest of those in her mess had to set to and clean it away. Some were better at that than others, and the whole company paid the price for inadequate swabbing with water. During the day, we walked about, stumbling, with some of the weaker ones among us unable to keep properly upright. From the beginning I didn't mind the motion of the ship and now I feel it mostly as a rhythm in my body. We women have become allies, if not exactly friends, even though there are still irritations and occasional quarrels between us.

When we first started working together, Miss Hayter handed out fabrics taken from the sacks the merchants had sent to the ship with the Ladies' Committee. Alice and Susan were put in charge of cutting the cloth into squares. Each has a template in stiff card and they're at work every day, making squares and triangles for the rest of us to stitch together. Miss Hayter also handed out a few fabrics of her own, some of which are prettier than the contents of our own bundles, patterned with flowers or leaf-bearing twigs. At first, I sat next to Alice but she seemed eager to talk to me and ask me questions. I prefer to do the asking. After a while, I moved to sit next to Joan, who is the opposite of a blabbermouth, which pleases me. I'm hard at work on my sewing, doing my best to make my stitches as neat and small as everyone else's. It's been a long time since I picked up a needle. Threading the cotton through its eye is hard, with the ship's movement unsteadying even the hands of the more experienced women. And I'm not used to matching colors or patterns according to what pleases me, or the edges of one piece of fabric with another, binding them together tidily so they'll lie flat. I understood, even after only a few hours of the work, that in another life, beside a fire in a comfortable room, this would be a pastime I might grow to enjoy. Aboard the *Rajah*, it's more a task than a pleasure, but it passes the time and takes my mind from my worries.

Some of the others are laughing. Tabitha has made a remark that has them clutching their sides. I don't draw attention to myself by seeking to know what was said. Alice and Susan seem angry. They're frowning, so the joke was probably lewd. Even Joan is smiling a little.

Joan's happier. I see this in the way she stands, walks and talks to the women she thinks of as her friends. I'm one of these, simply for speaking kindly to her as we sailed out of London. Her shoulders, as she walks on deck now, aren't bent under the weight of her sorrows. Joan's skilled with her needle, and she's often set to help the strugglers. She finds the right piece of fabric for them, the best one to sit next to the one they have in their hands. Ruth and Susan sometimes draw blood, which falls onto the cloth and marks it. Miss Hayter encourages them, and others like me, who aren't as neat as the rest, to choose dark fabrics and avoid visible stains. Perhaps Joan's been sent to sit next to me so she can help me, but she hasn't yet said anything about my sewing. She's humming a tune under her breath. I say, "You're happy," before I've even thought what I'm saying. I regret the words almost as I speak them. Who am I now? The woman who isn't Clara Shaw, not a bit like her in any way, wouldn't say such a thing. She'd make a quiet joke, or keep her own counsel.

"I am," Joan answers. "More than I was when we left England."

I think she'll go on sewing and say no more, but she continues. "You don't gossip like the others."

I nod. She whispers, "Then I can speak of this to you, can't I?"

I nod again. She's going to tell me a secret. "I won't tell anyone else," I mutter, under my breath, and feel a little ashamed of myself for being so eager to find out what she has to tell me. When I was Clara Shaw, I heard many confessions from the poor young women who begged me to release them from their predicament. I kept the secrets men whispered to me in bed. What I most miss is gossip, confidences and womanly chatter. Others on the *Rajah* never stop whispering in quiet corners, but because I have too much at risk— too much for others to discover—I try to keep away from such talk.

"D'you know who Isaac is? Isaac Margrove."

"I do," I say. Everyone knows Isaac. He's a presence on the ship, seemingly always at hand when there's work to be done. We convict women like him because he makes no difference between us and anyone else, greeting everyone just the same. "Morning, all," he says sometimes, or "A fine morning indeed!" as though we were his shipmates, not criminals condemned to transportation.

Joan leans toward me as I bend over my sewing. Anyone looking would think she's helping me.

"He's declared himself to me," she says.

I'd like to ask a thousand questions. How could it have happened so quickly? I say, "We've been at sea scarcely more than a week, Joan."

"But I met Isaac before we sailed," she answers. "He gave me a kerchief when I was crying. Don't you remember?"

I don't reply. Isaac must have found a way to speak to her. I know nothing, I realize, about what kind of person Joan might be when it came to men. I'd have wagered she was modest and shy, but I've learned that you can't guess how a woman will behave when it comes to lust. But what form did their meetings, their friendship, take? If the captain found out that one of his sailors was close to a convict woman, he'd surely be punished severely. And when did the two of them find the time to be together often enough for a declaration? Joan's with us in our living quarters on the lower deck. She sews with us and eats with us and sleeps beside us. Could she climb the companionway when the rest of us are asleep? During exercise, as we walk the deck during the hour set aside for this, who would notice if one of our number slipped away to . . . to where? Where to hide? As I think about it, I realize that if I'd made up my mind to disappear, I'd find somewhere: between huge coils of rope, behind large trunks and boxes stowed on deck. And I would find a moment here and another there, and soon I would find more . . .

"He's a good man," she adds. "He was kind to me from the beginning of our voyage. He makes me happy."

How has he made her happy? I wish I could ask but I've found that if you wait, and keep your lips sealed, someone who wants to confess will often spill out the whole story with no need for prompting.

"We've spoken often since then. I haven't been in any conversation with a man since my husband died. Years, it's been. I'm not accustomed to their ways, but he's made me . . ."

A silence falls between us. Joan is stitching at her patch, but she's frowning and her lips have tightened. She's trying to find a way to say what she wants to tell me. I've seen this look many times.

Women who were ashamed of what they'd done but longing to confess; women who wanted to talk about their child had told me of the better life their baby deserved, that he or she was worthy of special treatment. I wonder if I ought to say something and decide not to. It wouldn't do to appear too eager.

At last she says, "It started with talking. He seemed to want to know my thoughts. About ordinary things. No man's ever asked my opinion before about anything. My Jack was a good man, a kind man, as far as he understood kindness, but he never wanted to know my thoughts on any matter. He loved me, but maybe in the way you'd love a dog you were fond of, who could cook and clean for you. He spoke to give instructions or ask questions about the running of the household. Isaac . . . takes account of me."

I long to tell her what I've learned of men. Of how they want us chiefly to quench their lusts. Of how lucky and rare it is to find one who sees you as an equal. I say nothing. Around us, the others are chattering and working.

"I tried to keep it to talking but it soon . . ."

She falls silent. I say nothing but fix my eyes on the cloth I'm stitching: a red background with a pattern of dark blue squares. One stitch. Two stitches. Will Joan say more?

"He kissed my hand at first. As if I was a lady. I let him. That was how it began. I tried to see harm in it, but I grew fond and silly."

I nod. More stitches. In and out with the needle. Joan has slowed the rhythm of her sewing. I haven't. I am doggedly stitching in and out of the cloth, a trail of thread growing shorter by the minute. My needle will soon need threading again.

She sighs. "I can't help myself with him. It's like being drunk. Not in control of my senses. I don't know what to do now. After last night."

"What happened?" I say, hoping she'll go on, although I can guess.

Joan's face and neck are scarlet now. Her voice falls. She whispers a few words, and just at that moment, Tabitha says: "Oi, Susan, you clumsy baggage! Mind where you're putting your elbow!" Her brassy voice rings out, drowning whatever Joan's tried to say.

I catch the end of it. ". . . he kissed me. We were in the shelter of the boxes stowed on the afterdeck. It's so many years since anyone has kissed me in that way . . . I would wish him to kiss me again, on other occasions, but it's wrong and if we're caught, he'll be . . . punished dreadfully. And me? I don't know myself when I'm with him . . ."

I speak gently. "I'm sure you've nothing to be ashamed of, Joan."

"I didn't stop him."

Silence. I go on stitching and she speaks at last. "I let him put his hands on me and I should have stopped him. I'm not some young thing, but a grandmother. But it was good to be kissed. I liked it, and I like the way Isaac talks to me. I didn't want him to stop kissing me. I was happy." She takes her scissors out of her bundle and snips the thread. "I've not been with a man for so long. I'd forgotten. It was . . ." She cannot find words to describe it.

"I won't tell anyone," I whisper, while Joan is threading her needle.

Her eyes are shining. "He's fond of me, you know," she adds. "He told me so. No one has said such words to me in years."

"I'm sure he is," I say. I'm threading my own needle now.

"I could love such a man," she says wistfully.

"I wish you both well," I tell her. I mean it, though I fear they may be acting rashly. Many things could spoil what they've found together.

✦

When I was very young, after my parents died, and after the brother I thought would take care of me showed himself uncaring and turned me out of his house, I was taken up by a gentleman in his middle years, called Samuel Leigh. He found me alone and shivering with cold on a bench in the street and offered me shelter. I say I was young then, but not too young to know what he'd expect from me. I hadn't led a sheltered life. My parents tried to hide from me the worst things that went on in the streets around our small draper's shop, but I saw what I saw and my childhood companions talked constantly of this woman or that being "on the town," and every one of us knew what that meant.

In those days I had a certain look about me, though I may not have been beautiful. The girls and women I noticed back then, disappearing into dark alleys and coming back dishevelled and sometimes bruised, were not who I wanted to become.

"They're not all drunken sots and dirty with it," a woman called Margaret told me once. "If you catch a gentleman's fancy," she said, "why, you could be set up for life in a grand house." She laughed. "Anyone who'd feed me and clothe me and keep my feet out of the mud in fine shoes could do anything they wanted with me. Anything at all . . ."

Samuel *did* do anything he wanted with me. The house he lived in was far from fine, but it was respectable enough and there was food every day and best of all, I didn't have to deal with my hateful brother. Also I made sure that I was paid in coin for my pains.

"Why, you little minx," Samuel said to me the first time I asked him for money. We were together in his bed. "Don't you realize that I could throw you back into the streets you came from? Don't I feed you and give you shelter? You have an uncommon impudence to ask payment for something that you might do well to consider part of your duty . . ."

"But if you throw me out, there'd be no more treats on tap for you," I told him, as sweetly as you please. "Would there?" That settled it. I'd be paid for my work in his bed.

Well, women have been paid for such things since money and warm bodies have been in the world, but I learned soon enough that better lies brought better money. The more I praised and flattered Samuel, the more I pretended to be in awe of him and of his money, the more coins I could bury in my purse. So over and over again, I moved in certain ways and cried out loudly, while he was in his paroxysms, and this show I acted out every night gained me more pennies than I could ever have earned if I'd worked in a shop or as a servant.

I could have gone on like this for years. Twice, when I fell pregnant, he took me in his own carriage to a woman whose name I never learned, who, as he put it to me, "would return me to myself." The second time was the last, and I was never pregnant again. I think now, because I was so ill for such a long time after my body had rid itself of the small creature growing there, that there must have been something in the potions I'd been given to drink that made me ill forever. Some poison that made me barren and dry inside. I try not to dwell on this, for it's a sore place in my thoughts.

When I was well again, I went back to work, as I thought of it. I put up a good show for Samuel, but in time, he wanted more from me.

"Do this for me, dear Clara," he whispered, his breath, stinking with the fumes of wine he'd drunk, on my face, in a bed rumpled from what we'd been doing. "Let Mr. Carson have some of your attention. Only Mr. Carson, I promise. If you please him, he'll pay you handsomely. I've made it quite plain that you must be paid. I'm in his debt in several ways and he's often admired you . . . told me so. Please, dear Clara. I will give you a new dress if you agree . . ."

That was how it started. I was surprised at how hurt I was when Samuel asked me to do this. I didn't love him, nor he me, but we'd grown affectionate in some way, I thought, and I was grateful to him for his care of me. I'd thought he valued me, but he didn't. I was nothing but a doll, after all, to be used for pleasure. Mr. Carson, of the yellowing teeth and the hands that couldn't keep from hitting me, and the unspeakable things he made me do to his rank body . . . he was only the first. Samuel watched everything I did with other men, and seeing this made him grow hard. He hid behind a silk hanging at the head of the bed, and sometimes he couldn't contain himself and then he reached his climax with a loud groan and a series of disgusting panting sounds. After Mr. Carson, others appeared as the months went by: Mr. Black, Sir Stephen Flinting, Micah Garder and more. I noted their names and took what they gave me and put it away in my purse. This went on for some years. It wasn't me, there in my own skin while the sweating (I could hardly call some of them men. I thought of them as a kind of animal you'd never meet in any farmyard, a cross between a bull and a pig with a touch of serpent about them, too. . . .) *monsters* lying on top of me flapped and gasped and writhed and shouted out and blew blasts of sour horror into my face and spilled quantities of their slimy seed on my sheets, on me, on my skin, in my mouth till I gagged and spat. But I lied and went on lying, because to lie was not just to survive but to thrive.

When Samuel died, he left his property and possessions to his children, but he'd marked out a sum of money for me. I was described in his will as his housekeeper. Together with my own private earnings, the bequest was enough for me to buy my own small house at 57 Wellington Road, south of the river, near Putney, a house with two white lilac trees growing, one on either side of the small wooden gate. What has become of it now? Would Nora, my

maid, be living there? She'd known of my imprisonment, and I saw
her crying in court when I was sentenced, but I know nothing more
after that. What would she be thinking of my disappearance?
Would she ask after me? She wouldn't dare to do that, I think, for
fear of being turned out of the house. I don't think about her, because there is nothing I can do to help or harm her. I must forget
her, as I've tried to forget everything.

*Night sailing. The Rajah sets a course through small,
white-flecked waves, her prow breaking the water,
sending ripples in diagonal lines to each side of her hull.
Lantern light from small windows is faint, and the
pinpricks of light are swallowed by the
surrounding darkness.*

18

THEN

Cotton patch: mauve background, scattered with white flowers in an intricate, lace-like pattern

April 1841
HATTIE

"Pigs' trotters. In a lovely thick jelly," said Ann. "Oh, Lord, grant us the nourishment that comes from your bounty." Her dark hair was pulled back from her brow to reveal a plain face. She didn't often join in the conversation. The others poked at their squares of fabric with needles trailing cotton, and chatted, but today their breakfast porridge was horribly burned, food was much on everyone's mind, and work slowed as the women, even Ann, spoke of what they were missing. *Rajah* food was tasteless for the most part and endured rather than enjoyed.

"Plum pudding," said Elsie, joining in the litany of delicious things. Her companions knew she was a little slow, but she was a good worker. Her understanding was mostly in her fingers, with little enough finding its way to her brain. "I love that . . . with custard. Yellow, like the sun."

The others sighed. "I miss Christmas altogether," said Ruth. "I could do with Christmas dinner every night. With brandy on the pudding, mind."

"And set alight . . . bit of holly stuck on top! Berries and all," Beth said. "And a coin for the bairns to find—fat chance of finding anything in hardtack and ship's biscuits."

"There's rum, though," said Ann. Every ordinary utterance from her surprised her companions. They didn't trust her, for she was the first to tell Miss Hayter of something another had done of which she disapproved. A telltale, she'd have been called, if she was a child.

Phyllis said I borrowed her scissors and I didn't. It was Louisa and I told her so but she didn't believe me . . .

Dora took two of my squares for herself, just because she likes blue . . .

What Susan said about Ruth wasn't true. Ruth never ate her rations. It was Elsie. She's the greedy one . . .

"I'd give my teeth," said Tabitha, "for sugared almonds."

"You've done that, madam," said Phyllis, red with delight at her own wit. "Lost a good few already, I'd say."

Tabitha could be seen considering whether to rise to this bait or let it go. She looked around at the other women in the group, but they were giggling and clutching their sides, so she thought better of it. Not worth bothering with them, she decided. Their teeth were nothing to shout about, nothing to be proud of as far as she could see. Crooked and dirty, most of them, just like hers. Probably just as full of holes. Sugared almonds, though. Pale blue and white and pink and mauve . . . She'd happily give another tooth or two to be sucking one now.

"What about you, Marion?" Dora asked.

Marion looked up from her work. She was making tiny stitches along the edge of a mostly green square and seemed far away from them in contemplation of it. Miss Hayter had taught her how to lose herself in the colors of the fabrics, to keep tormenting thoughts far from her mind. She blinked. Her skin was pale, almost greenish, and she was trembling a little as she spoke. "I don't feel very hungry today," she said at last.

"You sickening for something?" Joan asked.

Marion shook her head. "An apple. A russet apple. I could eat a slice from one of those, I think."

Sobbing woke Hattie, who hadn't even realized she was asleep. The unusual motion of the ship, rocking and pitching on the water, was hard to get used to. At first it was a pastime for her and Bertie, practicing how to move on the decks, bending to keep their balance, but in the end, Hattie tired of it.

"I wish it would keep still, I do really," she said to her son, as they made ready for the night. They'd eaten a meager supper of tea, dried meat and some biscuits that were like breakable flat stones, and now it was time to lie down. The movement Hattie had felt through the soles of her feet while she was upright was now spreading through the wooden berth and the thin mattress, rocking her as if, she told herself, I was a baby in a cradle.

But now someone was shaking her shoulder. *I must be asleep* was her first thought and her second, *Is it Bertie?* Hattie sprang up and looked about her. Someone was beside her bunk, babbling so fast that Hattie could hardly take it in.

"Come, you must come. She's poorly. She's really poorly, Hattie. It's Marion . . . She's over there."

The speaker was Beth. She'd told Hattie she'd been at Newgate, but Hattie hadn't known her there. She couldn't have been more than twenty years old. From the sewing sessions, Hattie knew that

Beth was given to drama and exaggeration and there wasn't a situation that she didn't interpret as either a disaster or a miracle. "Hurry," Beth said now. "You must help her. She's bleeding really bad."

As they moved to one of the furthest corners of the living quarters, Hattie whispered, "Why me, Beth? What d'you think I can do if someone's bleeding? I'm not a doctor. Why d'you not go and find the surgeon? Or Miss Hayter."

"I daren't, Hattie," Beth said. She thinks I do dare, Hattie told herself, and she's right. The thought pleased her. "There she is, Hattie. She won't die, will she?"

Hattie knelt down next to Marion, who was biting on a rolled-up piece of cloth and twisting her body from side to side. There wasn't much light but she could see dark stains of blood on the blanket and mattress.

"Oh, Lord, Lord, what's to become of me?" Marion cried out.

"Shut yer mouth," said someone lying nearby. "Some folk trying to sleep, much good it'll do them."

"Shut yer own face, bitch," said Beth. "She's sick, can't you see? She's bleeding. What're you going to say if she dies?"

Hattie hushed Beth. "Stop your noise! D'you want Marion to hear that? How'd you think she'd feel if she heard such things?" She leaned closer to Marion. "Is it your monthlies, Marion?" She had no idea what to do. How could she stem the bleeding? No water anywhere. No cloths.

"What's happenin'?" A pale, straw-headed woman, who'd been snoring nearby, woke suddenly and sat bolt upright. Hattie recognized Annie Cooper, who was a kindhearted, not very intelligent woman of about thirty.

Beth, seizing on her new audience, whispered so loudly in her ear that Hattie could easily hear words like "blood," "agony" and "dy-

145

ing." Her fury at Beth was even stronger than her fears for Marion. "Shut your damned mouth. Just shut it. You're helping no one."

"But—"

"Shut it, I said." It was the voice Hattie used when she was scaring children out of their pretty clothes. She turned to Marion again as Beth subsided in a mess of gulped-back sobs.

"Is it your monthlies, Marion?" Hattie asked again.

Marion shook her head. "Not had them last three months," she said.

Hattie understood then. She took a corner of her nightgown and stroked Marion's brow, which was streaming with sweat. "Don't you know what that means? No monthlies?"

"Well, I was sick. I thought I was sickening with something or other. Could be sick from anything, couldn't you?"

"But, Marion, did you . . . have you . . . have you been with a man?"

Marion shook her head. "Can't remember the last time. Maybe in January. I don't remember rightly. Oh, it hurts so bad." She clutched Hattie's hand. "Help me, Hattie."

Hattie reckoned the time in her head. January was three months ago. Marion was pregnant, had been pregnant, but the baby would be no size at all, hardly even deserving to be called a baby just yet. She stood up. "I'm going to fetch Miss Hayter and Mr. Donovan. You're losing a baby, Marion. That's what's happening. Annie, see if you can find some water. Or some more cloths to soak up the blood. Beth, if you want to be more use than a straw barrow, hold Marion's hand and sing to her. Keep her as warm as you can."

She left before she could hear Marion's response. Other women sleeping nearby were waking, disturbed by the commotion. Some people were relieved when their bodies rid them of a child but others were sorely wounded. Hattie had no idea how Marion would be, but if the bleeding didn't stop, she'd die. Hattie knew this was possible in spite of what she'd told Beth. A picture of Marion's skinny body slipping over the *Rajah*'s rail into the endless dark water came into her mind. She pushed it away and climbed to the upper deck.

Once she was up there, she peered around in the half-light till she saw one of the men on watch. "Sir! Please, sir, help me."

"Sir, is it?" said the man, hurrying to where she stood clutching the rail. "Not been called that before. What's the matter with you, pretty maid?"

Oh, God, not here. Not now.

"Nothing's the matter with me, but you must tell me where Miss Hayter's cabin is. There's someone very sick below . . . one of the convicts."

"Right you are, then," said the man. "But while you wake the matron, I'm off to fetch Mr. Donovan. If there's someone sick, he's your man."

"Good," Hattie said. "Thank you."

"Follow me," said the sailor. He strode off along the deck, and Hattie almost ran along behind him.

He jerked a thumb at something that looked like a small hut built on the deck. "She's in there, the matron. I'll fetch Mr. Donovan down to the lower deck. Daresay we'll be there before you."

He disappeared and Hattie stepped over a low wooden barrier and found two doors facing one another. Which opened into Miss Hayter's room? The other might belong to an officer, or perhaps even the captain . . . No, he had his own quarters. Hattie knew that much. No good dithering, she told herself, and knocked firmly on one of the doors. No answer. She knocked again, harder this time. She also called, "Miss Hayter? Please, Miss Hayter, wake up!"

The door opened quite suddenly, just as Hattie was about to knock for the third time.

"Hattie!" cried Miss Hayter. "What's the matter? Is it Bertie? Are you ill?"

"No, Miss, not Bertie or me. It's Marion. She's—she's bleeding badly. I think she's losing a baby . . . I'm so sorry to wake you, Miss, really, only I didn't know what to do."

"We must fetch Mr. Donovan," said Miss Hayter.

"A sailor's gone to find him."

"Good. That was well done, Hattie. Wait here for one moment. I'll dress myself and come with you."

Miss Hayter looked different in her nightgown. With her hair down and a dainty pink knitted shawl round her shoulders, she seemed quite pretty. Hattie, standing by the door, could see a slice of Miss Hayter's cabin. A chest of drawers with a basin set into it, and a jug standing next to the basin. A lantern and matches. A small window. It was a grand thing to be able to look out, even if you saw nothing but sea and more sea. Before she was confined in the *Rajah*, Hattie had never realized how much she loved windows, how much she missed them. The ones on the lower deck were small and inadequate. She could see an embroidery frame leaning against a chair, with a canvas already in it, ready to be worked. A tapestry bag beside the frame had a few threads of silk poking out of it.

When Miss Hayter was ready, they hurried back to the convict quarters. Miss Hayter went first, with her lantern. Mr. Donovan was already there, with a lantern of his own.

"Good evening to you, Miss Hayter," he said, all good humor as if being woken from his sleep in the middle of the night wasn't the least bit of trouble to him. He'd been kneeling beside Marion's bunk and rose to his feet when he saw them approaching. "Or, rather, good morning, for I fear we're not far off the dawn, dark as it may seem to us." He chuckled. "That's what they say, don't they? That the darkest hour is before dawn."

"Is she . . . is the bleeding . . . ?" Miss Hayter's lips were pressed together and she was frowning but she spoke calmly to Mr. Donovan.

"I think I've managed to staunch the bleeding enough to move her to the hospital. I'll keep her there till she's more recovered. I'll give her something for the pain and to make her sleep. There's much to be cleared up here. I'll send a man down to fetch the bedding. The clothes can be washed, of course, but the mattress will have to go."

"I'll come with her," Miss Hayter said, and turned to Hattie. "She'll need help to walk." She knelt next to Mr. Donovan on the filthy floor and together they raised Marion to her feet. "Can you look to the cleaning, Hattie?"

Hattie would much rather have gone with Miss Hayter and Marion to the hospital than clear up bloodied sheets and tidy a place that she could not imagine being anything other than horrible. Many women were awake now, and coming closer to see what had happened.

"What's all that blood?" someone asked.

"None of your business," Beth said.

"Get back to your beds, you nosy vultures!" Hattie added. "None of you ever seen someone in pain before? Marion's lost a baby. Now clear off back to where you came from."

Somewhere in the darkness there would be—Hattie felt sick thinking about it—the remains, however tiny and however awash with his mother's blood, of a real person. Someone who might have given Marion as much joy as Bertie gave her. No point thinking like that, she chided herself. Get on with the work. Pretend it's just blood with nothing in it of a child. She looked for Beth and saw her sitting on the edge of her mattress with her head in her hands. The other women had returned to their own bunks.

"Help me with this, Beth." Hattie spoke as kindly as she could. "No good brooding about poor Marion. She'll be looked after."

"I didn't think of a baby," said Beth, getting to her feet. "That's bad. I feel sad for her."

"Perhaps it's for the best." Hattie remembered Miss Hayter's voice, when she read to them from the Bible, how strong it was. How the fine words had made her feel calmer, even though she found it hard to believe in God as completely as she should. She said to Beth, pretending to be as devout as Miss Hayter, "It was God's will, Beth. Marion will go to her new life now, without having to worry about caring for another person. She'll be free."

"That's not right. She wouldn't think like that. What mother thinks of her child as a burden? You don't, and don't pretend you do."

"We're not talking about Bertie. Or me. World's not like that. Don't you know about the women who stick knitting needles and worse into thousands of young girls to rid them of their babies? Or the ones who take away newborns and charge their mothers good money for dosing them with killing drugs or chucking them in the river? I thought everyone knew about things like that, once they were out of the nursery."

"Course I know." Beth sounded sulky. "Don't think Marion'll see it like that. That's all I'm saying."

As they spoke, they rolled items of clothing into a bundle for washing. Hattie hoped Beth wouldn't ask her what had become of the bloody stuff that at one time held the power to grow into a person. She'd lie. She'd say she didn't know, though it was probably there, under their hands, bound up in the sheet they were bundling to be rinsed clean in the stinging seawater that flowed past the hull of the ship. The mattress was black with blood and stank of rusty metal. Hattie hoped Mr. Donovan hadn't forgotten about the sailor he'd promised to send. She pictured him sliding the mattress over the rail and into the sea to float away, the water soaking the drying black stains, so that streams of red drifted into the water. She thought of fish, swimming through smoke-like trails of diluted blood, Marion's own and that of her growing child.

19
THEN

Cotton piece: white ground with large turquoise spots, ringed with black

April 1841
CLARA

Word has spread: Marion is in the hospital, having lost a baby. If you ask me, the loss was a blessing in disguise: the work I did in my past life has left me thinking that pregnancy is, more often than not, a nuisance—or even a curse. I listen to others talking.

"Mr. Donovan was so kind," Beth says. "And Hattie went to fetch Miss Hayter. Went right to her cabin. In the middle of the night. In the dark."

The young ones are sadder than the older women. Izzy Croft and Becky Finch, her constant companion, are sitting together, speaking about it to Rose Manners. Izzy's in the middle, with Rose on her right, Becky on her left, and Rose's hand goes often to Izzy's arm, then her shoulder. She touches Izzy very often and looks at her while she's speaking. Izzy pretends not to notice the attention but I see her eyes move and I see her smile, and she is falling for Rose. I know the signs. She lights up when Rose says anything, and then she's brushing some speck of dirt from Rose's shoulder while Rose preens and twists herself so that she can be closer to Izzy. I watch Becky especially, and she is suffering. Her face is pale and she speaks more to catch Izzy's attention than because she has anything to say.

"I feel sorry for poor Marion," she says quietly.

"She'll leave men alone from now on," Izzy says. "Learned her lesson." She giggles. "She'll have to console herself in other ways." Rose smiles and leans forward, touching Izzy on the wrist. She whispers something I can't hear, but Becky clearly does because she draws back as if someone has hit her, gets up and walks away. I watch her dragging her feet, her shoulders bent under a burden of misery I can almost see.

The Newgate Nannies have appeared and taken over the conversation.

"Didn't even know she was up the duff," says Selwood.

"She got off easily," Dwyer says. "I had it harder. Blessing to lose it before it's born—stops you having to get rid of it after."

Izzy laughs. "What would you know? No one'd want to touch you, would they? Not if they had eyes in their head."

Everyone falls silent. How did Izzy dare? Everyone knows Dwyer is not to be crossed. I can tell she's doing it to impress Rose, to seem brave.

Dwyer turns her wandering eye on Izzy, like a cat considering how exactly to rip off a mouse's head: slowly or quickly? Then she shivers and seems to think again.

"Wasn't always a fat old hag, was I? I was young and tasty once, too . . . I had a baby from my grandfather. That's right. Think of it. My own father's father. Baby almost killed me coming out. Ripped me apart and I couldn't even look at it when it was born. My ma and me took it to a woman in Seven Dials. Filthy house. Screaming babies in every room. My poor mother knew the woman and she took my baby without no money. Felt sorry for me, I daresay. Well, she wasn't the only one. Until you've got a child on your hands when you're not even eighteen and she's off someone who should've protected you from harm, not had his way with you, well, shut your mouth is what I say. You don't know *nothing*. Nothing."

Silence follows Dwyer's speech. No one can find words to say what they're feeling. One by one, we return to our bunks. From my mattress, I can see Rose and Izzy, heads together, moving toward the dark corner where Izzy's berth is. I look for Becky. She's lying down, her whole body curled away from the light. She's lost Izzy's affection, that much is clear. It crosses my mind to get up and speak to her, try to console her, but I don't move. I think of Dwyer, of all people, using the services of the kind of person I could understand. But women who sought my help came to a pretty, well-kept house. They were treated kindly. They left relieved. That was what I told myself—what I had to tell myself every time some poor creature crossed my threshold. Would these women forgive me if they knew how I'd earned my living? They might. Some might have sought my help. Every one of them is guilty of something but I am guilty of worse, and what I did . . . well, perhaps they would even forgive that terrible thing. Perhaps they would have acted as I did. As I had to act.

20
NOW

7 July 1841
Ninety-three days at sea

"Pass it to me," Emily said. "I'll do it. My eyes are better than yours."

"No, they're not," said Dora, a skinny woman with pinched lips and black hair. She was shy, but eager to please. "Just got a bit of something in one of mine, that's all it is. But here, take it. I don't mind if you fancy doing a bit of my work for me."

"She can't help herself, you know," Ruth said. "Always helpful, Emily is. Didn't you notice?"

"What's wrong with being helpful, tell me that!" An edge of temper had crept into Emily's voice and she was frowning. "Better than sitting there like a pile of potatoes and doing nothing for no one, like you."

"Don't hold with interfering in other folks' business, that's all." Ruth was a plain, heavy woman, with strong features and thick eyebrows. She didn't speak much, but when she did, it was often to complain about someone else or something that had struck her as unfair. Now she said, "Trouble with you, Emily, is that you're too busy currying favor with people. Want them to like you."

"Nothing wrong with that," said Emily. "It's good to be helpful."

"Well, it's not done you any harm. Miss Hayter favors you, and you're helping the children with lessons and that. Not bad for a scrawny baggage like you."

Emily leaned across and stuck the tip of her needle into Ruth's hand. Ruth sprang up, letting the work drop from her lap, and slapped her, her palm hardened and coarsened by scrubbing. She had worked for years as a laundress, and the blow left a red mark on Emily's cheek.

"Shut it, both of you," said Phyllis. She'd appointed herself a kind of under-matron, ever since the *Rajah* had left London, just because, in Izzy's words, she was big and bossy and far too interested in everyone else's private business. "Sit down, Ruth. Emily, what d'you think you're doing? As if we need any more trouble on this ship than we've got already. A stabbing ain't enough for you? That it?"

Ruth muttered something that sounded like "Sorry." She sat down again and turned her attention to her work.

"I forgive you, Ruth," said Emily, smiling. "I don't want trouble, not me."

"Then stop smirking all the time," Ruth said, but she said it under her breath and there were sailors laughing nearby, a breeze was blowing, and only Sarah heard it and she said nothing.

Emily took up her work again and began to stitch one side of a mostly gray square to one of deepest crimson. As she worked, tears gathered in her eyes, spilled over, and she brushed them away with the back of a hand. Lottie, who always noticed everything and was sitting directly opposite Emily, saw that. "Emily? Why're you crying?"

"Not crying."

"You are. Spit it out, woman. What's wrong with you now?"

"Thinking of my boy." Emily sniffed. "I've stopped crying."

"Miss him, is it?" Beth asked. "I'm like that. Can't get over missing some people. I spend hours crying. Every night since we left England I've wept into my pillow."

Ruth smiled and patted Beth's hand. "God, you're a lying little bitch, you are! You're snoring loud enough to wake the dead five seconds after you've lain down."

Everyone laughed at this, and even Beth had to smile. "That's as may be. I still spend hours shedding tears, I do."

"I don't," said Emily. "I'm not a crier. Not me. But today he would have been four years old. He died."

The women fell silent. You could make remarks about anything you liked, but a dead child trumped the lot. Silenced everyone. Nothing worse in the world than losing a child. Die a hundred times over, you would, before you chose that for yourself.

"What happened?" It was Marion who asked. She was not very sharp, but she was kind. Small spaces still frightened her, though she'd become sufficiently used to the lower deck not to shriek and moan every time she was shut up on it.

For a few moments, Emily sat stitching. Then she said, "Smallpox," and continued working without another word.

Marion broke the silence again. "Is that why you like teaching the children?"

Emily looked at her as though she'd taken leave of her senses. "The opposite," she said at last. "It's hard for me to be with the little

157

ones so often. It reminds me of my boy. Close to them. With some of them too attached to me, as well. But don't tell anyone I said that. It's probably best for me to be among children. The world's full of them and I have to live in the world, don't I?" She sighed. "I told Hattie about it, early on. But she promised not to tell . . . and she hasn't. Not a single one of you knew about him. Not till today."

Ann said softly, "Where d'you learn to read?"

"Wasn't always a thief," Emily answered. "We're country people. Farmers, my dad and granddad were. My ma wanted me to be a lady's maid. Sent me to the village school and I learned to read and the teacher liked me. I did well . . . I liked reading. I loved the stories in the Bible. Loved going to church and singing the hymns. Then I fell with child. My ma fought for me to stay at home, but my pa threw me out. Said I'd shamed the family. Choice was sell my body or steal things, so I stole. Good at it, too. Stole anything from stalls that I could and sold it. Then my boy fell sick and died and I lost all my reason. Not enough of a lunatic to be locked up, but the world became full of darkness and horror. Monsters everywhere. That was what I saw. Blood and fire."

"Oh, that's sad, Emily," said Marion, frowning in sympathy and reaching out to touch Emily's hand. "So sad . . ."

"Well, everyone's got something, haven't they? Something bad they're going away from."

"We have," said Joan. "We've all got something."

"Then I say put miserable things out of mind for a bit and think of good things, things we'll be seeing soon, when we land. England's gone, hasn't it? Bad memories should be left behind, too. We've got another chance now," Louisa said. "Truth is, I'm glad to be away from my family."

"Me, too," Alice agreed, and everyone laughed.

"Not my ma or sister," Izzy said, "but some are right horrible and I don't miss 'em a bit. Glad to be far away from the lot of them."

"We're better than family now," Phyllis said. "All of us doing this together." She stabbed her needle at the cloth. "Even though you try my patience often enough."

21

THEN

Cotton piece: Turkey red ground with yellow ferns widely spaced

May 1841
HATTIE

At first Hattie wondered what Emily was doing, peering behind a stack of wooden boxes, then retreating, peering over again—as though she'd lost something and was searching for it. From this distance it was hard to tell what was happening, but as she came closer she heard a child's voice and Bertie emerged, giggling.

He and the other children were sitting on some wooden crates and boxes that the sailors had found somewhere aboard the ship. They'd brought them into the living quarters and arranged them in a short row in a corner, from which the belongings of several women had been moved, amid much grumbling.

"Oh, shut your noise," another woman shouted. "You can push the boxes away when they're not using them. D'you fancy brats running about freely every minute of the day? Let them be schooled while there's someone crazed enough to try—give the rest of us some peace."

Some of the children on board the *Rajah* were too young for lessons. Those little ones clung to their mothers' skirts, and when their own flesh and blood grew weary of looking after them, plenty of others were willing to cradle and play with them, either because they were missing their own children, or because they'd never had care of an infant for more than a few hours and relished the novelty.

"I don't mind looking after them, doing lessons with them," said Emily, who had come up to stand next to Hattie, as the children took their places.

Emily seemed always to be at Hattie's side. Was she currying favor? She seemed to like Hattie more than any other woman. I was kind to her, Hattie thought. Or perhaps she thinks I'm grand in some way, and wants to be my friend for reasons that have more to do with bettering herself than any real liking.

"I saw at once," Emily said, "when I spotted you both coming aboard this ship, that the two of you were . . . superior to everyone else. Better. More respectable than most. Prettier than the rest of us. And your Bertie's a clever child. I could see you were . . ." She searched for the right words. "I could see you weren't brought low by being among convicts. By being labeled a criminal."

"Emily," said Hattie, "you're very kind to speak so, but I must correct you. I *am* a criminal. Unlike many here, I don't protest my innocence. I'm guilty of the things I was charged with and won't deny it. And thank you for what you say about Bertie."

Hattie wouldn't have confessed it to anyone, but part of the pride she took in Bertie was pride in herself. Her own mother had taught her to read and write, and she was determined that Bertie would have all the advantages she could possibly give him. The Whitings, when she went to work for them, were startled by her proficiency and Hattie felt sure that her education had helped her in life almost as much as her physical charms. She'd always been good at copying the manners of her betters, and the Whitings set a good example in such things. Bertie, she'd been determined from the day he was born, would have every advantage she could give him. The boy knew his numbers and letters, and Hattie had helped him. Looking at his companions fidgeting on the upturned boxes, she felt sure that Emily would find him among the best and most obedient of her pupils.

When she'd left the Whiting house, pregnant and in disgrace, she'd found a room in a huddle of mean dwellings. She had said, to anyone who asked, that she was a widow. There was no one near her who could prove she wasn't and she was determined that Bertie would never be known as a bastard. She bought herself a cheap wedding ring and told the story of her poor husband's demise so skillfully and dramatically—he had been ill with a fever that would not abate, in spite of her careful nursing—with so much sighing and looking Heavenwards that no one who saw her felt anything but pity for the pretty redhead with the creamy skin and her even prettier baby.

Hattie had realized long before Bertie was born that men would come to her assistance. They couldn't help it. She'd seen the effect her bosom—often displayed to show promise of better things to come—had on even the most level-headed of them. Patrick Sheenan was far from level-headed. Hattie had agreed to accept his offer so that she might move from the hovel in which she was living, but soon regretted it. She might have been willing to put up with his boorishness, drunkenness and even betrayal, but not his unkindness to Bertie. At first, it was only remarks. Patrick called him names like "brat" and "worm," but one night he told Hattie that Bertie should be sent away.

"Where would he go?" Hattie was aghast. She would have

picked Bertie up and fled the house then and there, except that she was almost naked and the night outside was freezing and wet.

"To my mother's house, in Suffolk."

There were no words Hattie could find to express what she felt. It was as though a huge stone had been placed on her heart, to weigh it down and hurt it. At last she said, "He's never met your mother. *I've* never met your mother."

"She's a bit of a hag, to be honest," said Patrick, "but kind at bottom. And a very good cook."

He fell asleep then and was soon snoring. He had, Hattie knew, drunk enough beer to lay him out till late the next day. She stared into the dark, wide awake and planning. Before dawn, she rose from the bed, dressed quickly, picked Bertie up, swaddled in his bedclothes, and bundled him under her arm as she let herself silently out of the house. He was grizzling a little but that was one noise she knew would not trouble Patrick or wake him. He was deaf to any sound that came from a child. Once she was out of the house with Bertie, she fled, as quickly as she could.

Before she'd left the bedroom, she'd had the presence of mind to empty Patrick's pockets of every coin that was stuffed into them. It wasn't much, but it was enough to find a room in another part of London. Patrick won't bother to look for us, she told herself. He's too lazy. He'll find another woman soon enough. And if he does come after me, I'm ready for him. She'd used part of her stolen money to buy a small, sharp knife and knew with some certainty that she'd be quite capable of using it in defense of her precious child.

Now, not wanting Bertie to be distracted by her attention, Hattie sat down, took out her knitting and began to work on a sock, pretending she was not listening to what Emily was saying. She felt flattered to be so admired by the woman, but it was tiring. There's no real harm in her, she thought, and I shouldn't be so uncharitable.

Emily was telling the children the story of Noah's ark. "And the waters rose and Noah called the animals, every one, and they came and lined up on the shore and went into the ark, two by two. Elephants and lions and tigers and dogs and cats and horses and chickens and every single other creature you can think of . . ."

"Flies, Miss," said one child.

"Fleas," said another.

"Rats," said Bertie, and Emily held up her hand for silence.

"Yes indeed, all of those. And the animals lived on the lower decks."

"Like us!" Bertie cried.

Emily smiled. "Very like us, Bertie. When everyone was safely aboard, the Flood came . . ."

Hattie stifled a yawn. It was muggy on the lower deck, and last night she'd hardly slept. She allowed herself to drowse and the needles fell from her hands. She woke only when Bertie shook her arm.

"Wake up, Mama," he said. "I've learned a new story. About a man called Noah. And Emily can cluck just like a chicken. They had chickens on the ark, you know. Emily, show her!"

Emily was standing behind Bertie with a hand on his shoulder. "Another time, Bertie. Another time."

Bertie wandered away, and Emily sat down beside Hattie.

"He's a very sharp little boy," she said. "Perhaps you've taught him a lot yourself."

"I've tried. I learned my letters from my ma when I was a very small girl and, more than anything, I want Bertie to read and learn, and be"—she hesitated—"better than me. I want him to do well."

"He will, I'm certain." She leaned forward and touched Hattie's hair. "He's fortunate in his mama. Such hair!"

When she was a girl, Hattie sometimes wondered why people exclaimed over her hair and pronounced her pretty. Others shunned her on account of it, calling her a "witch's brat" and worse. By the time she was twelve, she was used to the remarks that came her way, whether unkind or admiring. Now she said to Emily, "When I was a girl I longed for golden hair. Kitty would have grown up to be fair, I'm sure . . ."

"Kitty?" Emily asked quietly, sitting down beside her, ready to listen.

As she answered, Hattie reflected that it was years since she'd spoken of her. "My sister, much younger. Ma called her 'a mistake' and I cried when I heard her say that. How could such a pretty baby be a mistake?"

"Many of us are. I was . . . and my mother never let me forget it. Never loved me properly. I think many mothers are less loving than they might be. That's what I've learned." Emily was frowning. "They don't realize what they have. Also, for how short a time. Children leave you."

Hattie nodded. "They do. You know it, more than most. Ma couldn't care for Kitty. There were so many of us . . . four children and my father good for nothing but drinking money away . . . Oh, I suppose she acted for the best but I couldn't bear it. Saying good-bye to Kitty."

Emily turned a little toward Hattie. "Good-bye?"

"We gave her away."

"To a relation?"

"No . . . not a relation. A woman south of the river."

"Who was she?"

Hattie shook her head. "I don't know. A woman who helped anyone in trouble. Ma said Kitty'd be well taken care of. We were told she'd be given to a lady who couldn't have children of her own. Grow up to be rich and well dressed, sent to school and fed. All the things Ma feared she'd not be able to give her . . . She told me on the way home. 'It's a chance for Kitty, don't you see? To be something. Something better.' I didn't understand. I cried every night for a month, but in the end, you have to stop, for it's doing no good. But I don't forget her."

In sympathy, Emily put a hand on Hattie's arm. "I'll ask God to look after her, your sister."

"That's kind of you." Hattie was trying to smile, though this talk of Kitty had opened a wound in her heart: a wound that Bertie's presence eased a little. Since his birth, something like a scab had grown over the place where memories of Kitty used to be. Hattie could go for days without feeling sad, but when she began to re-member, the pain was as fresh as if her little sister had been given away yesterday.

They'd gone to the house in the rain. The parlor there was much grander than Hattie was used to. A big oil lamp with flower pat-terns etched on the glass that surrounded the flame stood on a table next to a sofa covered with dark green plush. The woman was dressed in a day gown with lace at the collar and cuffs. She wore an elaborately patterned Indian silk shawl that shone where the light caught it. The curtains were drawn . . . It must have been afternoon. November—Hattie remembered treading on golden leaves on the way home. Ma had been silent as they strode away through the dark, every lamp in the street lit, but Hattie could tell that each step was hard for her. She'd moved stiffly and kept her eyes fixed on the ground in front of her. She hadn't said a word to Hattie, not for more than an hour. But Kitty hadn't seemed to mind being handed over to a stranger. She'd rested in the woman's arms and smiled up at her.

"Such a bonny baby," the woman said. Hattie never did catch her name, or maybe it wasn't spoken. "You mustn't worry in the least. I will find her the perfect home. I know of several ladies who'd be only too happy to take her. She's delightful." The woman seemed kind and, for a few moments, Hattie was almost comforted. She had fine dark eyes, and her hair was carefully dressed, with curls falling over her left shoulder from a lace cap. She brushed them away from time to time with her left hand in a gesture that seemed to Hattie the height of elegance.

Kitty, Kittycat, Kitty, Kittycat . . . Hattie repeated in her head, over and over, as she walked. Her mother couldn't speak aloud and neither could Hattie. If the words were unspoken, maybe the sadness would disappear after a while.

When they reached home, Ma went immediately to look after the others. Food for everyone had to be prepared and put on the table. The boys never asked about the baby. Truly, they seemed not to see her while she was in the house, so her absence would not be noted. Pa took a bite from the hard end of a loaf, and said only, "Done, is it?"

"Yes," said Ma, and that was an end of it.

No one mentioned Kitty in the house until, just before Christmas, Ma fell ill with a fever and spoke of Kitty often in her delirium, begging Hattie to find her. She promised she would. What else was there to say? Maybe, she thought, the lie would make Ma feel a little better, but it didn't. She died on Christmas Eve. Ever since, Hattie had detested everything about the festive season.

"I pray for her, too," she said to Emily. "And for my mother, who lasted only weeks after she lost her." She shook her head. "I was soon out of the house, working for a family called the Whitings."

She turned to Emily and smiled. "Then I had Bertie, and now I have someone to love properly as I loved Kitty once. No good, I think, comes from looking back."

"That's true. We must always look forward." Emily rose from the bench. "We'll be sewing again soon. I'm happy we've both been chosen for the patchwork, aren't you?"

Hattie hadn't given any thought to this but Emily seemed so eager—like a rather ragged dog asking for a pat on the head—that she said, "Yes, indeed."

Once she was alone again, Hattie told herself that Emily was being friendly toward her and taught the children well, so it was unkind and uncharitable to think of her as ragged, with untidy hair, some markings from the pox and a smile that revealed uneven teeth. No one could help looking as they did and it was wicked to judge people by their appearance. The Newgate Nannies put it about, for instance, that Emily was sweet on a young sailor called William, who worked in the galley and didn't look old enough to be away at sea.

Dwyer had chuckled. "I'm told he peels potatoes and thinks of her."

"Maybe," said Selwood, "he'll carve her initials on the mast with his knife. Same knife he uses on the potatoes." The Newgate Nannies had laughed at that.

Beauty, thought Hattie, must truly be in the eye of the beholder, or half the human race would be quite alone forever. Very few people are lovely.

22
NOW

7 July 1841
Ninety-three days at sea
KEZIA

"Come in, please," Kezia said, holding the door open, and Emily Paxton stepped into the captain's cabin. She looked terrified, for no good reason that Kezia could think of. Of course, a certain nervousness before the inquiry panel was understandable, but Emily was very pale and biting her lips. She was someone whose cast of features fell naturally into a rather cowed and sullen attitude, while her extreme thinness and the nervous twisting of her hands didn't help her to appear innocent. Still, Kezia knew that she was, of all the women, friendliest and closest to Hattie and the one who, everyone agreed, was furthest from where Hattie had lain on the deck.

"Good afternoon, Emily," said Kezia. Mr. Davies was writing Emily's name. Charles and Mr. Donovan had indicated that Kezia should talk to her because she looked so frightened. "Can you tell us why you did not run toward Hattie when she fell?"

"I was too far away," Emily answered. "I was nearly at the entrance to our quarters. I turned to go back but the others were already shouting at me to fetch Bertie."

She paused and looked at Kezia. "I would have gone to Hattie . . . I couldn't bear to see her lying there . . ." She wiped away a tear with her sleeve. "I love Hattie, Miss Hayter. She's my closest friend on this ship."

"Thank you, Emily," said Mr. Davies, looking up from his writing. "May I ask who called to you to fetch Bertie?"

Emily thought about this for a moment. "I think Sarah was the first. She said, 'Bertie—go and fetch him. She wants Bertie. Quickly, Emily.' Then Marion called, 'She's crying for Bertie. Get him, Emily!' So I went. As fast as I could. I ran down there. I did."

"And you fetched Bertie?" That was Charles.

Emily nodded. Mr. Davies put down his pen in a way that made it obvious he was impatient and considered the question ridiculous. Kezia could somewhat understand it. No one had uttered a single word that indicated one of the others was lying. We are, Kezia thought, being thorough and careful. So far, the only doubt was about Hattie's actual words. Was it possible that she really did say *Not Freddie* rather than *Not ready*? She must have known she was in danger of dying and was clinging to her life. Did it matter in any case? Kezia felt increasingly baffled. Maybe someone had been hiding, waiting to attack poor Hattie, someone no one had considered till now. And I'm to blame. May God forgive me.

23

THEN

*Cotton piece: geometric groups of four squares in dark blue and red on
a drab ground, each set of four squares arranged to form another square*

April 1841
KEZIA

All afternoon Kezia had sat with her needlewomen, watching them
piecing together triangles of cloth. She listened to their chatter.
Beth was talking about her sister, who'd gone to work for a milliner
in Edinburgh and found the weather very chilly. Elsie was having
difficulty in keeping her stitches small enough and Kezia had
helped her to achieve a slightly improved effect.

They're becoming a group, she thought, whatever their differences. And there *were* differences. Some of the women, happy to
be doing something useful, enjoyed talking to their companions.
Phyllis, Beth, Rose, Hattie, Dora: they were the talkers. Izzy and
Rose seemed to be friendlier than usual. Izzy looked at Rose constantly, and it was true that Rose was certainly the prettiest of the
women. Beth made a scene of the most trivial pronouncement.
Rose could say nothing without taking the Lord's name in vain or

cursing in a way that wouldn't have disgraced a sailor. Phyllis liked others to follow her suggestions. She had her own way of doing things and tried to impose it; some heeded her, others didn't.

"I think we can finish now, everyone," she said. "Let us put our work away and those who know it can join me in the hymn."

Several women were now adding their voices to hers, she noticed, when they bent to pack away their work. Then they stood, with their hands folded over their stomachs and their eyes closed, in imitation of Kezia. She said the prayer she sometimes added at the end of a day's work: "Lord, we thank you for guiding us in our labors today and pray that you will guard us through the night so that we may continue with it tomorrow. In the name of the Father, the Son and the Holy Ghost, amen."

Once the wavering chorus of amens was over, Kezia watched them returning to their berths and felt a pang to think of them lying in the near-darkness of the lower deck, while she went to her tidy little cell of a cabin. Whatever efforts the sailors and the women made to keep it clean, the place was still a foul-smelling large box and there was little to be done about it. Prison cells were not fragrant, but this was much worse. Perhaps we've all grown used to it, she thought.

Kezia was making her way along the deck when the captain appeared, walking toward her. "Miss Hayter," he said, bowing.

For a few moments, they stood in silence. Kezia searched her mind for a topic of conversation. She was about to ask him to identify a seabird that had flown over them, when he said, "D'you think that the prisoners in your care are by nature bad, or that their circumstances have led them to crime?"

Kezia faced him. This was a subject she'd often discussed, and it was close to her heart. "God says we will be forgiven our sins if we repent sincerely. If He can forgive the most terrible sins, then I'm sure we can try to understand lesser crimes. Most of the women below would have been driven to crime by impoverishment, in money and in education. One generation of the poor passes its troubles to the next. A woman steals to feed her children, and if she's caught, she may be transported. That leaves the children to fend for themselves or be taken into the care of the parish, so they grow up poor, with no instruction to better them." Kezia stopped. She felt that perhaps she had spoken too frankly.

She was on the point of apologizing when the captain said, "That's true. I've often noticed it. But do you not think that some people, women as well as men, are born more malevolent than their fellows?"

"There is the devil to be reckoned with," Kezia said somberly. "If I believe in good, I must also believe in evil, but I have seldom seen it in my fellow humans. I've seen stupidity, poverty, madness, malice and the terrible effects of jealousy, but pure evil? I haven't seen that."

"What about murder? Is that not evil? In all circumstances?" They were leaning over the ship's rail.

Kezia paused. "No," she said at last. "I can think of circumstances in which killing a person might be justified."

"Really? You surprise me, Miss Hayter."

"I might be kept a prisoner by my husband. I might kill him to escape his treatment of me. No one can tell how they'd behave," Kezia answered. "It's hard to imagine the situation, but I've seen it. I've spoken to women who didn't have a free moment in their lives. Whose every breath was drawn in fear of the consequences."

"I am sure you're right, Miss Hayter. I bow to your knowledge of these women."

A gust of wind buffeted them. Kezia said, "The weather will be so much warmer soon."

"It will. You and your sewing companions will be as brown as nuts if you work out here on deck. The sunlight can be very strong."

Kezia frowned. "What's to be done, though? To sit in the convict quarters all day long would be . . . very uncomfortable. And it's much easier, too, to sew in good light."

"I can have the crew rig up an awning for you, to provide some shade." He smiled at Kezia. "A spare sail or a sheet of canvas. I'll attend to the matter at once."

"That would be very kind," she said, and smiled in return.

He made no move to leave her and instead said, "I would advise you to keep to the shade as much as possible. The sun can be blistering in this part of the world."

"I will," Kezia said. "Thank you. And I shall warn my women."

"It would be a matter of deep regret to me if a face I so admire were as sunburned as any sailor's by our journey's end." He bowed stiffly and strode away.

"Thank you," said Kezia. He had said he admired her face. Had he? Could she be sure that that was what she'd heard? Perhaps she'd misunderstood. No one had ever said such a thing to her before. She went over his words and still wondered if she had been mistaken.

24
THEN

Cotton piece: white ground with sprays of black and white leaves widely spaced on the cloth. Each leaf bearing a pattern designed to make it appear like lace

April 1841
CLARA

I remember Hattie Matthews. I remember her from long ago. I didn't recognize the name, at first. "Harriet Matthews" meant nothing to me. Even when she came forward, that first day, to join those of us who'd been chosen, I didn't know her. For weeks I've sat near her without a thought, but today when I heard her story, what she said, and looked at that red hair, gathered at the nape of her neck and curling down to her shoulders, a memory returned to me. I know who she is now and, even worse, *how* we met. My heart's almost stopped beating from the shock. What if she recognizes me? What if she says, out loud for all to hear: *I know her. I know what she did.*

I can feel myself trembling. I bite my lip hard to bring my feelings under control. I cannot flee. Where to go on a ship in the middle of the ocean? Should I turn to Miss Hayter and beg her to let me be excused from the small group of helpers? I worry about drawing attention—I have to pass unnoticed. I force myself to stay calm. The meeting between us lasted less than an hour and was many years ago. Maybe it's a different Hattie Matthews. But that hair! I'm in no doubt. Stop worrying, I tell myself. I'm changed. *You're not what you were then. She won't know you. She'll have forgotten. She was no more than a young child . . . And, look, she hasn't screamed out in horror yet, has she?* But I can't stop fretting. We've arranged ourselves into smaller groups and Hattie's not one of my nearest companions. I must keep my distance, I tell myself. Keep my face turned away. I glance across at her. She's talking to Emily and Lottie. They're laughing. Even when they're in a dreadful situation the young can find something to cheer them, if they have their friends around them.

As I sew, with my eyes turned down to my work, I repeat to myself that, with every day that passes, there's less danger. We are putting a greater distance between ourselves and England, which has to be an advantage to me. I'll deal with Hattie if I have to. I've dealt with difficult things before and this'll be the same. She may never notice me.

Sarah asks to borrow Marion's scissors. "Mine are below," she says, and Marion passes her the scissors to cut a stray thread. "Thank you," Sarah says, and Marion dips her head, making no answer. She is low in spirits since her miscarriage.

I distract myself by talking to Joan, who sits beside me.

"You're quiet, Joan," I say. "Is anything the matter?"

She shakes her head. "I can't speak of it," she says. I know that if I say nothing, the words will come.

She goes on sewing for a few more moments, then puts her work down on her lap and hides her face in her hands. When she looks up at last, her face is pale.

"I believe him when he speaks," she says, and I know she means Isaac. "He says it makes no difference and that's the worst of all. It makes a world of difference to me."

"What do you mean?" I ask her.

"He's a married man," she whispers, and uttering the words undoes her. Her hand forms a fist, which she drives into her mouth to stifle the sound between a shriek and a groan that has risen to her lips.

"Joan," Miss Hayter says, for she has noticed her distress. "Would you like to withdraw for a while?"

"I'll go with her," I say, glad of the chance to leave the others.

"Come and find me, please, if Joan needs me," says Miss Hayter, and I lead Joan away, like a small child. I know the others will be staring after us.

Joan and I go to stand at the stern, looking over the rail at the ocean disappearing behind us. The wake is like lines of lace on a darker fabric.

"Tell me about Isaac," I say. "I won't speak of it to anyone else."

"Yes, I know that. You're very careful with what you say, but still . . . I feel . . . Well, there was hope for a short while and now there's none. He's married. He's a wife in Portsmouth. And three children from her."

Because I don't know how to answer, I put my arm around her. The only thing that surprises me about this news is that Joan hadn't taken it into account from the beginning. It stood to reason that a man like Isaac Margrove wouldn't have reached the age he is without entering into some sort of bond with a woman.

"Isaac is very well set up," I tell her. "I suppose it's to be expected."

"I don't expect lies," she says, a touch of vigor entering her voice. "I don't expect to be led down a garden path as if I was a silly young thing, not a grandmother."

"Did Isaac lie to you? Tell you at any time he wasn't married?"

"No, but . . ."

"But what?"

"He made me believe he loved me."

I sigh. "Did he say it? Did he speak of the future?"

"No," she admits.

I turn her to face me. "Joan, if he told you he is married, maybe it's because he is growing more and more fond of you. Do you see? He *could* have lied. He could have *deceived* you, but he didn't. Surely it's best always to know the truth."

"I would never have let him kiss me and lead me on, letting me think he loved me, if I'd known," Joan whispers. "I'd not have spent so much time with him, telling him things I've not told anyone else."

I say nothing. Can Joan not see that, out of her own mouth, she'd given Isaac good reason to hide the truth about his wife in Portsmouth? He'd judged her very well. Anyone could see that Joan's morals were far stricter than those of most aboard a convict ship. And perhaps it's possible that Isaac likes her more than he thought he would at first and acted accordingly. He might have strung her along till we reached Van Diemen's Land.

"I'll put all thoughts of him behind me," she says at last. "He stopped me thinking about the rest, my children and grand-children . . . That's the truth of it." She turns to me. "Do you believe me? When I speak?"

"I do," I say. "You're not a liar and, believe me, I've dealt with liars my whole life. I recognize a lie better than most."

"I did it for her, you see. My daughter, Meg. They caught her with stolen things. Her husband, a brute called Peter, he was the real receiver, but he would've lost what work he had at the butcher's, and then what would they have lived on? Meg takes in washing and that's the best she can do with the children so small. She didn't want to let me do it, cried and tore her hair and grew sick, but still I couldn't let her be sent to jail or away on a ship like this, so I said I'd do away with myself if she didn't let me take the blame. Poor Meg, what could she do? I told her, 'You can't die. You can't go to prison. You have to be here for the children.' What I didn't tell her was that she had to protect them from their horrible father but I think she knew my mind. Even shared my opinion. She kept quiet and I confessed, and they took me in front of the judge and here I am."

What to say? "You *will* go back, you know. To England. After you've served your sentence."

"I'll be old. I'm already old. I feel so ill . . . so muddled. I can't govern my thoughts, and they run all over my head and trouble me."

I look at Joan. Her color's high and, though it's true that the weather is growing warmer, she oughtn't to be quite so flushed. I put out my hand and touch her brow. It's burning hot.

"Joan," I say, "you must go to Mr. Donovan and tell him you're sick."

"But I'm one of his helpers," Joan says. "I have to be there for others."

"You can't help in this state. If you don't go and find him, I'll go myself."

As I speak, Joan slumps down to the deck and sits there, her head hanging. "Maybe," she says, "if I could lie down for a while, I'll be better soon. And a cool drink."

"Sit here," I tell her. "I shall fetch Miss Hayter and Mr. Donovan."

I go quickly to where the others are still at work on the sewing, relieved that Hattie has her back turned to me. "It's Joan," I say. "She's not herself. I think she has a fever." Was it a fever? Or could someone have given her a drug, such as the one I'd used to silence the real Sarah Goodbourne? Could one of the sailors . . . No, I told myself. She's simply ill. Perhaps it's something she ate.

Miss Hayter springs to her feet. "Rose," she says, "go and find Mr. Donovan." She has chosen her messenger wisely. Rose is the youngest of us and the prettiest. Mr. Donovan will be happier with bad news delivered by her than any of the rest of us. I find myself filled with apprehension. What if Joan is mortally sick? She has become the nearest thing I've had to a friend for many years and I'm frightened at even the slightest prospect of losing her.

25

THEN

Cotton piece: dark ground, patterned with blue-green flowers resembling chrysanthemums

April 1841
HATTIE

"Bertie? Where d'you think you're going? Come here this minute. Come here . . . Are you listening to me?"

Bertie was making his way across the convict quarters, toward the companionway. Hattie stumbled out of her berth and went after him as quickly as she could.

"What d'you think you're doing? Come back here. Now." She spoke sharply.

"I want to go out there. To see the storm."

"Wait!" Hattie said, and almost fell over as the whole ship seemed suddenly to rear out of the water and lurch to the left before crashing down again. Everyone screamed in unison. The ship was rolling so far from side to side that clothes, slop buckets, bundles of belongings and even benches were sent sliding toward one side of the space, then the other. From time to time there came the sickening lifting of the whole wooden frame of the *Rajah*, up and up until it seemed that the ship might be taking flight.

"What's happening?" Phyllis screamed. She'd been deeply asleep and sat up in a rush only to see bodies, possessions and furniture being tossed all over the living quarters.

"Don't be so stupid," said Tabitha. "It's a storm coming, you silly baggage."

Hattie pulled on her skirt with trembling hands and wrapped her shawl around her. To Bertie, she said, "Why'd you want to see the storm?"

"Don't like it here. Everyone's screaming. Smells, too."

Hattie looked down to where a slop bucket had turned over, spilling its contents on the planks. Every timber was creaking and groaning. No one was going to sleep while the storm was raging. And how long would that be? Bertie was right. The deck might be better. Hattie wanted it, too—to be anywhere but here. They would be tossed about and perhaps someone might see them and stop them, but she couldn't bear the prospect of staying in the convict quarters. The deck had to be better than that. The noise of women wailing was so great that she had to lean down to speak directly into Bertie's ear. "I'll take you out there. But you're not to go anywhere near the rail and if you don't hold on to me every second, you'll feel the back of my hand. Every second, mind. Promise?"

Bertie nodded. Hattie pushed against the door with all her might until at last it yielded and they came out onto the deck, then climbed the steps of the companionway. On the upper deck, they struggled to stay upright as the wind pressed them against a wooden partition.

Hattie clung to Bertie's hand as if her life and his depended on it. Perhaps it was wrong of me to leave shelter, she thought. How can we be so wet already? Where can we hide from the rain out here? Bertie's hand was slippery. She put one foot in front of the other, and for every small progress she made, the wind drove her back to where she'd come from. Around her, the air and wind and rain were like a black whirlpool, and in the whirlpool, men were sliding and shouting orders at one another, dealing with flapping canvas and tying up sails. No one was looking in her direction. The captain would be in the wheelhouse, guiding the ship.

Hattie glanced down at Bertie and saw that he was gawping at the storm, his mouth open and his whole face awestruck. She followed his gaze and watched the water coming nearer and nearer as the *Rajah* slid onto her port side and the rail seemed only inches from the waves. She pulled Bertie closer to her with one hand and, with the other, clung with every bit of her strength to a rope tied to the partition.

One of the crew, someone she'd never seen before, appeared beside her, shouting into her ear. "You can't be here, Miss," he said. "We're battening down the hatches. No one allowed on deck. How'd you get out?" He picked Bertie up and the child clasped him round the neck, both hands tight. The man pried Hattie's hand off the rope and pulled her along the deck to a small space out of the worst of the storm. He shouted, over the noise of the waves: "Stay here for now. Don't you move." He took Bertie off his back and handed him to Hattie, who pulled him close and pushed his wet hair off his forehead.

As the ship plunged into mountains of water, over and over again, then started the long climb up and up, Hattie's eyes closed. How long had they been shut when the voices woke her? The worst of the tempest had passed. The *Rajah* had returned to her normal rhythm, back and forth on a much gentler swell. The rain had stopped, though the deck was still wet and shining in the first light visible just above the horizon to the east. Someone was speaking just behind her, and Hattie froze. Who else had come up on deck? Had they seen her? It wouldn't matter if they had. She'd not done anything wrong, not really, and though it was understood that the women kept to their quarters after dark, the captain hadn't given an order that Hattie had heard. She leaned close with her ear almost against the wood of the crates, trying to overhear the conversation. Anyone would, she told herself. It's only natural to want to know.

"I can't tell her. Not yet," said a voice, speaking quietly.

"You must. I'm not having her go anywhere near you. Not ever again."

Hattie recognized Rose's voice. Who was she with? Who was the other person not wanting to tell? Tell what? At that moment, two women walked round to her side of the crates, but they were so absorbed in one another that they didn't see Hattie and Bertie in their dark clothes against the dark wood. Once they'd passed her, Hattie leaned forward to look after them. They stood at the head of the companionway, with their arms around one another. They were kissing, not in the friendly way that two women might kiss goodbye, but lost in one another. Hattie understood then that Becky Finch was the person who had to be told, the person whose happiness Rose Manners had ended during the storm. Izzy and Rose were lovers now. That much was as clear as the daylight spreading across the pale sky.

She was absorbing this new knowledge when she became aware of someone behind her and turned swiftly, still holding Bertie in her arms. She saw no one, but someone was looking at her. She'd felt the cold crawling of her flesh, the discomfort in her bones that you only feel when eyes are upon you. She'd have sworn to that.

184

Hattie peered into the gloom and wondered if she should search more carefully behind bulkheads, crates and coils of rope lying on the deck, but she didn't dare to do that for fear of what she might find. She hugged Bertie even more tightly and went down into the stench of the lower deck.

26
NOW

✦

8 July 1841
Ninety-four days at sea

Because the women were so worried about Hattie, because they wanted more than anything to know what was happening, both in the inquiry and in the hospital, where Hattie lay, they were often distracted, not attending to their stitching with much concentration. It was fortunate that the work was almost done. Some had stopped stitching entirely and were stroking the work in front of them, admiring it.

Lottie was supervising them today but she wasn't as strict as Miss Hayter. She said, "It's a properly pretty bit of stuff we've made here, and no mistake, but no excuse not to be working." But Joan was with them now, not tending Hattie, so their attention wandered from the work, and the questions she faced were endless.

"Does Bertie speak to her?" Alice wanted to know. "Can she hear him?"

Joan shook her head. "I think she hears nothing. She says a word from time to time but no one's made sense of them."

"Is he sad? He must be."

"I try to be cheerful for him and explain that she has to sleep a great deal if she's to be well again," said Joan. "Sometimes he seems to understand, but at others he's still crying when he leaves his mother. It's dreadful. Horrible."

"He's bearing up," Emily said. "I haven't made him come to his lessons with the others but he seems to want to be with them. It cheers him, I suppose, to see them playing. And I try to be as kind to him as I can. It won't help him to brood over his mother."

"What did they say to you, Tabitha?" Ruth asked.

"Same as they did to Marion. Wanted to know what went on. What I saw. What I heard. And what Hattie said to us. So I told them."

Phyllis shivered. "It gives me the creeps, really." She looked around the circle. "There's seven of us being questioned. Still, my belief is it could be one of the crew but they reckon one of us's done it and we don't know which it is." Her gaze fell on Sarah, Emily, Joan, Marion and Tabitha.

"Who's innocent here? Eh?" Tabitha bared her teeth and glowered at Phyllis. "We're on a transport ship. There's not a single one of us who's blameless. Go on, deny it! We'll wait and see what they decide in their wisdom, those men."

"And Miss Hayter," said Marion. "She's there, too."

"No more use than a fart in a thunderstorm, her being there. That's for show. Those men'll judge us in the end."

"Didn't she speak?" Susan asked. "Did she not say anything?"

"This and that. But it's mostly the men. Always is. Fat lot of good she'll do in that company."

"What if," said Beth, "they can't find out who did it by the time we land? What then?"

"They'll hand the seven of us over to them in authority and let them deal with us."

"But what if Hattie dies?" Beth asked.

"No need to look so bloody eager!" Izzy shouted. "She in't dead yet. You look as if you're longing for that, you brainless whore."

Beth kicked Izzy in the shins. "I'm not! I'm not!" she said, looking around for confirmation. "Someone'll be in for the long drop if she does." She shivered.

"Stop fighting, both of you," Ruth muttered, through gritted teeth. "Miss Hayter's over there, talking to the gentlemen. She'll be here soon."

Beth wiped her eyes and, with trembling hands, picked up her needle to thread it. The others were quiet, and the ship moved silently through the water in what little wind there was.

27

NOW

✦

8 July 1841
Ninety-four days at sea
KEZIA

Kezia went to the rail of the ship and stared toward the horizon.
After a stormy night, the sun shone weakly from behind thin
clouds. The sea spread away to what might have been a coastline,
but that, Kezia knew, was an illusion. The ocean went on and on
and she was uncomfortable when she considered how far away the
Rajah was from any land.

"Good morning," said a voice, and Kezia turned to see the captain striding along the deck toward her, with the Reverend Mr.
Davies and Mr. Donovan. Charles was smiling as he stopped to
talk to her, and she was surprised by how much it pleased her to see
him. All thoughts of how lonely the *Rajah* was on the vast ocean
left her. The captain's solid presence made her feel safe.

"Good morning," she answered.

"Please walk with us," Charles said, and they continued to walk together. Mr. Donovan was speaking, and the men seemed intent on continuing the deliberations of the inquiry. The clergyman in particular seemed eager to contradict almost everything Kezia had told them.

He hates what I'm doing with the women, she thought. And because of that, he has a very low opinion of me. If he knew that I'd like to run away from him and not have to talk to him, he would think even worse of me. She was determined to speak up for herself and for her women at every opportunity.

"I think," said Mr. Davies, "that Miss Hayter has a rosy vision of what these women are capable of. It is a question not of their characters but of passions brought on by their present circumstances. Don't you see?" He turned to Kezia, for, clearly, she needed to understand his version of the truth.

The four stopped walking and leaned against the rail, keeping their voices down, for the women were busy working not far away. Mr. Davies continued: "Kept in convict quarters, the women's minds may have been swayed and altered by being so far from home. Or perhaps they may have come into possession of strong spirits."

"You are not kept in convict quarters, sir," said Kezia, "but you are still far from home and your sherry every evening is strong drink, is it not? Is your character altered?"

Mr. Donovan laughed. "She's got you there, Davies," he said. "And I must add that I've treated a fair few women for one thing and another throughout the voyage. I still maintain that not one of them seems dangerous."

"Very well, then," said the clergyman, stiffly. "I can see my words are falling on deaf ears. Good day to you all." He strode away toward his cabin and Mr. Donovan followed him, pleading that he must work.

"Please, may we walk again, Charles?" she said. "There's something I want to say away from my women. I don't want them to overhear us." Or see us, she added to herself. They would notice my anger.

"Very well," said Charles. Then: "Is something wrong?"

"I am very . . . I'm very perturbed by your attitude to me in the inquiry."

Charles stopped abruptly and Kezia turned to him as they stood together, out of sight of the women.

"My attitude to you is of the utmost respect." He moved a little toward her, and seemed about to say more when Kezia interrupted him.

"And yet," she said, "you pay less heed to my advice and opinion than you do to those of the men."

"I assure you, my dear, I do not!" His face was a picture of indignation.

"That is how it often appears to me. All of you dismiss my knowledge of the women's characters and behavior as though it were of little account."

"I'm sorry. In future I will ensure that your views are given as much weight as anyone else's."

"Thank you," Kezia said. "I must go to my women now." She turned and walked quickly away. She should have felt grateful for what he had said, and perhaps it was wrong of her to judge him harshly for not addressing her main irritation. She should have made a point of mentioning it directly. *Why*, she'd thought of saying to him, *do you put up with that man being so dismissive of me?* But she was glad she hadn't. She didn't need others to speak for her. She was perfectly capable of telling Mr. Davies her opinion without the captain's help, and she was determined to do so when the time was right. He would never admit that he was wrong, but perhaps he would cease to cleave so fervently to the belief that he was always right.

28
THEN

*Cotton piece: white stripes on a brown background, each stripe pat-
terned with leaves in red and blue, alternating*

April 1841
CLARA

It wasn't only our belongings that were tossed around in the storm,
trodden underfoot and vomited on. We are feeling shaken, too. It's
hard on this ship to find anywhere to be private, away from prying
eyes, but now that every corner's being sluiced down, now that piles
of bedding have been taken up to the deck to be brought down
again when they're dry, it's even harder.

Small groups of women are talking as they work. Miss Hayter's
among them, coming and going, offering encouragement to everyone, putting things to rights. Women who'd be sewing on an ordinary day are busy down here, but not everyone's working. Izzy
Croft's speaking to Becky Finch, and Rose Manners hovers nearby.
I can't hear what she's saying but Becky isn't happy. She's sitting on
a bench with her bundle beside her, the one we were each given
when we came on board the *Rajah*. Izzy's speaking urgently, eagerly,

waving her hands about. Becky's not moving. Not talking, just staring at the floor. Rose comes closer and puts her hand on Izzy's shoulder. She leans forward, and speaks over Izzy's head. Some people have voices that pierce the air and carry more than others. Rose's voice is like that. She's almost spitting into Becky's face and I hear what she says. "She's told you. What's she just said? She doesn't love you no more. Wash your fucking ears out."

She and Izzy go off together, arm in arm, and join a gaggle on the other side of the convict quarters. Becky doesn't move for a long time. Then she reaches into her bundle and finds the scissors. She sits with them on her lap for a moment, then opens them as if to cut away a stray thread. I watch as she pushes the filthy cuff of her dress a little way up her arm and, with one of the scissor blades, scores a line in the flesh above her wrist. Not exactly a cut, but enough to scratch the skin and leave a thin line of blood. Has anyone else noticed?

I don't want to call attention to myself but what if Becky doesn't stop? What if she keeps scratching at herself till she bleeds properly? I get up and go to sit next to her, saying nothing. Perhaps having someone beside her will be enough to stop her. Maybe she'll put the scissors away when she sees me.

She takes no notice of me. I look down at her wrist. A lattice of fine dark lines crisscross one another from where her thumb joins her wrist almost up to her elbow: old scars of attacks she'd made on her own flesh. As she begins to add another line above the first, still showing red, I can't help myself. I put out my hand to stop the scissors doing their work.

"Becky," I say, "stop. Stop doing that."

The blade hangs in the air above her arm. "Why?" she says. Her face is like a plate: flat and white and round. She speaks with no emotion.

"You're hurting yourself," I said.

"It's good if it hurts. Stops you thinking. Done it for years."

"But the scars . . ." *How can it help to scratch a map of bleeding lines on your arms?*

"Doesn't matter about scars. No one'll see them. Izzy never minded the scars."

Becky applies herself to the next cut. I want to grab the scissors and take them from her, but how can I? She'd hang on to them. There would be a fuss. Everyone would come running and I'd be in the middle of it. I say, to distract her: "What was Izzy saying to you? I saw her and Rose Manners talking to you."

Becky puts her scissors away in her bundle, and I'm surprised at the relief I feel. "Rose stole Izzy away," she says. "Izzy said it was me she loved, only she doesn't. Not anymore. Rose stole her." She sounds matter-of-fact.

"You'll find someone else who'll love you, I'm sure."

She stands up. "More fool you if you think so," she says. "And, besides, I'll never love anyone else. Not ever. Only Izzy."

She walks away. I watch her go to her bunk and lie down. What would she be capable of doing? How much is her reason affected by her devotion to Izzy? I don't leave the lower deck for a long time, and whenever I look she's still there, exactly the same, like a stone carving on top of an old grave.

In the dark, the worst things come to my mind. I can't sleep. There's too much to remember.

The nights are much worse than the days. Some of the foul messes that spilled from the slop buckets during the storm haven't been cleaned away properly and the smell is vile. Some women here have been in prison often but I'm not used to the stench. The troubled ones are at their worst, shouting and moaning coming from every side. Marion weeps every night. Well, I tell myself, as I listen to her sobbing, there are those who give thanks for being rid of a child and those who mourn a scrap of nothing much more than blood as though it were a living, breathing person. Other women turn on their thin mattresses and mumble, snore or cry out in their sleep. I lie in the dark and imagine the fathoms of black ocean moving under the *Rajah*, and it unsettles me. During the storm, I saw what the sea could do, and now even gentle rolling frightens me.

Joan is still in the hospital, not restored to herself yet. I'm sorry for her but can't bring myself to condemn Isaac completely. On a long voyage, what could be better than finding a companion of sorts? Someone to talk to, to kiss, to laugh with sometimes.

I try to comfort myself with past memories. My own little house pleased me more than anything ever has before or since. Two rooms downstairs and two upstairs, but they were enough for me. I loved the roses in the little front garden. Two lilac trees, full of fragrant white blossoms in May, grew one on either side of the wooden gate. I lived alone. I was determined, after Samuel's death, never again to wake up with a man's head next to mine on the pillow. There was no one to please and I loved my freedom. If I ever felt lust, I knew ways of quenching it quickly without welcoming a man into my bed.

My bed was my sanctuary and I saw to it that whatever else I had to deny myself (and there was much I couldn't afford in the early days) my linen would be the best I could buy: lace-trimmed and as glowing white as scrubbing, bleaching and careful ironing could make it. I had quilts and knitted shawls to cover me, and many small cushions piled high, covered with satin and plush in every shade of pink and red that I could find. I bought material in the market from a stall owned by Mrs. Bee, a fearsome creature whose daughter, Nora, was a cowed, skinny thing with magic fingers.

Nora made my fabric into cushions and delivered them to my house. Whenever she came I brought her into the parlor to pay her. She would gaze, awestruck, at my warm fire and comfortable chairs, as if unable to believe such luxury existed.

What would my life have been if Nora hadn't come knocking on my door, that dreadful November night? The fog was so thick around her that, at first, I didn't know who she was. I hadn't visited her mother's stall for months. Nora was as thin and small and pale as ever, but that night she was holding a tiny baby in her arms, wrapped in bits of flannel and knitted fabric. A picture of misery, that was what she was.

"Please, Miss," she said. "Please let me in . . ."

I let her in. I fed her. I listened and she told me her story. How her mother had thrown her out of the house when she knew about the baby. How, now it was born, she didn't know where to turn, who to go to for help. The baby was vermin, Mrs. Bee said. She was washing her hands of Nora and her child.

"I wish she'd never been born," Nora sobbed. "I wish I could go back to when she wasn't there . . . I don't want her. I can't look after her . . . I wish . . ."

She was frantic.

I said, "When did you give birth?"

"Yesterday. Or maybe the night before . . . I don't remember. I don't want her. Oh, God, forgive me, but I don't want her. What can I do? Some say there are those who'd pay for a newborn baby . . . You've lived a little in the world—d'you know of such people?"

She looked at me with such swimming eyes, with such sorrow in her voice, that I made myself sound stronger than I felt when I spoke. "It's true. I do know of such people. Why have you come to me? Why do you not go to one of them?"

"I've not a penny. I don't know where to find such a person . . . I couldn't think of where to go for help but to you. You've always been so kind to me."

"There's people who'd pay for a newborn," I said. "I can ask, but for now, you must eat and sleep and clean yourself. I'll boil a kettle."

Why did I take her in? She was nothing to me, not really, and I might have shut my door against her. But I didn't. I was flattered, I suppose, that she'd come to find me, when her own mother had been cold and unforgiving. She must have thought of me as someone who'd help her, and that pleased me. Also, I saw that she'd always be in my debt if I helped her now. If I employed her, she'd do her best for me, and I could see how useful it would be to me to have someone in my house who owed me so much. I regret it now, thinking back, but then I told myself she could be a maid and do my bidding for very modest wages. It also came to me: if Nora's desperate, she's not the only one. There was a trade in infants; I knew that. Till that night, I hadn't thought I could be a part of it. The money I had would not last forever and I needed employment. Nora had been so grateful and others would be, too. I was sure of it.

She was the first. It didn't take me long to learn how things were managed. The poor creature was right. The truth was, there were often those who'd pay for a healthy child. I did well from them, too. And when all else failed, there were many other ways to dispose of unwanted children, as I discovered that night. Once I was sure that Nora was asleep, I wrapped myself in my warmest shawl, took the silent baby from her arms, went out into the fog and walked and walked more than two miles till I came to a very lonely place on the river, far from Putney. Damp and yellowish mists clung to my skirts and muffled the sound of my shoes on the pavement. I saw no one. When I reached the water, I put the baby in the shelter of an old boat, pulled up on the mudflats. Then I turned and walked away.

Was that crying I heard? I closed my ears. I might have imagined the noises. I put one foot in front of the other and bent my head to stare at the ground, all the way home. The clock on the mantel in my parlor stood at three o'clock. I'd been out for less than four hours. I was too exhausted to do more than sink into my armchair, fully dressed. I fell asleep at once, but woke soon after, uncomfortable and stiff. I took off my clothes, washed, put on my nightgown and climbed into my soft white bed, and when I was there, I couldn't sleep. I lay unmoving till dawn, trying not to think of the baby, trying not to recall where I'd left her. Making up a story to tell Nora about the kind woman who'd taken her child . . . comfortably off, pleasant, and sad after the loss of her own daughter. Perhaps, I told myself, someone would find the child. Rescue her. I fell asleep just before it was time to wake up.

Since that night, I've not slept well. I've been back too many times to the same question: what would have happened if I'd said no? Did I ruin Nora's life or save it? I left her child to die but what would that baby's life have been? I found it easier to deal with the others who came after Nora. I found other, kinder ways of ending a tiny life.

Nora stayed with me. She was grateful for my help and also happy to be released from her mother's constant moaning, happy to be away from brothers and sisters who were piled on top of one another in a house that was no better than a slum, happy to be in charge of her own life, happy to be in her own bedroom, however small.

As my maid, she sewed my curtains and bed hangings, and knitted pretty garments. After some time, she began to help me in finding homes for the babies of other women as desperate as she'd once been. After that first night, she never asked again about her own child, but she knew that sometimes, when homes couldn't be found, you could get rid of babies in ways no one would choose but which sometimes you were forced into using. Nora learned quite quickly what had to be done in such cases.

This was what I did. What many did, to earn a living. We took the babies of young, poor, unmarried girls who'd become pregnant and, for a fee, we cared for them. I told the girls that everything would be for the best, and they believed it. Dead bastards mean little to the law. Babies are frail, and some families would pay hand-somely for a healthy child. I might have been helping young women even now, living in my pretty house, but I did something worse and could not deny it. I stuck a knife between a man's ribs, and would do it again if I had to, even though it took me straight to the gal-lows.

Dawn sailing: the sun comes up behind the Rajah as she makes for the west. Her unfurled sails are tinted mauve and pink. Birds, inhabitants of small and distant islands, visit the ship for scraps and perch unsteadily on the masts. The sea is calm and every wave is edged with gold.

29
NOW

✤

8 July 1841
Ninety-four days at sea
KEZIA

The weather was growing colder as they moved across the water.
We are all thinking of Hattie, Kezia told herself. Haunted by her.
The women are worrying for poor little Bertie. How can he visit his
mother every day and not despair to see her there, drained of color
and talking nonsense when she did speak?

As the women took their place on deck, they wrapped their
shawls around themselves. The wind was quite sharp but, still, it
was better to be out there, and not in the stuffy convict quarters.
The days had been passing too slowly. The women had gone from
speculating about who had stabbed Hattie to fretting about everything. Three groups of women were sitting close to one another on
the deck, and Kezia felt momentarily heartened. Perhaps they
found it distracting to work. Perhaps it helped to go on stitching

when thoughts were unbearable. And it was possible to see, Kezia thought, that the patchwork was becoming something beautiful. There was harmony here, and even evidence of careful needlework, but also places where the pieces had been rushed and squeezed in, so that the stitches puckered. Several of the women she'd chosen hadn't been as skilled as she'd thought. But they'd been making something together, and in these darker days that seemed to count for something. For a fleeting moment, Kezia wondered what her mother would have thought of their accomplishment, if she could see it. All through her childhood, her own handiwork had been compared to Henrietta's and found wanting.

She sighed. The distance between Kezia and her mother had grown as the years had passed. It gradually became clear, even to Henrietta, that their mother's irritation with Kezia had become stronger. After being presented with a series of young men as possible suitors, Kezia had not only set her face against every one but had also felt a growing distance from her mother. One particular gentleman presented to her was, her mother explained, very wealthy. She did not seem to notice how ill-favored and sullen he was. Kezia tried to explain herself.

"I'm not interested in marrying, Mama," she said.

"Nonsense," Mrs. Hayter replied. "How can you say such a thing? A young woman in your situation can't afford to be 'not interested.' You haven't considered how you will live, after my death."

They were sitting on either side of the fire, and the tea table between them was laid with fine china and a large teapot patterned with garlands. Mrs. Hayter lifted it and paused as she poured tea, then passed the cup and saucer to her daughter. "Who will care for you? You'll have no position, no money, no influence, not to mention no children if you constantly set your face against any young man to whom I introduce you."

Kezia could hear the exasperation in her mother's voice. She sipped some of the hot tea but tasted nothing. Placing her cup and saucer on the table, she took a deep breath and made another effort to explain. "Mama, I'm not eager to have children—" she began, but was interrupted.

"You *think* you don't want children! You say that now, when you're young and vigorous." Mrs. Hayter leaned over the table and shook a finger in Kezia's face. "You'll be of a different mind, I promise you, when old age comes upon you. A woman must have children to care for her in her dotage." She sat back and folded her hands on her lap. "Why, without my sons, what would become of me, when I'm unable to care for myself any longer? I would be out in the cold. And there's dear Henrietta, of course. She won't leave me to die all alone. But you, Kezia, you are so caught up with Mrs. Fry and Mrs. Pryor and their care of prisoners that I would not be certain of any attention from you, if you remain single."

"You wish me to marry someone—anyone—in order that I may care for you at some future date?"

"How dare you?" Mrs. Hayter shouted. She rose from her chair, and swept away from the tea table. At the door, she turned. "You are a foolish girl," she said coldly. "It's your welfare I'm thinking of. *Your* future. Well, I've always known I couldn't trust you. Not to look after me, and not to make me proud."

Kezia found herself unable to utter a word. What she wanted to say, what was screaming somewhere inside her, bottled up behind years and years of silence, rose within her, though she said nothing. *You!* she thought. *It is you who doesn't love me. You've never loved me properly and I've always known it.* She had been howling thus, silently, since early childhood. Her mother had never noticed.

After that day, after those words, Kezia could no longer remain at home. She asked to stay with relatives, saying she needed to be nearer the prisons she would be visiting, alongside Mrs. Fry and Mrs. Pryor.

"Criminals and fallen women," her mother muttered, on the day she left. "You're more concerned with the welfare of such creatures than that of your own mother. I am ashamed of you."

"Good-bye, Mama," Kezia said, kissing her mother's cheek. "I will remember you in my prayers."

And so I have, she reflected now. *I've said a prayer for you every night since I left.*

Kezia's belongings stood by the front door, packed into two valises. She had picked them up and made her way down the short drive to where a carriage sent by Cousin George was waiting to take her to his house. What she had learned from her cousin and what she'd seen of his work were as important to her as her love of God. He'd allowed her to consider the possibility of making something beautiful, and Mrs. Pryor, when she grew to know her, had shown her practical ways of achieving worthwhile things for her own pleasure at the same time as she was helping others to find a better way of living, a way down a path of righteousness.

Now Kezia approached a few of the women, sitting down beside Izzy and Rose. Some women spoke ill of these two, and Kezia had had to reprimand the Newgate Nannies for laughing at their habit of always being arm in arm or hand in hand and calling them dabblers. Early in the voyage, Kezia had heard Dwyer use the word and asked what it meant. Immediately, she wished she hadn't. "It means," said Dwyer, taking pleasure from Kezia's discomfiture, "that they like paddling about in one another's fannies. Dabblers, we call such women. Or paddlers, if you like it better."

Kezia tried to appear unflustered but feared her blush had given the lie to her apparent composure. She'd fixed her gaze on Dwyer's one good eye and said, as firmly as she could manage, "If I hear such words uttered once more on this ship I'll report you to the captain." And she hadn't heard any, though she was perfectly sure that worse was said out of her hearing.

As she regarded Izzy and Rose, she was struck by how close they were, their heads together, their giggles meant only for one another. Rose was so pretty that it was easy to see why Izzy might want to be her friend, but even though Kezia never judged anyone by appearances alone, Izzy seemed to her much less appealing. She was a gawky young woman, with coarse, pockmarked features and a tactless tongue. She was also sly, coming to Kezia often with tales about other women in the circle. Louisa had helped herself to Izzy's scissors without permission and now wouldn't give them back. Phyllis was always telling her off for nothing. It was hard to deny that Izzy was a complainer, and Kezia was not sure why Rose put up with her. But she did, and when they were occupied with one another there was less opportunity for them to make mischief among the rest of the group.

As Kezia sat down next to Dora, the women began to ask questions.

"Have you seen Hattie, Matron?" Alice wanted to know. Kezia liked Alice, a plain woman with dark hair, for her religious devotion; she was one of many convicts on board whom Kezia found hard to imagine involved in any crime. Alice had, however, stolen three pork pies from a market stall and was in the habit of receiving stolen goods from others.

"Yes, Alice," Kezia answered. "I've visited her every day, though Bertie and I only stay for a moment. Rest is what Hattie needs. She says nothing but lies in a state of unconsciousness for the most part. As soon as she's more herself, I'll visit her for longer and see if there's anything she can tell us."

"She might die," said Elsie, a slow-thinking woman who didn't often speak. "And then she won't be able to tell us anything."

Beth sighed. "D'you remember what she said on the night of the storm?"

"What did she say?" Kezia asked. "If you remember something, Beth, you must tell me."

"She said someone was following her. When she was out on deck. Said, *There's someone watching me, Beth*. Her very own words. But she asked me not to say. So I haven't. Not till now."

"I've not felt safe since she was stabbed," said Phyllis. "Often feel as if someone's behind me."

"We're all in danger, when you think of it. Aren't we?" That was Susan.

"But why was Hattie followed? Why would someone pick on her?" Phyllis asked. "Or watch her, for that matter."

"To plunge a knife into her, of course," said Beth, ever one to see the most dramatic aspect of every event. "They didn't succeed then, but someone's done it now, haven't they? Found a way . . . Don't know why . . ."

Ann, who was not normally given to uttering kind thoughts, said what Kezia was thinking: "Hattie's a lovely girl and there's no reason on God's earth why anyone should want to hurt her."

"You don't know that," said Rose. "Handsome isn't always as handsome does. People are deceiving. Can't go by looks. Hattie looks as if butter wouldn't melt, but she can be fierce, can't she? We don't know what she was before, do we? Not really."

No one said anything further, though Kezia could see some heads nodding. Hattie was popular with many, but she thought of the blue cotton piece with those words stitched on it. *Speak & you die*. Kezia felt a tightening in her chest when she thought about the patch. She should have done more.

30
THEN

Cotton piece: bright green printed with a closely spaced pattern of four-leafed clovers

May 1841
HATTIE

"He's sweet on me," Emily said, under her breath, as she and Hattie sat near one of the masts, joining squares together as neatly as possible. Hattie's stitches were almost invisible while Emily's were bigger and more careless, possibly because she was more interested in talking about William and less interested in the way one square was joined to the next. The wind was blowing a little more strongly today, too, and the women stitching the coverlet had tried to place their bundles in such a way as to stop them flapping. Phyllis was as cautious as ever. "I'm not trusting that wind," she said, and she began to put every piece of fabric she could find into her bundle.

Hattie rolled her eyes and pulled her needle through the cloth. She looked at Emily and laughed. "You're sweet on him, you mean. He's even younger than you are and you're pulling the wool over his eyes."

"No!" Emily said. "I'd never do that, Hattie. He gives me titbits from the galley. We've not snatched more than a kiss or two. I daren't walk about like Miss Hayter."

Hattie nodded. Miss Hayter had begun walking the deck with the captain, toward sunset, like an elderly married couple, which was strange because neither of them was old. Perhaps, she thought, it was this liking that led to stitching being allowed on deck when the weather was fair. Hattie loved such times, even when the wind made sewing more difficult. It was easy to imagine a different life, a warmer life under the Antipodean sun, and as her tiny stitches bound together two pieces of fabric, she had time to enjoy her own handiwork, and that of her companions.

Hattie had come to admire Miss Hayter very much. She was calm in all her dealings and was ready to listen to anyone in the company who went to her for help. Now, as she stitched two brightly colored pieces of chintz together, Hattie glanced at the whole coverlet, and felt her heart lift at how the colors were beginning to come together.

"Look at Bertie," Emily said. He was rolling about on the deck with one of the other children and the little ones were watching. Something like a shadow fell over her face. "It's time I brought them to the benches for a story. Or perhaps a few songs today. And the alphabet . . ."

"That sounds like hard work to me," said Hattie. "How lucky that you're here to keep them occupied. When they're with you, they don't have to be watched in case they fall overboard."

"They won't fall overboard," said Emily, laughing. "One of the sailors told the bigger ones such stories of drowning, and the monsters that lurk in the depths of the ocean, that they hardly dare look over the rail at the water."

Hattie was fond of Emily even though she thought her a little silly. Bertie liked her, too, and Emily enjoyed teaching the children, in spite of the complaints she sometimes made about them. That, at least, reassured Hattie that she was sensible underneath the grumbling.

Hattie listened to the children chanting the alphabet in unison and the sound of their voices soothed her. She looked out over the sea, blue today under a blue sky. Sometimes the water seemed angry to her, but now, whipped by the brisk and playful wind, the mighty ocean was dotted with white-crested waves. The motion when she walked the deck felt no more threatening than that of a rocking horse.

A creak, someone trying to step quietly, woke Hattie from a dream. She sat up, going at once to look at her son's small mattress, but he was asleep and lay quite still. She could see his sweet face in the first traces of daylight. The night was over. There'd been darkness in the dream, one darkness falling over another, like a length of black silk rolled out on a black table. Something had fallen on her face. A leaf? A feather? Had something touched her?

Hattie shivered, then ran her fingers over her forehead and through her hair. Looking down, she saw something pale caught in the folds of her blanket: a square of pale blue cotton. Someone had crept up to her mattress in the night. She'd been half aware of it. They'd left a square of fabric on her blanket.

As she turned the square over in her hands, she didn't understand what she was seeing. Who would have taken the trouble to make such a thing? She took a deep breath, closing her eyes briefly. The message was still there, stitched roughly on the cloth in black thread, clumsily executed. Even in the dim light, she could read the letters clearly and a chill closed round her heart. *Speak & you die*.

The words swam under her gaze. Who would put such a thing on her pillow? What did it mean? What must she not say? She sat in the cold dawn light and searched her mind for any secret she knew . . . There was nothing. Nothing she could hide, even if she wanted to. Terror washed through her, leaving her for a moment almost unable to draw breath.

Miss Hayter: she'd know what to do. I must go to her now, Hattie decided. Before she's up and about her business. Otherwise the whole ship will know of this. She took her shawl and wrapped it round her shoulders. Bertie stirred on his mattress.

"It's not time to get up yet, Bertie."

"But you're getting up, Ma," he murmured, and rolled over, fast asleep again. Hattie looked at him. How could she leave him here by himself, with such danger lurking close by? Emily—she'd wake Emily and ask her to keep an eye on Bertie. She'd tell her why later and think of some excuse. Emily wouldn't mind and she'd do it for her. Hattie stared into the darkness and wondered which of the sleeping bodies had left the fabric square. The *Rajah* was rocking gently tonight, and she lay for a moment listening to the creaking of the timbers. The sun would be up soon. I must be quick, she thought. The rhythmic groans and snores of the women rose and fell around her as she tiptoed over to Emily's berth.

Hattie stood in front of Miss Hayter's door and tried to work up the courage to knock. Then she looked down at the piece of fabric in her hand. *Speak & you die*. I can't hide this, she thought. I can't walk about wondering what I mustn't say and who is going to kill me. Perhaps someone had lost their reason, or why would they threaten her? She knocked and, after a few moments, Miss Hayter opened the door.

"What's the matter, Hattie?" said Miss Hayter. She was holding her embroidery in her left hand. "Is someone ill again?"

"No, no, Miss Hayter." Hattie knew they were both remembering the night of Marion's miscarriage. "Only I must talk to you, please. Away from company."

"Come in," said Miss Hayter, and held the door open. Hattie came in and stood awkwardly next to the chest of drawers.

"There isn't very much space, I'm afraid."

"Thank you," said Hattie, and glanced over her shoulder, as if someone might have followed her.

Miss Hayter was already dressed, which surprised Hattie a little, though she was too preoccupied with her own troubles, too terrified of what she held to take time to wonder why she was awake so early. She stood, hesitating, at the door, till Miss Hayter put out a hand, drew her in and closed it behind her. "Tell me what's wrong," she said. "Come in and sit down . . . here." She guided Hattie to a chair and sat on the bunk, close enough to put out a hand and touch Hattie's knee to comfort her.

"I'm so sorry, Miss. It's this, you see." She held out the square of blue cotton. "Someone put this on my pillow . . . You see what it says . . . I can't speak of it to anyone . . . Please say you won't tell anyone, please . . ."

Miss Hayter looked both vexed and worried.

"I must tell the captain," she began, but Hattie interrupted her, horrified.

"Oh, no! If I thought you'd tell anyone I'd have—I wouldn't have come to you. I thought you'd be willing to keep my secret. You'd not want to see me in danger. See what it says, Miss. *Speak and you die.* Maybe I shouldn't have come to you. Please say you won't tell anyone. Please."

Hattie felt her heart knocking in her chest. A chill fell over her.

If Miss Hayter told the captain, he might announce the threat to the whole ship, and Hattie would be done for. What would happen to Bertie if she wasn't there to look after him?

"Do you think"—Miss Hayter sounded doubtful—"that this could be someone's warped idea of a jest?"

Hattie shook her head. Who'd go to this trouble to stitch these horrid black words in secret if they weren't serious? There had been times when she'd thought she felt the force of someone's gaze on her back, but she'd dismissed it.

"No, I can see that it's not . . . I'm sorry." Miss Hayter looked distressed. She said, "Very well, Hattie. I'll do what I can on my own. But first of all, you must tell me the truth, Hattie. Is there something, something in the past? Can you think of anything?"

Hattie went through in her head everything she'd done that could in any way be called bad. Her crimes . . . By the time her young victims reached their parents, Hattie was far away. What about Patrick? Could he somehow be taking his vengeance, punishing her for running away from him? Of course not. He'd have been furious for twelve hours, then drowned his sorrows in another glass and found another gullible female to enchant.

"No, I swear, Miss Hayter. Nothing. I can't think of anything. As far as I know, no one who knew me before this voyage is aboard this ship. Who could possibly know what I've done and not done?"

"Someone clearly thinks there's something others shouldn't know . . . Perhaps you've seen something done by someone else. Someone who wants their deeds kept secret."

"No!" Hattie was firm. "Nothing like that. I've not seen anything." Hattie wailed, "I don't know . . . I really don't, Miss Hayter."

"Well, then," said Kezia, "you must put on a brave face and see to it that no one suspects you're troubled. But you *must* be on your guard. See if anyone around you behaves in an unusual way that makes you uncomfortable. You must undertake to tell me if you see anything."

Hattie nodded. "I will, Miss, I promise. Thank you. I'm so sorry."

"There's no need to apologize, Hattie. None at all. I'm sure everything will turn out well."

As she left Miss Hayter's cabin, Hattie felt a little better. Part of her longed to say something; to gather her friends about her and spill out her fears to them. Maybe she ought to speak to Emily or Rose or Izzy. But, no, the threat was there: *Speak & you die.* The other side of that was *Keep silent and you'll live,* and Hattie knew that not a word, not a syllable about the square of blue cotton would pass her lips. She was happy that Miss Hayter had the care of it now.

On the way to the lower deck, Hattie heard stifled noises coming from behind an enormous coil of rope lying on the deck. Her heart jumped. Who was that? Was it one of the crew? She paused, listening. It was still very early. No one but a few sailors would be up at this hour, and that was a woman's laugh, suppressed, not very well. Hattie tiptoed carefully around the rope, and there, squeezed between the rope and the side of the ship, was Emily. William was emerging from her skirts, his face flushed and his mouth hanging open. Hattie swiftly moved away and came across Sarah Good-bourne, standing by the ship's rail. She often rose early and walked on the deck.

"Quick, Sarah, move away. Emily's there with William," Hattie whispered. She put out a hand to draw Sarah back toward the companionway.

Sarah cast a glance in the direction of the rope. William emerged onto the deck and vanished in the opposite direction. There was no sign of Emily.

"Did you see them both?" Sarah asked.

"Yes, I did. Emily was . . . well, she was . . ."

"I can picture the scene, Hattie. Don't bother describing it."

Sarah walked away and Hattie stood still to collect her thoughts. Should she say something to Emily? She'd been preoccupied to say the least, and might not know, even now, that she'd been seen.

"Hattie . . ." That was Emily, emerging onto the deck, hair hanging down and face flushed. "Did you see?"

For a split second, Hattie thought of lying. "Yes, Emily. I asked you to look after Bertie. Don't you remember? How could you leave him? You're at William's beck and call. You're a fool, you know. If you're caught with one of the crew, I don't know what'd happen to you but he'd be punished severely, I'm sure."

Emily was shamefaced. "I know. But I couldn't help it. He's so . . . I'm so . . . When he looks at me, I come over funny, and when he touches me, oh, Hattie, I want him to touch me so very much and he does and I touch him and I can't stop wanting that. I can't."

"Then you must be more careful. Sarah was here, too, you know."

"Tell her to say nothing, Hattie. Please tell her. For me. Explain to her, please. Will you? It would be the ruin of us both, me and William."

"You could tell her yourself."

Emily looked so alarmed at the prospect of doing this that Hattie took pity on her. "Very well," she said. "I'll talk to her. No one'll find out from either of us."

In that moment, Hattie determined never again to ask Emily to look after Bertie. She'd been frightened and desperate to talk to Miss Hayter but she wouldn't do that again. Bertie would never again be left unsupervised, however terrified she'd been by the words embroidered on the patch. *Embroidered*... Someone had sat down in a hidden spot, taken out her needle and made those stitches. There was work in those stitches. Someone had had to *work* to make that abomination. The thought buzzed in her head like a wasp.

31
THEN

Cotton piece: pale green and madder red stripes printed with large red flowers and thick darker green leaves

May 1841
KEZIA

"In some ways," Kezia said, "I've grown used to it. Being at sea, knowing that whichever way I look in any direction there's no sign of life." She corrected herself almost at once. "I mean, apart from all of us on board. No other sign of human life. I love the porpoises and the seabirds . . . but we are the only people. It can seem"—she paused to find the right word—"precarious. As if we might at any moment disappear . . ."

"I will ensure that we do not," the captain said, and he seemed a little amused at Kezia's fears. "But you are right in one way," he went on. "We are alone together for a few months and, because we are, we have sometimes to . . . We might perhaps run more speedily through the manners we'd be following on shore."

Kezia said nothing. They were walking along the deck. Groups of women were sitting together, talking and laughing. The day's work on the coverlet was done. Sailors were engaged in tasks Kezia knew were important for the smooth running of the *Rajah* but which she did not fully understand: moving barrels and boxes, coiling ropes, climbing up and down the rigging and all at great speed. When they reached the stern, Kezia leaned over to watch the wake, frothing out behind the ship.

"Miss Hayter," the captain said, "I would like to call you by your Christian name. Would you allow it? When we are on our own? And will you call me Charles?"

Charles . . . Kezia did not know how she would summon the courage to address the captain by his given name. But she liked the sound of her own name when he said it. She nodded. "I will try," she said. "And, yes, of course you may call me Kezia."

"Thank you," the captain—*Charles*—said, and he was smiling at her.

Just then, a gust of wind began to blow away her shawl. The captain—*Charles*—reached out to catch it. He placed it around her again and his hands lingered on her shoulders. Kezia's own hands, in the act of going to tie the ends of the shawl together, met Charles's fingers and she blushed.

"It would be a shame to lose such a pretty shawl overboard," he said.

"My sister is a great knitter," Kezia said. The memory of his hands on her shoulders was with her still. "I have many shawls."

"But this color becomes you," said Charles, and then, as if somewhat regretting such a personal remark, he added, "I must take my leave now and let you go to your cabin. Good-bye, Kezia." He bowed again and walked away with his back very straight.

This color becomes you . . . Kezia had never considered this before, but it was true that Henrietta had chosen a particularly delightful shade of blue for the shawl.

My dearest Henrietta,

Today I was called by my Christian name for the first time since I left London almost a month ago. I did not realize how much I missed hearing it spoken. The captain, who has said that I may call him Charles, asked if I would allow this. I was happy to do so. I've always trusted him in matters of managing the ship safely and well, but he has shown himself very understanding of the women and of the work we're engaged in. And he admired the blue shawl you knitted for me, which shows he is a man of taste . . .

32
NOW

✦

8 July 1841
Ninety-four days at sea
KEZIA

"Are you perfectly certain, Miss Hayter," said Mr. Donovan, "that you are not tiring yourself unnecessarily with this inquiry? You seem to be . . ."

"What? What do I seem to be?" Kezia was standing at the foot of Hattie's bed in the hospital and Mr. Donovan was at his desk.

"Forgive me, but you seem to be . . . irritated with the way things are progressing. I suppose we all are, in a way. It ought not to be proving so difficult to find the guilty party, yet we're no closer to an answer than we were when Hattie was stabbed."

Kezia moved the blanket that was covering the end of Hattie's bed and sat down. "You're very kind, Mr. Donovan. And you notice things that others don't see. May I speak to you frankly?"

"Of course." He pushed his chair back against the wall and looked steadily at Kezia.

She dropped her gaze. "I fear Mr. Davies has a low opinion of me, my intellect and my motives." Seeing that Mr. Donovan was about to answer, Kezia held up a hand to stop him. "Let me finish, please, because I don't know if I will be able to say these things again." She stood, and began to pace up and down between the end of Hattie's bed and the door. "He never listens to a word I say without a sneer on his face. He does not give any weight to the fact that I know these women."

"Perhaps he thinks he has greater experience because of his age and station," Mr. Donovan said mildly.

"And because he's a man. He does not believe that a woman might be his equal in intellect or feeling." Kezia frowned at Mr. Donovan. "For all I know, you agree with him."

"I judge each person as I meet them, man or woman."

Kezia sighed. "I know you do, and I am sorry I spoke so carelessly. You have always been kind and fair to me and in your dealings with the women. He cannot see that women often commit their crimes for good reason. They're hungry. They're poor. They steal to please their husbands. They are taken advantage of in so many ways." Kezia's voice was raised now, and Hattie stirred, muttering. Immediately, Mr. Donovan sprang from his chair and went to stand beside the bed. Kezia fell silent and turned to see if Hattie was awake.

"It often happens," Mr. Donovan said quietly. "She moves a little, says something unintelligible and my hopes rise, but they are always dashed."

"She couldn't have been better cared for."

Mr. Donovan seemed about to speak, then thought better of it, and leaned forward to smooth Hattie's pillow. "It's kind of you to say so, Miss Hayter," he said. "Very kind indeed."

"You're distracted, Kezia," said Charles. They were walking as the sun was setting behind banks of cloud, tinged now with purple and gold. The air was cool, and Kezia had put on her cherished finger-less gloves, knitted by Henrietta in dark green wool, as well as a shawl.

"I am," she said. "I saw Hattie today and she looked so ill, so pale and still. So very unlike herself."

"We mustn't despair. And I know . . ." He paused.

"What?"

"I know you're often impatient with what Mr. Davies says to you. He's a man who believes he knows best. There are many like him. He does it to me, too, and to Mr. Donovan. If he could come up to the wheelhouse and steer the ship, he would. He can't help it. I'm sure he has the best of intentions."

"He treats you quite differently. I'm a lesser creature because I'm a woman, even though he gives me some credit because my cousin is a court painter. It's the convict women he thinks of so dismis-sively. That's what I don't like in him. He considers them lost souls, incapable of any change or improvement. He treats our work to-gether as frivolous and useless, of no spiritual help whatsoever."

They had reached the stern. Lacy trails of foam streamed out behind the *Rajah* and it seemed to Kezia in that moment that they were the only people on the ship. The rigging and the timbers creaked around them; the wind and the water were always there, in the background, but between them, there was silence.

"Should I speak to him?" Charles asked her. "Tell him to keep his opinions to himself?" He put an arm around Kezia's shoulders and she leaned against him, enjoying the wind blowing the hair forward onto her face, wishing she could always stand close like this, in the shelter of his arm.

"No," she answered. She had no intention of allowing another man to speak up in her defense. "I can speak for myself."

"Please sit down, Sarah." Kezia watched her lower herself onto the leather seat of the chair presented to her. She might once have been a handsome woman, but it was hard to tell. Frown lines marked her brow and her gray hair hung down to her shoulders, covered with a scarf in a color that was no color at all. A hue into which her eye sank without seeing it properly.

"Now, then, Sarah," said Mr. Davies. "There's no need to be frightened. We're here seeking the truth, that's all. Your matron has given a good report of your work and diligence. I hope your answers will prove that your powers of observation are likewise to be commended."

Kezia smiled inwardly. How easy it was, if you knew how to do so, to turn words this way and that so that they caught the light and glimmered! Kezia had told the others that Sarah Goodbourne worked well but was hard to get to know, and now the clergyman's added "diligence" gave her an air of obedience to duty that was not part of her character, as far as Kezia had been able to tell, though it was true that no one could have called her lazy.

"Where were you, Sarah, when Hattie cried out?"

"Still sitting on the bench. I'd only just put my work away."

"And did you run to her side when she called?"

Sarah thought about this. "I was the last one to get there, I think," she said at last.

"Did you hang back for some reason?" Kezia asked.

HOPE ADAMS

"No, Miss. I was putting my pieces of fabric in my pocket. I didn't want them to fall on the deck and get dirty."

"Most commendable," murmured Mr. Davies. "So, when you reached Hattie's side . . ."

"Others were holding her up, speaking to her. I kept quiet. I didn't have anything useful to add to the clamor."

"Did you hear Hattie say anything?" Kezia smiled at Sarah, trying to make her feel more comfortable. She looked as though she were longing to get up and run from the room.

"She was asking for Bertie," said Sarah.

Kezia heard Mr. Davies sigh beside her. He was, she knew, impatient for some new development. All the women questioned so far had said the same thing: Hattie had called for Bertie.

"What exactly did she say?" Charles asked. "Her very words, if you can remember them, please."

Sarah waited for a few moments, then said, "I heard the name *Bertie*. She said that several times."

"Did she say, 'Not Freddie'?" Mr. Davies asked. "Or perhaps something that sounded like those words?"

"I couldn't swear as to that, sir. I only heard 'Bertie.'" The clergyman sighed again.

"Thank you, Sarah," said Charles. "You may go now, if you've nothing else to tell us."

"I haven't, sir. Nothing else."

"Thank you," said Kezia, and watched as Sarah rose to her feet, her eyes fixed firmly on the rug. She left the room, and Mr. Davies, who had been recording the last few remarks in his elegant hand, threw down his pen. "There must be something else," he said. "They're all saying the same thing. We'll never come to the truth in this fashion."

"Perhaps Hattie herself will be able to help," said Mr. Donovan. "Though she's not recovering as I would have liked . . ."

"I know I ask it every time we speak, but is she still not responding to visits from her child?" Charles wanted to know.

"It's pitiful to watch them. He sits beside her, holding her hand, with one of the other women beside him to cheer him. I tell them she's sleeping. She has to sleep, I say, in order to mend, but after a while Bertie becomes restless and they leave."

Kezia shivered. During the inquiry, it had sometimes seemed to her that they were about to discover the truth of what had happened on the night Hattie was stabbed, but most often, at the end of each session, she was filled with a mixture of anguish and fear. The knife was doubtless at the bottom of the ocean, but the person who had wielded it was still on board the *Rajah*.

Dull sailing. The Rajah moves in the direction of banks of cloud on the horizon as though the gray masses were a longed-for harbor. Fog hangs in the rigging, veils the decks and masks the outline of the vessel.

33

THEN

Cotton piece: eccentric pattern of bows and diamonds in dark brown

May 1841
CLARA

Sitting in the sunshine, listening to Miss Hayter read aloud from a book of Bible stories intended for children, has made my head ache. She means only to teach us as we work, and some of the women, the ones who can't read or write, look forward to the readings. The stories they've heard from other women, the gossip and scandal of the streets: that's what they're used to, so tales of men being swallowed by gigantic fish or killing giants with a single shot from a catapult excite them and they sit with their mouths open in wonder, a lot of them, while Miss Hayter reads, stopping occasionally to urge her listeners to sew. I like the readings. I can stop worrying for a few moments while I'm distracted but always in my thoughts is the fear that Hattie might suddenly remember who I am. Today I feel far from my usual health.

"May I be excused, please?" I say.

227

Miss Hayter looks up. "Is something the matter? Are you ill?"

"My head aches a little. I'd like to lie down, please."

"Of course," she says. "But if your head isn't better soon, you must report to Mr. Donovan."

"Yes, Miss Hayter," I say. I leave them, and go down into the convict quarters. Many women are there, talking in small groups, knitting or sewing their own small pieces of patchwork. Mr. Donovan's there, too, bending over someone I can't see. He comes quite often to the lower deck, with his bag of remedies for ordinary complaints, like constipation or red and irritated eyes.

When he stands upright again, I see he's been looking after Becky Finch. She's in her bunk and he's looking around for someone to help him. I go up to him at once. "What's the matter with Becky, sir?" I ask. "Can I help you?"

"Thank you, yes. I'd have brought Joan with me, but she's busy in the hospital. Two sailors have eye infections. I didn't know this would be so serious. If you could take her other side, we'll help her to walk."

I'm shaken to see that Becky's bedclothes are stained dark with blood. Her arm is bandaged roughly and her face is gray. We stumble in silence along the deck and up to the hospital and there is Joan, who takes charge at once, leading Becky to one of the bunks and fetching wet cloths and clean bandages.

"Here's a lucky woman," says Mr. Donovan. "If Nathaniel hadn't been returning some slop buckets to their places," Mr. Donovan says, "she'd have died for certain. Blood pouring out of her wrist. Self-inflicted, clearly. The scissors were in her hand."

He turns to me. "Thank you," he says.

I nod and am about to leave when I decide to speak. "Have you seen her arms?" I ask him.

"I have indeed." He sighs. "This poor young woman wanted to

end her life. I'm sure of it. I can't let that happen on this ship." He goes to his desk and begins looking at his log.

My heart begins to beat very fast and my throat is dry. Surely he won't put me in charge of looking after her. I couldn't bear it: someone else's life dependent on my care.

"Lily Hughes," he says at last, looking up at me. "D'you know her?"

"I haven't spoken to her, but I know who she is," I answer.

"She's in the log as a nursemaid. Does she seem steady?"

Lily Hughes is a stolid, silent, unremarkable woman, who seems dull to me. She's one of a gaggle of women who are also dull. Birds of a feather flocking together. "I'm sure there's no harm in her," I say.

"I would've asked you," he says, "but I know you're one of Miss Hayter's company and I felt sure other women would be willing to help in this matter."

I go back to the others, who are still sewing on deck, relieved that I'd been spared the care of Becky Finch. Miss Hayter has already left. I sit down among my companions, feeling fortunate to have been chosen to spend my days stitching together squares and triangles of cloth for hours on end. The other women fill their days as best they can. They knit, gossip, quarrel and doze. They work on their own small patchworks. But for those of us in Miss Hayter's company, it is a great relief to have a daily obligation.

"Where you been, then?" says Rose.

"Helping Mr. Donovan with Becky Finch," I answer. "She was half dead when he found her. Cut her wrists."

The others want to know every detail.

"She's a cutter," Ruth remarks. "They're funny. Don't seem to feel the pain."

"Pickpocket," Tabitha adds. "Seen many like her at work. Lots

HOPE ADAMS

of them quite handy with a knife. Not often on themselves, though. More on others. Cut a pocket from a dress in an eyeblink."

I let them talk. When the speculation dies down, Susan says, "Well, you going to tell us then? What'll happen to Becky now?"

"Mr. Donovan told me to keep quiet," I answer, "but he's seeing to it that she's looked after." I bend my head to my work. The others start to chatter and mutter. Izzy and Rose aren't feeling in the least guilty, that much is clear, but Phyllis leans over and points her threaded needle at Izzy.

"It's you two made Becky do that!" she announces, in the ringing tones of a judge speaking from the Bench. "You were hand in glove with her, Izzy, weren't you, to start with? Then you went all soppy about that madam there." The needle swings round to point at Rose.

"Shut your face," says Rose, quite calmly. "Becky's feebleminded. Anyone who slices into herself over and over's feebleminded. That's what I think. Izzy don't want no feebleminded friends."

"Cruel as well as stupid," says Dora, who doesn't often speak. "That's what you are, Rose Manners." We all turn to her to hear what will come next. "You don't know what's led her to cut herself. She may have had dreadful things done to her. You can't say she's feebleminded. Maybe she thought being hurt or dead was better."

"You're the stupid one," says Izzy. "How can being hurt be better than being not hurt? How can being dead be better than being alive?"

Dora doesn't answer and neither does anyone else. I could tell them the answer, though I don't. Being hurt in a small way is a distraction from an injury that's even more painful. And being dead might be preferable to being alive and unloved. I can understand not wanting to be in the world. I've never had the courage to end my own life, but I understand Becky perfectly.

230

34
NOW

9 July 1841
Ninety-five days at sea
KEZIA

"You're sad, Kezia," said Charles. He was sitting at the table, and Kezia was in one of the armchairs on the other side of the cabin, staring at her lap. Mr. Donovan and the Reverend Mr. Davies would arrive at any moment. "It's to be expected, with Hattie showing no signs of improvement, but you must be brave."

"It's when I come from taking Bertie to his mother that I feel it most. He asks and asks when she'll be better. What if she dies? What then?"

Charles left the table and knelt down near Kezia, putting his hand on the arm of the chair. "We must be hopeful. What's the point in going through every bad thing in advance, when it may not happen? When Hattie may live?"

"Your optimistic outlook is admirable," Kezia said, though she couldn't help feeling that a little pessimism might be more appropriate in this case. She was losing sleep, worrying about the outcome of their inquiry. How could they get to the truth if every woman came forward with a version of the same story? Whenever she sat with the circle of needlewomen, sewing on deck, she listened for what the others were saying.

No point looking for a knife . . . Whoever it is will've chucked it over the side . . . Someone was jealous of Hattie. Has she been after Isaac, Joan? Don't speak to Joan like that . . . Rather remarkably, it had been Sarah who'd come to Joan's defense. She rarely took sides in any argument, but Joan was so obviously good that even Sarah was prompted to defend her.

It was Joan who was coming before them today.

"Joan Macdonald," said Kezia. "She is perhaps the most skillful of my women. She and Hattie are the most accomplished. Joan's older than many of the others and she's charged with disposing of stolen goods. I've seen nothing violent about her. She is quiet and careful."

"As far as you know," Mr. Davies added. "Appearances and utterances can be deceptive. There are times when we have to suspect a person isn't speaking completely honestly."

Before Kezia could summon an answer to convey her irritation without being openly rude, there was a knock at the door and two sailors brought Joan into the cabin. She walked with her head bent, and her hands clasped together at her waist.

"Good day to you, Joan Macdonald," Charles said. "Please sit on the chair there."

Joan did so, and folded her hands in her lap. She was staring straight in front of her.

Kezia said gently, "Joan, we're only trying to find out exactly what happened to Hattie. Were you close by when she fell to the deck?"

"I was quite close. I didn't see what happened, not really. Only when Hattie fell down . . . she cried out so loud that we all turned to look. She was lying doubled up. I could have seen the person who did it if I'd been looking in her direction, but I was not. I was putting away some of my own things. We'd just packed away our work . . . I was, I confess, lost in my own thoughts, and I regret that now, very much."

"We have been told repeatedly that you all went straight to help Hattie," Mr. Davies said wearily. "Do you confirm that?"

Joan nodded. "Me and Marion and Tabitha ran to her. Phyllis and Ann were still further back, and Sarah was there, too, somewhere."

"What about Emily Paxton?"

"She was nearer to the companionway than the rest of us. We called to her because Hattie wanted Bertie. We called to Emily to fetch him from below."

"Ah," said Charles. "That is why you called Emily to fetch him? Because she was nearest to the companionway already? The furthest away from where Hattie was lying? It would therefore be sensible for her to bring the child for that reason?"

Joan seemed to consider. "Yes," she said at last. "That's true. But we all thought . . ." She fell silent.

"What did you think, Joan?" Kezia asked.

"We thought those around her were calling Emily to fetch him because Emily was Hattie's friend."

"Were not all of you friends of a sort?" Mr. Donovan said.

"Emily was closest to Hattie. Emily is very fond of her. She admired her." Joan spoke quietly but firmly.

"What did Hattie say?" Kezia asked. "When she called out for Bertie."

"She said, 'Bertie.'" Joan's voice shook and she wiped at a corner of her eye. "Then . . . something like 'Not Freddie.'"

"But are you sure that's what she said?" Kezia was insistent. "Was it truly 'Not Freddie'? Could it perhaps have been 'Not ready'?" As she asked the question, she was aware of the irritation of the others. They had, it was true, been over the same ground many times. But she wanted to be sure of everything and felt angered when Mr. Davies took a deep breath, as if to say, *What kind of question is that? We've already ascertained that there's no one called Freddie aboard this ship. What difference does it make? All that matters (and everyone is in agreement about this) is that Hattie wanted her son brought to her.*

"I can't remember. But we were crying out to Emily to fetch Bertie. It was pitiful."

"Perhaps," said Kezia, "Freddie is someone Hattie knew in London. Maybe she has a relation with that name."

Mr. Davies ignored this remark. "Go on," he said to Joan. "Have you anything else to add?"

"Fetching Bertie seemed to take a very long time," Joan answered. "Every second we waited seemed to be an hour. And when he arrived, it was too late. Hattie'd gone, taken away by Mr. Donovan and a few sailors."

"What happened when Emily and Bertie arrived?" Mr. Davies asked.

"Oh, that was the worst thing I've ever seen, sadder than anything. It was—I don't even like to think about it, that poor little boy."

"Can you think of anyone," Charles asked, "on board this ship who would profit in some way from Hattie's death?"

"Profit?" Joan gave a scornful laugh. "There's nothing among the lot of us anyone could profit from! We're convicts, not a penny to any of our names."

"Indeed," said Mr. Davies.

Once again, every woman has said the same things, Kezia thought. We know that Hattie was threatened with death. We know someone tried to kill her, so we're assuming whoever embroidered the threat also tried to kill her. That's not necessarily true. No one has asked any of the women about private patchwork they may have done. No one has tried to find out anything about the embroidered threat left on Hattie's pillow. Which may have nothing to do with her stabbing, but if that is the case, we have to assume that *two* women may want Hattie dead.

The very idea was beyond her understanding.

"Thank you, Joan," said Charles. "You may go."

Joan stood up and left the room. As she opened the door, one of the sailors who'd been waiting outside for her came forward with his companion and led her away to the living quarters. How old she looks, thought Kezia, her shoulders bowed, her steps shuffling and slow.

"I agree with Kezia," said Charles. "That woman doesn't look capable of violence."

"We are all," said Mr. Davies, "capable of violence if we're sufficiently provoked."

With this announcement, and a final blotting of his inky words, he stood up. "I must bid you farewell now. We will be in Van Diemen's Land in a few days and I've a great deal of correspondence to finish before we land there. Several important letters to be sent back to England. I'll return to speak to the women we're seeing this afternoon. Good morning to you."

"He knows his letters are more important than anyone else's, to be sure." Mr. Donovan's voice was full of wry amusement. "But we're no nearer to finding out the truth of this matter. I must go to Hattie. I still hope she will wake at any moment and tell us what happened. She does speak, but of strange things. Cats, for the most part."

Kezia was lost in thought. In all the days they'd been on board the *Rajah*, Hattie had never once mentioned cats.

35
NOW

✦

9 July 1841
Ninety-five days at sea

Through all the weeks they'd been aboard the *Rajah*, the women took turns to help Marion. Her anguish was always worst in the middle of the night, and it wasn't unusual for her to be accompanied out of the living quarters by one of her companions. The sailors had reported this to the captain, and he'd agreed that, in order to keep everything calm and quiet, Marion would be allowed to come up on deck for a while, even when the other women were asleep. Tonight, Sarah was with her. As they leaned over the rail, Marion said, "I have bad feelings in my blood."

"In my bones, you mean," Sarah said. "That's what you say. You feel something in your bones. My gran used to say that. Her bones told her things every day."

"No," Marion insisted. "It's in my blood. I can feel a burning in my veins. There's blood rushing round my head and it's heavy and dark."

"You're ill again, are you? Like before?"

"Not like that. I lost so much blood. This feels like there's too much blood in my veins, blocking them up."

Sarah decided to say nothing. Everyone knew Marion had suffered a miscarriage, because Beth hadn't been shy about spreading the story. Sarah liked Marion well enough, but no one would have said she was clever, and maybe she hadn't cottoned to the truth of things. Perhaps she'd thought her monthlies were a little heavy and no more than that.

"We're worried about Hattie," Sarah said. "That's why you feel like that, maybe. You were on deck, so you feel it more, I suppose. I do, I know that."

"I fear it, Sarah. I fear her death. They'll take one of us and hang us if she dies. What if it's me?"

"But was it you who stabbed her?"

Marion gasped aloud. "No, of course I didn't. How could you think that? But it doesn't mean I mightn't be accused."

"I know you didn't. I'm sure they know you didn't, too. Marion, they're good people. Clever people. They'll know you didn't stab Hattie, I'm sure."

"What if I stabbed her without knowing about it? I sometimes forget things, you know. But Miss Hayter won't let them hurt me, will she?"

Sarah sighed. Marion was a poor soul and she shouldn't be unkind but really . . . "No, Marion," she said at last. "Miss Hayter will see you right. She'll know you're innocent."

"But I feel bad, Sarah. Something dreadful's going to happen."

"Come back with me and sleep now," said Sarah. "You're tired. Come and lie down."

"In the dark. I hate the dark."

"But it's dark out here, too. Can't you see?" She waved an arm at the blackness that lay just outside the circle of light thrown by a hanging lantern. "A huge black sea out there . . ."

"The stars," said Marion, pointing up to where the sky was thickly scattered with points of light that shimmered. "I love the stars. Aren't any stars down there."

As she spoke, Sarah was leading her to the companionway. The salt smell of the ocean, the light breeze and the glittering stars were left behind as the women went down the steps and the stuffy blackness of the convict quarters enveloped them.

36
NOW

✦

9 July 1841
Ninety-five days at sea
KEZIA

Sitting next to Hattie, holding her hand as she lay feverish in her narrow bunk, troubled Kezia. It reminded her of days when her beloved papa was sick at home. Mama was always there next to him, with Kezia and Henrietta very often at her side. *I was only five,* she told herself now. *Of course I was frightened to see him so changed, so unlike himself, but I am grown now.* What had not changed, though, and was still just as dreadful as ever, was the knowledge that Death lurked in this small cabin set aside on the *Rajah*. Mr. Donovan kept the shadows at bay as well as he could, in a place that was as clean as possible, but still, Kezia was aware of Death's black wings ready to be unfurled, shadowing all with a special darkness. Mr. Donovan sat some way off at a small table. A cupboard was pushed up against one wall. In it he kept his medicines and potions. His instruments and bandages lay in a chest of drawers much like her own.

Hattie was mumbling again. Her eyes were closed, her lips parched and flaking. Kezia leaned forward to catch her words. She took her hand and began to stroke it. "Dear Hattie, are you better today? You're speaking. Bertie . . . Did you see him? He comes to see you every day, you know."

"Not Freddie. He's not." The voice was a whisper, less than a whisper, cracked and broken, too. It was hard to understand the words. Kezia felt an eagerness, an excitement, rising within her. What was she about to hear?

"Who isn't? Who is Freddie? One of your brothers? Do you know where you are, dear? It's the *Rajah*. You're on the *Rajah*, going to Van Diemen's Land . . . We're nearly there, you know."

Perhaps she can't hear me, Kezia thought, close to tears. Then, miraculously, Hattie spoke again. Kezia missed the words and was filled with despair. "What did you say, Hattie? Tell me . . . Please tell me," she said, trying to keep the frustration she felt out of her voice.

"Sarah . . ." Hattie murmured. "Not Sarah Goodbourne . . . I mustn't tell."

Kezia frowned. "What do you mean . . . about Sarah?"

"She isn't. Not Sarah . . . She's not her. Kitty. I want my little Kitty back . . ."

Mr. Donovan jumped up from his seat and hurried to join Kezia at the bedside. She said, "Did you hear what she murmured just now? Kitty was her sister and I believe she died . . . but what about Sarah?" Her voice shook and she clamped her teeth together hard, to steady herself.

"She's delirious, Miss Hayter. There's little sense in what she says. Or if there is sense, I can make nothing of it."

Kezia bent closer to Hattie again. "What d'you mean, Hattie dear? Say it again . . . Not Sarah? I don't understand."

Nothing but silence came from Hattie. Donovan sighed. "That's all the speech you'll get from her now. Maybe for the rest of the day. She's unable to say anything for the most part. I've asked her repeatedly who stabbed her, to no avail. This attempt at speech may be her last. She has been very weak . . . We must prepare ourselves for the very worst, I fear."

She turned to the bunk once more. There was no color in Hattie's face, and her breath was ragged and bubbling in her chest. Kezia closed her eyes and prayed. *Please, dear Lord, save Hattie. Don't let her die. Keep her alive for her child, for Bertie . . . and give me strength to deal with whatever may happen.*

Mr. Donovan stood suddenly. "I can hear the change in her breathing, Miss Hayter. I'm afraid that this is the end," he whispered. "Perhaps you should leave the room. Dying is never easy."

"Thank you, I will stay," Kezia answered. Sadness washed over her and the shock that always afflicts the heart at the approach of death. "I'll hold Hattie's hand."

She could not, later, have said how long it was, the time between knowing Hattie would die and the moment her spirit left her body. Each breath rose from her chest with a terrible bubbling sound. Her mouth hung open. Her eyes had rolled back in her head and Kezia wanted more than anything to close her own but found she could not. She stared down at poor Hattie, so pretty, so pale and weak. At last, after minutes that seemed to go on far too long, silence fell in the small cabin. *She's gone to our Lord*, Kezia thought, feeling again the numbness around the heart that she remembered from childhood. *She'll be in Heaven. I must believe that . . . far from pain and fear and every unhappiness.*

"Miss Hayter, I'm so sorry. I could do no more than I did."

Kezia shook her head, unable to answer. He nodded as he closed Hattie's eyes. Looking carefully at Kezia, he said: "Will you tell poor little Bertie? I'll do so, if you'd rather."

"No, no," Kezia said. "I'll tell him. Then I'll bring him to see his poor mother."

"I'll make her as much like herself as I can," said Mr. Donovan. "For the child. But then we must commit her body to the sea. Captain'll want to do things properly."

"And the women . . . There must be a funeral. Will you speak to Mr. Davies?"

"I will, Miss Hayter. Don't trouble yourself on that account."

Kezia walked slowly along the deck to find Bertie. She could see some of her sewing women under the awning, stitching diligently. Sarah, Rose, Tabitha, Susan and Ruth were adding squares to what would be the last border of the coverlet. Should she tell them first? Part of her wanted to, very much, wanted the comfort of other people, who would cry with her, and cling together. Maybe she could cling to them too . . .

But, no, Bertie should be the first to know. The others would find out soon enough. Kezia paused to look over the railing at the sea. She stared down at water that, in the bright sunlight, glittered like a metal sheet: gold, or bronze, broken into ripples at the hull. How peaceful, quiet and cool it would be to plunge down and down into its depths, away from everything. Soon, very soon, Hattie would be there, under its weight, surrounded by water forever, picked at by sea creatures, her bones white on pale sand, hidden by fronds of the slippery green weeds that grew below the surface. Oh, poor Hattie! Poor Bertie . . . Kezia closed her eyes briefly. Then she stood up as straight and tall as she could, trying to calm herself. I must be the steady one. The consoler. She sighed and went on, looking for Bertie.

Then she saw him. He was with the other children, sitting on a bench in the shade of one of the sails, and Emily was reading to them from the Bible. As Kezia came up to the group, Emily fell silent and stood up. *She knows,* Kezia thought. *She can see it in my face.* Bertie's hair in the sunshine was like a fiery halo around his head.

"Emily," said Kezia, trying to steady her voice, "please could you send the other children away? I must talk to Bertie."

"Go and find your mothers now, children," Emily said. "Miss Hayter wants a word with Bertie." She ushered the others away and Kezia was aware of her presence, standing some way off.

Was it the sun? The heat? Suddenly, the deck seemed to her as liquid as the sea around them, swimming under her gaze. Kezia felt herself trembling as she walked to the bench and sat down beside Bertie. All the words, all the things she thought she should say, left her. Flew out of her head. She turned the child to face her and put both arms around him. His little body was so thin, so thin. "Dearest Bertie, I'm very, very sorry to have to tell you . . . your mother has died. She's gone and she's at peace now, with no pain to suffer any longer, but I'm so very sorry, my dearest child."

Bertie looked at her and sat very still. "You said she'd be better, you and the doctor." He was whispering, hardly able to speak. "You didn't say she'd die. You never said . . ."

Kezia took his wrists and held them gently in her hands. "I know, Bertie, I know. We hoped. We prayed and hoped, and we thought she'd live . . . but she died. God's taken her to Heaven. She'll be with the angels. They'll look after her."

"But *I* want her. Don't want angels to have her. I want my ma. She's my ma."

"We'll care for you, Bertie. The captain will think very carefully and we'll find the best person possible to look after you. You mustn't fret . . ."

Bertie was weeping now. Kezia held him as he cried, and minutes went by as they clung together. At last his tears stopped and his small body trembled as he wiped his eyes with Kezia's handkerchief.

"Would you like to see her, Bertie? Your mother? Say good-bye to her?"

Bertie nodded, and as they walked along the deck, Kezia was aware of Emily, stiff and frozen with shock near the ship's rail. She could see the other women, too, now standing. *They all know,* she thought. *They can see. They must've heard Bertie sobbing.* As she walked, she noticed one of the women going down to the lower deck. Everyone would be told soon enough.

"Come, Bertie," she said, when they reached the hospital. "You're going to have to be very brave now."

Bertie had been holding tight to her hand, but as the door opened, he pulled away from her and ran straight toward the bed where Hattie lay. The sounds coming from him now were those of a small animal being tormented: a terrifying cry that she wished she'd never heard and which didn't stop but filled the small cabin and screamed in her ears. Kezia knew that *this* sound, *this* horror, would come to her in nightmares for as long as she lived. Bertie had flung himself on his mother's body and was sobbing into the sheet that covered her.

Mr. Donovan walked to the child and put his hands on Bertie's back. "There, there," he said, stroking him, soothing him in the way you'd soothe a frightened horse. At last Bertie was quiet. He sat back on his heels on the floor beside the bunk and Mr. Donovan knelt beside him.

"You're a big boy, Bertie, and you must know something. If she'd lived, your mama would have been very sick. She'd have been in great pain. She was very badly wounded and she wouldn't have been the same mama as you had before. She has no pain now. She's at peace. And she loved you so much, Bertie. She wanted only your happiness. She'd want you to be happy."

"I can't," Bertie wailed. "Not without her. Not without my real ma."

"Not today. Maybe not for a long time, but you must try to be brave. See, I have her tin label for you, Bertie. Take it and put it round your neck. Then you'll remember your mother and how she wore it and you'll feel some comfort from holding her name near your heart."

Bertie said nothing as Mr. Donovan put the tin ticket round his neck. For a moment, he paused in his crying and looked down at his mother's name. He picked up the label and turned it. "Harriet Matthews," he said.

"You've learned to read well, I see," said Mr. Donovan.

"It's my ma's name," said Bertie. "I can't really read it properly. But I know that's her name."

"Your dear mother will be looking down at you from Heaven and you must make her proud of you, Bertie. Be good and kind and brave."

Bertie started crying again.

Even though the news was known all over the ship, the captain himself came down to announce Hattie's death formally to the women in the convict quarters. Those who were closest to Hattie wiped their eyes. Bertie, exhausted by the events of the day, was asleep on his berth with Joan, Phyllis and Emily close beside him.

"Poor mite," said Joan, stroking his hair as he lay with his face turned into his pillow. "Motherless."

"She's here, though. Can't you feel her presence? She'll be here, near her boy," Dwyer said. "Her spirit will be haunting this ship, mark my words. She'll not lie easy till justice is done."

Everyone who heard her shuddered and gathered closer together on the bunks and benches. Hattie had been so lively, her hair shining like red gold, her laugh scattering the misery of the lower deck. Of course she would be missed. Some of the women felt real sorrow, but even those who wouldn't give her the time of day felt a kind of sadness simply because death, and especially murder, trumped what you thought of a person.

The Newgate Nannies had taken up a position on a nearby bench. Even they were uncharacteristically somber. "Can't get away from it. We're all looking behind us now. Who knows who's out there, thinking to do it again?"

"It ain't me," Tabitha said quickly. "No need to look at me, just cos I was on deck. Saw nothing."

"No one's saying it is, Tab," said Dwyer. "Only a fool would think that." She looked around at the others with her wandering eye, daring anyone to suggest Tabitha might be guilty. "Tab's one of us and no one'd better say the Newgate Nannies are stabbers. Looking at a murder charge now, and no one'd better say we're murderers. That's all."

"It's bad, a death on board ship," Selwood said. "Unlucky. Will they find who did it, d'you think?"

"Bound to. Maybe they know already." That was Phyllis.

"Don't be so daft. What'd be the point of carrying on with the questioning if they know already? Your head's full of bits of moldy straw—that's your trouble," said Ruth.

"What'll happen to the one who killed her? That's what I want to know," Izzy wondered. "Will she be taken back to England to hang?"

"Got gallows in Van Diemen's Land, ain't they? Why'd they

bother taking someone back? Nothing but a waste of space, that'd be. No, they'll hand whoever it is over to the Van Diemen's Land folk and let them deal with her."

"They'll bury Hattie tomorrow. *Commit her body to the deep.* That's what they say for a burial at sea," Emily said.

"That's sadder than anything," said Marion. "No grave for Bertie to visit. Nowhere to put flowers. Nowhere to go on special days. It's hard, that."

"Don't make no difference. An orphan's an orphan. Bloody great statue of an angel ain't going to cheer him up, is it?" Rose chipped in.

"But think of the water. Her body'll be all bloated and swollen. Horrible. I've seen 'em pulling suicides from the river. It's not pretty," Tabitha said.

"Shut your filthy mouth!" Dora was crying now. "I'm not going to think of her like that. Just shut it, if you can't say nothing good. It's a crying shame, that's what it is, her dying so young and so pretty."

One by one, the women returned to their own berths and lay down, but it was hard to sleep. As the night wore on, the *Rajah* began to roll and pitch as though the sea itself could find no rest.

When daylight came, the sky was black with storm clouds. By noon a squall was driving in from the east, and the women who'd gathered to pay their respects to Hattie as she was buried clutched their shawls around them and bent their heads. If anyone was weeping, their tears mingled with the driving rain. The whole crew of the *Rajah* joined the convict women on the deck to hear Mr. Davies say the words, fine words, to accompany Hattie Matthews to the bottom of the ocean. No one would have heard them, however grand they were, if anyone else had spoken them, but the wind was no match for Reverend Davies: *"Out of the deep have I called unto thee, O Lord. Lord, hear my voice . . ."* He stood, head held high, and intoned the psalm over the heads of the assembled crowd. Everyone listened to the mixed wailing and speaking and to the wind blowing.

A stillness fell on the crowd as two sailors approached the rail carrying Hattie's body on a stretcher. She'd been sewn into a piece of canvas, with metal weights, but it was easy to make out her shape, as the thick, wet fabric clung to it. Kezia prayed that God would look after poor Bertie, who had to see such a thing. He won't forget, she thought. Some things stick to the mind, and as long as he lived, at unexpected moments Bertie would see this: everyone in dark clothes, the rain driving down and pricking the surface of the water with a million small spears, and a horrible dun-colored thing with his mother's shape, sliding down to the sea where it made an almost inaudible splash and was gone.

After the women had filed away, Miss Hayter was left holding Bertie's hand.

"Come with me," she said. "We'll go to the captain's cabin, find a towel to dry you and rest there for a while. A drink of cordial . . ."

Of what use were all the sweet things in the world when your mother was lying on the seabed and you were sailing away from her last resting place?

Joan hung back when the others went down into the living quarters. The squall had passed. The rain had stopped and there was scarcely any wind. The sea was still choppy, each wave that passed marked with white crests. She looked over the rail into the water, thought of Bertie, all alone in the world. That reminded her of Lydia's children. My little darlings, she thought, my babies.

"Joan," said a voice behind her, and she turned to see Isaac Margrove. He held out his handkerchief. "Are you in need of my handkerchief again?"

"I shan't cry but I'm sad for Bertie," Joan said.

"He'll be well cared for, I'm sure," said Isaac, coming to stand beside her at the ship's rail. "The cap'n will see him right. And it's good to speak to you, Joan. I've missed our conversations."

Joan sighed. "I've missed them, too."

They stood awkwardly next to one another, not touching, both turning their gaze on the ocean, rushing past the hull. Isaac said, "I look at you women as I go about. I see the work you've done on that patchwork. That's fine work."

"Thank you," said Joan. "It's good to have that to do."

The two of them looked at one another. Isaac, so ready with the talk in the normal run of things, didn't know what to say and shifted from foot to foot. Joan knew that she could help him. All she had to do was smile, hold out her hand; he would take it and they could move to the space behind that barrel where he would kiss her and, for a moment or two, she could be happy. Would that be so wrong? Perhaps it wouldn't. Maybe, because they were only a few days away from land, it wouldn't matter. They'd be parted soon enough. I could forget myself, Joan thought. I could love another woman's man just for a little while, and how wrong would that be? She shook her head. Wrong was wrong and, as if it were a sign from Heaven, the boatswain came striding up the deck.

"I'll bid you good day," said Isaac, bowing. "Please keep the handkerchief."

"Thank you," said Joan. She watched him walk away from her and felt her heart shrinking. She tucked the handkerchief into her pocket. The second gift from Isaac. It'll remind me of a good man, she thought, as she went down the companionway to the lower deck.

Rain-soaked sailing: the Rajah passes through curtains of blowing rain, her decks awash, her sails sodden, the wood above the waterline as wet as the wood below it. She bends to the water enveloping her, and the horizon is dark and hung with cloud.

37
NOW

✦

11 July 1841
Ninety-seven days at sea
KEZIA

Sleep had almost deserted her. What would Bertie's fate be, alone in the world without Hattie? The poor boy hung around Emily and the women, unwilling to play with the other children, and quiet in every gathering. Who could be trusted to look after him once they arrived in Van Diemen's Land?

The inquiry had flagged. They had spoken with Ann, who merely wept and had very little to add. They would speak to Phyllis later in the day, but as outspoken as she was, they'd learn little that was new, Kezia was sure. And now they had a murderer to find, and the weight of this responsibility lay heavy on Charles and the others, too. Kezia's mind went back to Hattie's last words. What had they meant? She'd spoken to no one about those last words.

Mr. Donovan could not have heard them. *Sarah isn't Sarah . . . Not Freddie . . . She told me not to tell . . . Kitty.*

Sarah . . . What did Sarah Goodbourne, who was dull and quiet and altogether unremarkable, have to do with Freddie? She'd heard Hattie speaking of Kitty before: *I did have a younger sister, but I'm sure she's dead now . . . Kitty, she was called.*

She wished she knew who Freddie was. Charles had assured her that there was no one by that name in the crew. And, from what Kezia had observed, Sarah kept herself mostly to herself and showed no great interest in any of the women or in Hattie. Was Freddie something to do with Sarah? Was Freddie someone Hattie had to keep quiet about? Was someone telling her this when she stitched *Speak & you die* on that cotton square? Kezia sighed in frustration, slapping her hand against her pillow. I have to speak to Sarah, she thought.

Should she consult the men, she wondered, and tell them her intentions? *No.* Mr. Davies would immediately decide that the mere mention of Sarah's name from Hattie's lips meant that she was guilty of the stabbing. Charles and Mr. Donovan would probably agree with him. No, Kezia told herself. I must see Sarah on my own.

Thinking about Charles calmed her a little, and Kezia was struck by a surprising thought: whatever the situation, however troubling and difficult, the idea of Charles, the memory of his face, made her happy somewhere in her deepest heart, a place seemingly separate from the rest of her being.

But before she spoke to Sarah, she had to attend a meeting of the inquiry.

"Well, now," said Charles, to Kezia and the others gathered at the table in his cabin. He was frowning, and when he spoke, there was a heaviness in his voice. "Matters have, as you know, become more serious since we last met. We are now having to deal with a murderer in our midst."

"Indeed, and we must find her out," said Mr. Davies. "We must not land with this unresolved. The authorities in Hobart will want to know exactly what they're dealing with. Have you any suggestions, Miss Hayter?"

Kezia shook her head. "I will talk to my needlewomen again this morning, but I cannot see that someone will suddenly have anything useful to add to our deliberations."

"Perhaps we should bring our suspects together and ask them as a group," Mr. Donovan suggested.

"Let's wait and see what effect Hattie's death has on her companions," Charles said. "Someone might say something. Miss Hayter can ask what's being said by women in the convict quarters. If we're no nearer a solution tomorrow, we'll have them here again, and question them together. We're very close to our destination, no more than a week away, I'd say."

Kezia stood up. "I'll bring the women out on deck. We'll talk about Hattie, I'm sure of it." She wondered where she would find the occasion to speak to Sarah on her own, but was determined to do so. The men wouldn't understand why such a conversation was so urgent, or so necessary. I can hardly, she thought, explain it to myself.

38

THEN

Cotton piece: white ground, with block-printed three-petalled red flowers and brown leaves

July 1841
CLARA

Stitching allows you to think. The others talk among themselves and I join in from time to time, but mostly I'm quiet. Memories of the past come to me too vividly. Today, we're in the shade of the awning, even though it's no longer hot. Miss Hayter's not here, for now, and the others are speaking about their men. It's natural, I suppose, that some women have favorites among the crew. Keeping the men entirely separate from the women at all times would be impossible. The younger ones are sure that the captain is in love with Miss Hayter, and when the matron's not among us, they're free with their opinions and their language.

Beth says, "They're stiff enough when they walk the deck, but what happens when he gets her alone? Is he stiff, more likely?"

"When are they alone, though?" Phyllis asks. "I've only seen them walking about. What can you do when you're walking about?"

Izzy says, "I can think of things . . . They get to somewhere quiet and he opens his breeches. She's only got to put out her hand and there'd be spray all over the deck—and I don't mean seawater."

Rose and Ruth giggle at that, and Phyllis sniffs. "I can't imagine Miss Hayter—"

"Well, I can," says Ruth. "And there's the night, too. Just imagine Captain Ferguson, Phyllis, tiptoeing to her cabin, sliding in next to her on the bunk, lifting her nightgown, then sliding himself into her just like a slippery eel only made very hard . . ."

Ruth, Rose and Izzy are weak with laughter but Phyllis's face is scarlet.

"Never!" she says. "She's a God-fearing young woman, is Miss Hayter. She'd never let a man near her, not without no wedding ring first. Not her."

"That's far from the truth. I've known godly women," says Rose, "plenty of them, and they'd spread their legs quick as the next once they'd felt an itch."

"That's disgusting." Phyllis makes a face. "I won't believe it and I'd thank you to keep a respectful tongue in your head."

Izzy says, "I reckon Phyllis is right, though. I don't think they've got to that yet. I'd be able to tell."

"That's bilge," Alice puts in. "She might be better at hiding things than you'd reckon. May the Good Lord protect her from temptation, but it's the quiet ones you've got to watch." She nods firmly to emphasize the importance of this remark, which is one I've heard often in my life. What I've found is it's true sometimes and at others it's not. There's no way on God's earth of knowing what goes on between two people once lights are out and clothes are off.

The others go on talking. I say as little as I can, but make a remark from time to time. Mostly my thoughts go back to the past. I should never have let myself fall so much in love. My whole life I've kept myself removed from such emotions. I'd seen other women, watched the storms of feeling wash over them when their hearts had been stolen. Every bit of good sense they ever had disappeared overnight. I swore I wouldn't ever be like them. I've admired some men. I've been grateful to others, particularly Samuel and his friends. It was worth it—their attentions turned me into a person of property. I've desired others and let them fuck me. But Edmund wasn't like any other man. He knew nothing about me or my work.

I met him by chance, walking along the street. I tripped on a piece of wood lying in the road and he caught me before I fell. He'd pulled me toward him to set me on my feet again, and in that instant, I was lost. I didn't see it then, but as we began to know one another better, I liked him more and more. Two days from our first meeting, he came to my house and into my bed. After that, I spent hours dreaming about him when I should have been doing other things, going over the words we'd said, my flesh alive and throbbing when I recalled what we'd done in the dark. On days when I knew he would visit me, every part of me wanted him, wanted his hands on me, felt the need for him so much that every last part of me was on fire.

He had a wife. He had three small children. We never mentioned them. I wanted to know nothing about the rest of his life, because if he spoke of that, my conscience would be stirred and that was the last thing I wanted when I was with Edmund. I wished him mine. I wanted him to have no history and nothing else in his life apart from me. I didn't mind having only part of his attention. All I cared about was making our hours together as pleasant as they could be. What came over us, on the night we went into the Flag Inn, was a kind of madness. We should have kept to my house and not ventured out, like ordinary lovers. We shouldn't have drunk a single drop of anything stronger than cordial. And Edmund shouldn't have come to my rescue when a boorish, ill-favored dolt began to call me whore, drab and worse, as he reached out to touch me. I try not to think of what happened, but two men were dead by dawn and I'd killed one. The other drinkers at the Flag knew neither of them, and I pretended I'd never met them before that night.

I was caught and brought to Millbank, ready to stand trial for the death of a stranger. I mourned Edmund with all my heart and feared for myself, too. A gallows was where I'd end my days, as sure as dawn comes daily. Later, I remembered that three children would grow up without a father and my feelings of guilt and sadness nearly overwhelmed me. But after only one night in the cells, I made up my mind to escape. Others were going to be transported and I knew, as soon as I heard the word, that that was where I had to be: on a ship sailing away from my own execution, as well as everything I wanted never to think of again.

Miss Hayter has come back to tell us we must put away our work. The others have obeyed her and are packing their things. Hattie's quite close to me on deck, and I'd run away if I could, but she's talking to me. I've managed to keep my distance from her so far, much better than I could have hoped. And she's said nothing since I left a warning on her pillow. That was weeks ago. I've begun to feel almost safe. But she's going to speak to me, I feel, and I wish I could simply stand up and walk away. I don't want to talk to her. I don't want her to talk to me, but she's speaking to me and I can't escape. We are alone and talking.

"She looks happy, don't you think?" Hattie says. "Do you think she knows he loves her?"

"Maybe," I say. I bend my head to put my work away and my hair, which is uncovered today, falls forward onto my shoulders. I brush it away with my left hand. Then, not wanting to seem unfriendly, I add, "The captain seems happy, though." They are the first words I've exchanged directly with her for some weeks and I look up at her as I speak. She's stiff with terror, frozen. She stands, clutching her fabric bag to her breast with her mouth open. She's not breathing. And in her wide, wide horrified blue gaze, I see it.

She knows who I am. I've been recognized. We've been on this ship for weeks but only now has she realized who I am. Why now? What did she see *now* that reminded her of something that happened so many years ago?

39

THEN

Cotton piece: drab ground scattered with a pattern of widely spaced leaves and flowers in black and yellow

5 July 1841
Ninety-one days at sea
KEZIA

Kezia looked at the women sitting around her, each one with her head bent over her work. The last of the day's sunlight glanced occasionally from a steel needle, but the awning that had been put up to shade the women was no longer really needed in the cooler weather.

Phyllis, Marion and Ann had their shawls tied round them for warmth. Izzy was leaning over to whisper to Rose as usual, and they were having difficulty stifling their laughter. Joan was holding up her work, close to her eyes. Even with her spectacles, her vision was a little clouded.

How many thousands of stitches, Kezia wondered, are there in this coverlet that they've made with me? Eighteen women, gathering every day in small groups.

It was easier now to see the shape of what they were making. Smaller sections of the coverlet had been stitched together and now she could see lines of similar color spreading out over the women's laps: brownish patches and reddish ones next to paler greens and reds. Rows of triangles were sewn to rows of squares. Spotted fabrics lay next to striped, with flowered and plain ones adding variety and contrast. Here and there, a mark still showed where she'd tried to scrub away a bloodstain. Kezia touched a spot that had proved especially difficult to remove.

"You can't help but leave a mark with blood," Susan said.

"We've done the best we can," Kezia said. "It won't be noticed in the whole."

"So many other colors, no one'll see," Izzy agreed. "It looks grand. Never thought it would be as fine as this."

It would be dark soon, but the sun was emerging fully now, only minutes before it would set. The clouds that had been massing along the western horizon were swept away by the wind. "When you come to the end of your thread," Kezia told the women, "you may put away your needles."

Kezia watched as they cut their threads, tucked their needles carefully away and began to stand up and stretch their limbs. Tabitha shook out her fingers, muttering, "Stiff and cold. Feels like my hand's dead."

A bird, with wide white wings, suddenly swooped toward the women, cawing and crying, then rising again and making for the rigging. There it settled and looked down on them. Ann muttered, "Bad luck, that is."

"It's a bird," said Kezia. "Nothing more. Let us sing a verse instead of worrying about omens."

She began the hymn and as she sang, the others joined in:

"A servant with this clause
Makes drudgery divine.
Who sweeps a room as for thy laws
Makes that and th' action fine."

The voices floated up to tangle in the intricacies of the rigging and soar across the huge expanses of the sails. Kezia glanced to where the white bird had perched. There was no sign of it. When the singing was over, she rolled up the coverlet with help from Phyllis and Dora.

The women left behind after Kezia's departure picked up the bits and pieces of fabric that had fallen to the deck, and put them into the pockets sewn on their skirts. They walked slowly, reluctantly, toward the companionway, leaving behind the glory of a sunset that was marking the sky with wide stripes of apricot and mauve, laying a sheet of molten bronze on the water.

There were still a few women left on deck when the screaming began.

40

NOW

✦

12 July 1841
Ninety-eight days at sea
CLARA

The seven of us, one of whom might be guilty of murder, are working next to each other now, and the others draw away from us a little. They try to behave as if everything is as it was before, but they sit further away than they used to, and closer to one another, turning their faces from us. What are they saying about us? Which of us do they think it might be? If anyone had a motive, it's me. I'm the one who needed her to be silent. If they knew my past, these women would not believe I was innocent.

Miss Hayter sits down next to Tabitha.

"We're thinking about Hattie today," she says. "We're all very sad, but we have to find out the truth. And I'm sure we're close to an answer. We'll soon know who the guilty person is. She's among us, that's certain . . ." Miss Hayter looks around but every woman is staring at her work and won't meet her eye. She goes on to talk of other matters, and to move around the circle, admiring Izzy's work, helping Phyllis and Lottie to put the final touches to the last border, making sure that the stitches lie evenly. Silence falls, which is unusual, but as ever, the work takes us away from our thoughts for a short time. Miss Hayter goes from one of us to the next, examining our handiwork.

When she reaches me, she says, "Come to the end of your thread now, everyone. Finish as soon as you can, please, and, Sarah, if you could help me take everything to my cabin, I'd be grateful."

I push my needle through the fabric and run the thread through a few stitches on the back of the work. Then I cut the cotton, put my needle away and stand up, waiting for the others to do the same. When they've stopped sewing, they roll up the work in its cotton sheet and Miss Hayter and I pick it up. We haven't sung the hymn today.

Steady sailing: the Rajah has the sunset behind her. It's been a calm day and toward evening the sky was striped gold and pink. Pink has deepened to scarlet and the ship is entirely red as she sails toward the eastern horizon.

41
NOW

12 July 1841
Ninety-eight days at sea
KEZIA

"Thank you," said Kezia. "Please come in. You can put the work over there."

"Yes, Miss," Sarah said, bending over to place the burden carefully. Then she said, turning toward the door, "May I go now?"

"I'd like to ask you something first, Sarah. Please sit down."

Sarah seemed very pale. She went to perch warily on the only chair and Kezia sat on her bunk, facing her. "You look tired, Sarah," she said.

Sarah shook her head.

Kezia continued. "I have to ask you something now and I beg you to answer me honestly."

"I will, Miss," Sarah said, so quietly that Kezia had to lean forward a little to catch what she said.

"I was with Hattie when she died," Kezia continued. "I heard her last words. She was near death and not herself, of course, but one of the last words she spoke was your name. She mentioned you by name more than once. Is there something you want to say to me before I go on?"

Kezia watched Sarah carefully. Her head was bent, and she'd made fists of her hands, driving her nails into her palms. She didn't look up but spoke into her lap.

"If Hattie said I stabbed her, that's a lie. I never stabbed her, Miss," she said, raising her head a little and speaking more confidently. Her lips had narrowed to a pinched line in her face. "I'd not do something like that. Never. Not that. You have to believe me, Miss. I wouldn't."

Silence fell and Kezia waited. At last she said, "Hattie said something else."

Sarah looked up and her eyes were wide with fear. "What? What did she say?" Her voice had fallen again and Kezia could hardly hear her.

"She spoke of being told not to tell anyone something . . . Do you know anything about a warning left for Hattie?"

Sarah stood up abruptly, and turned away, facing the chest of drawers. She stood silent for so long that Kezia was about to ask the same question again, but then she turned. Her back, Kezia noticed, was straighter than before. She looked taller.

"Yes," she said, taking a deep breath and looking directly at Kezia. "I needed her silence." Her voice was different and stronger, but then she sighed and bent her gaze to the cabin floor. Kezia could see the torment and distress of her thoughts marked on her face. "I stitched some words on a square of fabric. And she said nothing; she must have kept quiet, because I've been left alone."

"But what did you need her to be silent about?" Kezia was bewildered. How would Sarah explain herself in a way that she could understand? "Hattie also told me that you were not Sarah Goodbourne. How can that be?"

Sarah covered her face with her hands and cried out, "Oh, dear God . . ."

"You're distressed." Kezia looked at Sarah and at the door of her cabin. Am I in any danger? she wondered. Would Sarah—would she attack her? Kezia looked at Sarah's stricken face and knew she was safe. "Come and sit down again," she said. "Sit down here, Sarah."

Sarah Goodbourne obeyed, but said nothing. She was still covering her face. The moments passed, each one, it seemed to Kezia, thick with foreboding.

"Speak to me, Sarah. Say something. Please look at me."

Sarah lowered her hands but could not look Kezia in the face. She turned away as she spoke.

"That's true. Hattie was telling the truth. Sarah Goodbourne isn't my real name. I stole it before coming aboard the *Rajah*. I'd killed a man. I'd been sentenced to hang. He'd've stabbed me to death if I'd not killed him first. I left the real Sarah Goodbourne drugged and tied up in Millbank and took her name to be my own. My given name's Clara. Clara Shaw."

"But how did Hattie know this? I don't understand." Kezia felt as if she were groping her way in a fog. "Had you met her before?"

Sarah's eyes widened, and for a moment she seemed unable to answer. She looked away from Kezia and fixed her eyes on her own hands, twisted in her lap. Then she said, "I knew her mother a long time ago—Hattie was no more than a child then. Her mother came to see me and brought Hattie with her. She must have been about twelve years old then, but still, she recognized me—I couldn't, *I daren't* be discovered. If anyone had known my real crime, I'd have been sent back to hang. I was not a good person, Miss Hayter. I have done everything since to become better, different from what I used to be."

Kezia was silent for a long time. Then Sarah spoke again. "I didn't stab Hattie," she said, more vehemently. "I promise I did not. It was on the day she was attacked, as we were finishing our work, that I saw she recognized me. I couldn't risk her saying anything about who I really was. I beg you to believe me." Sarah's voice was beginning to tremble. "I turned away from Hattie at once, and I was walking away, trying to think what to do, what to say for the best, when the screams came. I didn't. I couldn't . . ." Sarah fell silent and kicked at a loose plank, over and over.

Kezia closed her eyes as she tried to understand everything that Sarah . . . *Clara* had said. One fact stood out above the others. Clara was capable of killing. She'd admitted that she'd stabbed a man to death, and if she hadn't overpowered some poor creature in Millbank, she'd have been hanged by the neck. Kezia shuddered. There were laws, she knew. Laws of God and laws of man. There had to be punishments visible to everyone that told them: if you do *this* thing, if you commit *this* crime, then here's what you must expect. An eye for an eye, said the Old Testament. But what is merciful, Kezia had often wondered, about killing someone simply for having stolen goods or forged money? There were many crimes for which you could hang. She was certain of one thing in this moment: if the men knew of Clara's past, they would reach the obvious conclusion. Kezia could hear their voices in her head. *It must have been Clara who wielded the dagger. She's more than capable of it. Why, she'd stabbed a man to death not more than a few weeks ago. Said so herself. Admitted it. And hadn't she admitted to sending Hattie a warning?* Kezia stood up.

"Sarah . . . I will continue to call you Sarah until we have resolved this matter in the inquiry. I shall have to speak to the captain about it."

"No!" Sarah sprang up and her voice shook. "I implore you to say nothing. Please, for the love of God, have mercy. The captain will have no choice but to send me back to hang. I killed a man. Please. I beg you!"

"You say you had to kill him. I would like to know more about the circumstances, if you'll tell me."

"I've not spoken of it since that night," Sarah said. She twisted in the chair, as though to turn as far away as she could from Kezia's gaze.

"I will make no judgment," said Kezia. "I'll listen to you and that's all. I give you my word."

Sarah bit her lip and found it hard at first to speak. She hesitated for a time that seemed to stretch into minutes. "We were both—the man I was accompanying and I—a little the worse for drink. I admit that, and I'm not proud of it. It was a summer night and we were happy and the beer may have made us silly. No more than that, but not ourselves. Perhaps we drew too much attention. A man came up to me and began to paw at my arm. His hand was thick and none too clean, and I pushed him away. That angered him and he began to call me names. Dreadful words. Drab, whore and worse."

Sarah lifted her eyes and met Kezia's gaze. "He assumed I was on the town. A prostitute. He came to that conclusion because my companion looked like a respectable man." She sighed and continued. "When we left the inn, our path took us through some quiet streets and then through a park of sorts. We hadn't noticed anyone following us but there he was, behind us. He attacked Edmund first . . . my companion. Knocked him down with a blow to the head. Then he came for me."

Kezia wondered if she should stop the narrative there. Was it

270

right to make Sarah relive such a dreadful night? It seemed to her clear that Sarah was telling the truth. Her account was sincere and even the most skeptical of the men—even Mr. Davies—would believe her if he were present. She put out a hand but Sarah waved it away and leaned forward.

"You won't know such things, Miss, but they go on. Men acting as though you're there for their pleasure. Many thoughts were going through my head, and I was fuddled with the beer. I thought, Let him do his worst. Then it'll stop and this'll be over. Then I thought, I can't bear it. I'll fight him. I wanted him battered into pulp. Still, I wasn't entirely off my head. I knew that if it came to it, he'd beat me into the middle of next week. He'd torn off my skirt and my drawers and hit me about the head a little, getting me ready. I was flat on my back on the earth. He was talking about what he'd do to me, now, just as soon as he could, and pushing my legs apart with those filthy hands . . . well." Sarah paused and a long silence fell in the cabin. Kezia felt herself hot with the shame of hearing such a thing. Sarah went on. "Then he did. Didn't take long. After, he gave an almighty roar and rolled off me. But Edmund had come to his senses and he lifted the man to his feet before he'd quite recovered, and turned him round so they were facing each other. I got up as quickly as I could, too." Sarah covered her face with her hands.

"Would you like to stop, Sarah? I think I've heard enough."

"No, no, you haven't. It's taking time to tell it, but when it happened it was so quick. Over in a couple of blinks. He had a knife and stabbed Edmund. In the heart. I began to shriek. What's next is muddled in my head but I ran and sank my teeth into his disgusting hand. I bit him very hard on the hand that was holding the knife and he dropped it. He wasted seconds swearing and cursing and jumping about with pain. I took the knife from where he'd dropped it. I went for him. Got him in the neck just by his ear. Put the knife in up to the hilt. Did I want to kill him?"

Kezia said nothing and Sarah went on. "I did. At that moment, I did and I was happy I did. My love was dead and I cared nothing for anything else. My shouts brought the constables. The rest comes from that."

"I cannot imagine your pain, Sarah. You were provoked beyond reason. Wouldn't the Bench have looked favorably on you for that?"

Sarah shook her head. "Stabbing's stabbing, Miss. Death is death."

Kezia could find no answer to that. "I'll plead for you with the others, Sarah. I'll make certain the captain doesn't act hastily. I promise you that. Nothing will be done yet . . . We still, don't forget, have to find who killed Hattie. That's the most important task to my mind. I'm more concerned with that than I am with seeing you brought to justice, either for killing a man, or for impersonating someone. Though that, of course, was very wrong of you . . ." Kezia's voice faded to nothing. "Did it not occur to you that the real Sarah may have been hanged in your place?"

Sarah didn't answer. There were tears in her eyes. "I couldn't allow myself to think such things. It would have—it would have prevented me. I have had to make myself unfeeling. Uncaring. I am trying . . . I hope one day."

Kezia was not in the least certain that Charles would be as prone to mercy as she was. He would not be as sympathetic to Sarah's attempts to become a better person. She had no certainty that she could persuade him to her point of view, and in that case justice would take its course and she could not prevent it. A gallows would be waiting in Van Diemen's Land. Sarah, or Clara, would be handed over to the authorities and would certainly be condemned to hang. But she must know that, Kezia thought, so why would she protest her innocence in the matter of Hattie's stabbing? Kezia believed her. The truth seemed as far out of reach as ever.

"May I go back to the others now?" Sarah asked.

"Yes, of course," said Kezia. "Thank you for telling me what you did. I will pray for you. And please come to me with anything that you remember about the evening Hattie was stabbed."

Almost before Kezia had shut the cabin door, before she had properly collected her thoughts, someone was knocking on it again: a swift succession of blows on the wood. She went to open it, alarmed, and there was Sarah again, her breath coming fast, as though she'd been running.

"What's wrong, Sarah?" Kezia said. "Has something happened?"

"Miss Hayter, I must speak to you again."

Kezia stood aside and Sarah came in.

"It's only that I wanted to ask you . . ." She hesitated again before saying, all in a rush, "I want to beg you to say nothing to the other women about my real name. I'm sorry for what I did to Sarah Goodbourne but I have to forget Clara Shaw. I want to put her and everything she was behind me. Please, Miss Hayter."

"But wouldn't they understand your situation?" Kezia asked. "Just as I've understood it?"

"Some may. Others won't. But I don't want their sympathy. I want . . ." Sarah fell silent for a few moments, then said: "I would like to be invisible."

"Then I will say nothing for now," Kezia said. "Though perhaps you misjudge your companions in the convict quarters."

"Thank you, Miss Hayter." Sarah opened the door and left the cabin, almost running as she made her way to the deck.

42
NOW

✦

14 July 1841
One hundred days at sea
KEZIA

"But do you not *see* it, Kezia? Cannot you understand?" Charles
stood up from his desk and took the chair next to Kezia. As he
spoke, Kezia turned away her face. He went on. "This woman,
whatever her real name is, is a criminal. Quite apart from what she
did to gain a berth on this ship, she confessed to you two days ago
that she stabbed a man to death. It's true that the circumstances
were . . . Well, she was provoked. But, still, she committed murder.
What more evidence do you need, Kezia? Why d'you not *see* it?"

How to answer him? Anger and hurt rose in her so strongly
that she knew this: if she opened her mouth, words would emerge that
she'd regret. She took a breath to calm herself. She forced herself to
look at Charles. He would not, she knew, deliberately want to anger
her, and if she were honest, she could agree that, on the face of it,

Sarah, or Clara, *was* the obvious suspect. Kezia spoke as evenly as she could. Her fury felt to her like a rock in her stomach.

"Simply because she's the obvious suspect, it doesn't mean she is guilty. If you've done something in the past, it doesn't follow that you will continue to do those things in the future. Does it? Is there no hope of redemption? I believed her. She was sincere. I'm sure of it."

"Forgive me, Kezia." Charles was looking at her with a wry smile, which made her want to kick him. "You are a kind and virtuous person and can't imagine, I've no doubt, the sort of mind that finds it easy to lie and continue lying. Why would Sarah change? She's been used to lying throughout her life. Why should she not go on thus, especially when her life is in danger?"

Kezia stood up and faced him. "Because she has nothing to gain from lying, *that* is why! She'd already told me . . . simply by confessing *she knew*, she must have known, that she'd signed her own death warrant. Knowing what you know of her, will you not give her to the authorities in Van Diemen's Land for them to deal with her according to the law? Is she not *already* likely to end on the gallows? Why, in such a case, would she need to lie about Hattie?"

"Perhaps . . ." he conceded.

"What possible advantage would come to her from denying a part in Hattie's death? Why would she hide her guilt in this, when she's already confessed to so much?"

"As to that, I can't say." Charles strode over to the window and stared out of it.

"You're walking away from me"—Kezia was almost shouting now—"because you don't want to admit that I may be right. That someone else killed Hattie. If you tell Mr. Donovan and Mr. Davies about Sarah and what she's admitted to me, we lose the chance of discovering who it was. The others will see nothing but a culprit when they look at her. They'll stop thinking about anyone else being responsible."

"But which of the other women could it be? We have no idea. No one's obviously guilty, are they? Every one of them was there and not one with the slightest motive." He came up to where Kezia was standing, biting her lip and frowning, and took hold of her wrists. Very gently, he said, "That is the main reason, Kezia. The motive. These women are criminals, to be sure, but they aren't murderers. Not one of them, except Sarah. I will call her that. *See* it, Kezia. See the truth. She had the motive. She's killed a man. What do you have to put against these facts?"

"My heart. My instincts. She threatened Hattie, it's true. She was fearful of being discovered, but almost a whole voyage has passed quietly since then, and Hattie had said nothing. She had no idea that Sarah had killed a man. Why, so near our destination, would she put everything she'd been striving for in jeopardy by stabbing Hattie?"

"We don't know, Kezia. How d'you know that Hattie hadn't said something to her? Sarah may not have meant to do more than threaten her again. Matters spiral out of control. I can think of a dozen ways in which it might have happened."

"Then will you wait? For now, let me talk to the women again. I beg you . . ."

"I cannot," Charles said. "It's my duty to tell them. They'll be arriving in Van Diemen's Land very soon and they must be told."

"But we're so close to land. They'll put Sarah under guard. Let her at least be free till we land."

"I cannot. She may throw herself overboard, evade justice. I will have to put her under guard."

A knock came on the door. Kezia sank onto a chair and tried to compose herself, to no avail. He would not bow to her pleas. He would do what he wanted to do and the devil take her opinions. They were of no importance to him. This thought fell on Kezia, like a pall, and weighed down her heart with sadness. The door opened. Mr. Donovan and Mr. Davies came in and solemnly took their seats. Kezia realized they must have overheard, if not the angry words, then certainly the tone of the conversation. The fury she felt must still have shown in her face. Her hair had come unfastened at the nape of her neck and she concentrated on that. She could feel her heart hammering in her chest and a drop of sweat making its way down her spine.

"Well, now, Miss Hayter and gentlemen," said Mr. Davies, rubbing his hands together. "Where do we find ourselves this morning? Has the dawn brought enlightenment?"

He's cheerful, Kezia thought. He's closer to home, eager to take the money he'd brought from London to his congregation. He'll have friends there, she told herself. Well, we are all, also, eager for land. For a moment, she allowed herself to think of a time when her feet would always be steady, when walking wouldn't involve balancing her body and a negotiation of some kind with her surroundings. Then Charles spoke.

"We have a confession from one of the women . . ." he began.

"Indeed?" The other men beamed at him.

"Not to the stabbing, alas," he said, and the others sat back in their chairs, crestfallen. "Sarah Goodbourne has confessed two things."

Kezia let him continue, wondering at how little he took her opinion into account.

"Well," Reverend Davies said, after Charles stopped speaking, "it seems we have found our murderer. What say you, Miss Hayter? Has the captain convinced you?"

Kezia stood up and pushed aside her chair. "No, sir, he has not.

I am convinced that Sarah Goodbourne is innocent of this crime, though guilty of much else."

Kezia looked around at the others. They seemed embarrassed. "But I ask all of you one favor. If you come to the conclusion that Joan Macdonald is not guilty of Hattie's murder, and I'm sure that you will"—Mr. Donovan and Charles nodded, though Mr. Davies simply folded his arms and looked at her searchingly—"then," she continued, "I think Bertie would not only thrive in her care, but also provide as much help to her as she would to him. She, more than many others, feels the loss of her family most deeply. Looking after Bertie would provide some happiness in a life she feels has been emptied of joy. I have been watching her dealings with the boy. She is very kind to him."

"I agree," said Mr. Donovan. "I'd come to the same judgment myself. She was most tender with him whenever she brought him to visit his mother. Most tender."

"I'm glad," Kezia said, "that at least on this matter we're of one mind." She looked at Charles and Mr. Davies, as if daring them to contradict her, but they both murmured assent, nodding and smiling at the happy resolution of at least one problem.

"Unless, of course, in spite of all our good opinions of her, Joan *was* the person who stabbed Hattie," Mr. Davies added. "Miss Hayter, after all, is trying to persuade us that someone other than Sarah Goodbourne may be guilty of murder." There was laughter in his voice and Kezia felt rage rising in her again.

"If Joan turns out to be guilty, I'll tear up my master's ticket and never go to sea again," said Charles. "But whatever is the case, we can, I think, wait a little while to put Sarah Goodbourne under guard."

Dizziness overcame Kezia and she closed her eyes. "I am withdrawing from this inquiry," she said. "You may now do as you see fit."

She heard nothing but silence behind her as she left the room.

The stars in the southern hemisphere shone much brighter than Kezia was accustomed to. The sky above the *Rajah*, as she sailed through waters ruffled by a light wind from the west, was studded with them and they burned as brightly as lamps. They seemed so close that she wouldn't have been surprised to see one impaled at the top of the highest mast. Everything is always different at night, she thought. She recalled how frightened of the dark she had been as a child.

Once, her mother had put her to sit on the stairs outside her bedroom for shouting at Robert. He'd taken one of her dolls and removed an arm, playing at soldiers. As far as Kezia remembered, he had received no punishment beyond a scolding. For shouting at him and pummeling him with her fists, she was put to sit on the stairs in the dark. Henrietta had come out of their bedroom to keep her company for a while but Kezia had sent her back to bed when she saw that her sister's eyes were closing. "If Mama catches you here, we'll both be in trouble," Kezia said. "Go to sleep. I'll be there soon, I'm sure. I'll be taken from this dark step and sent back to bed."

How long did I sit there? she asked herself now. She couldn't remember, but Mama's words when she'd come up still sounded in her head. "You won't be so eager to shout at your brother in future, missy," she'd whispered, as she'd pushed Kezia into the bedroom with a hand in the small of her back, and neither a good night kiss nor a kind word before she closed the door behind her. Also, there was the darkness, waiting for Kezia in her own bedroom: thick and suffocating, to be dreaded.

The sailors on the watch said, "Good night, Miss," as they passed where she was standing at the rail. The *Rajah* creaked and rolled, and Kezia understood how a ship could become like a living soul to those who had care of her. In spite of the dirt, the gloom and the pervading smells of the convict quarters, there was, beyond that, something noble and inspiring about what was, when all was said and done, nothing but wood and canvas, rope and nails, yet able to move so swiftly over the water, to carry so much.

They'll notice, thought Kezia. Every one of the women will notice. Even Isaac, bringing her breakfast, had remarked on her condition.

"Are you feeling quite well, Miss?" he'd asked. "I can come back later if you'd rather wait a little."

"No, thank you, Isaac," she'd answered, with as steady a voice as she could muster. "The porridge is most welcome."

As she struggled to swallow spoonfuls of the cold, gelatinous mess, Kezia went over everything she knew. Something that one of the women had said came to her. Which of them had said it? She couldn't remember. Was it to do with fetching Bertie?

Her face in the looking-glass was pale, dark shadows scored deep under her eyes. As she closed her cabin door behind her and made her way to the lower deck, she felt as if the wind would blow her away. She glanced at the sails, billowing, bearing the ship ever closer to its destination, and bit her lip. I must find out the truth.

The fiery white light of the sun brightened the convict quarters a little, and it was some moments before Kezia's eyes grew accus-

tomed to the dimness. She peered into the distance and saw someone sitting on a bunk, idly twisting a strand of hair between her
fingers. She had to be sure it wasn't any of the women who'd been
in front of the inquiry, so she walked up to her. Maud Ashton was
a mousy woman, but she had a curious streak.

"Are you quite well, Maud?" Kezia asked. "Many of your companions have chosen to go up on deck."

"I hide from the sun, Miss," Maud said, and it was true that her
skin was very fair. "Even in cold weather, the brightness is bad for
me. I'd best keep in, I think."

"I hope you'll allow me to ask you something, Maud." The
woman nodded, sitting up straighter and biting her lip. "It's nothing you've done," Kezia said quickly, trying to reassure her. "I'm
only seeking information. May I sit down?"

Again Maud nodded and Kezia sat beside her on the bunk, quite
close, because others had come in from the deck and she didn't
want their conversation overheard.

"Then there is a particular question I want to ask you about the
night Hattie was stabbed, and I beg you to be truthful when you
answer me."

Maud nodded a third time, to give added weight to her words.
"I'd never lie to you," she said. "Cross my heart, Miss, and hope
to die."

43
NOW

✦

15 July 1841
One hundred and one days at sea

They were gathered on deck, eighteen women under the shade of the awning. They'd been stitching since daybreak, in the cool of early morning. The sky was pearly-white, the color fading out of it as the sun grew stronger. A stiffish wind was blowing and the sea was deepest blue, each wave crested with white and all moving in lines along the side of the ship. Miss Hayter was with them, sitting between Lottie and Joan. Sarah was on the other side of the circle, Emily on her left and Phyllis on her right.

"Look, Miss," said Rose. "The captain's coming . . . and the minister. And Mr. Donovan. They've got Bertie with them."

"Indeed. I've been expecting them." Miss Hayter stood up and turned to face them as they approached.

"Good morning," said the captain. "A beautiful day, is it not?" Everyone nodded and looked to see how Miss Hayter would react.

Since yesterday a kind of gloom had descended on the company, all of them aware of the matron's unhappiness. It showed in her every movement and utterance. The only thing that brought light to her eyes was the coverlet. She was pleased with that at least.

"You've worked very well," she said, as the final border was being carefully stitched to the rest. "Each and every one of you. The Ladies' Committee will be delighted, I'm quite sure."

"I have something to say to you," said the captain. There was a wooden crate nearby; he pulled it toward him and sat on it. Miss Hayter gave a signal and the women rolled up the work in its sheet. She took it and placed a box on top of it to keep it from unrolling. Mr. Davies and Mr. Donovan stood behind the captain, and Bertie, whose hand he'd been holding, stood in the crook of his arm. "We have, as you know, been considering the death of Hattie Matthews, and I can tell you that we're near to a decision on that matter. But today we've something else to consider. Or, rather, someone. We—Miss Hayter and the three of us—have been thinking of what might best be done for Bertie. I've spoken to the boy, haven't I, Bertie?"

"Yes, sir," said Bertie. No one but those closest to him heard his words. They were blown away by the brisk breeze, though he was nodding in agreement.

"This boy's mother has gone to her last rest," the captain went on. "No other person will ever replace her, of course, but we're agreed that another kind person, who'll love him and care for him, will be the nearest he can come to receiving a mother's love. Not everyone feels they can carry the burden of someone else's child, and please tell me if these are your feelings, and we'll think again, but it's our settled opinion that you, Joan Macdonald, would be the right person for this undertaking. If you agree—"

He hadn't finished speaking. Everyone could see that there was more he intended to say, but at that very moment Emily opened her mouth and shrieked, like a soul escaped from Hell. She clasped her arms around herself and began to rock backward and forward.

"No, no, no!" she cried, and then, "You can't! He's my Freddie. Tell them, Freddie. Tell them about our game. Tell them. He's mine, not yours! He's my angel and you can't—he isn't hers! Mine! I wanted to tell her but she wouldn't listen. She wouldn't listen to me. He's mine!" She ran to the captain, spitting in her fury and trembling all over, then seized Bertie and pulled him away. Demons, they say, can possess a body and give it strength, and if they'd not seen it for themselves, the women would never have believed Emily capable of such power. Within seconds she'd put her arms around Bertie and had lifted him almost over her head. The captain moved swiftly to remove him from her grasp, but she ducked. At one moment she had been upright, the next she was down low, near the deck, and Bertie seemed to be tucked under her arm. She ran with him, quick as lightning. There was a gap between Ann and Rose on the other side of the circle and she made for it.

"Catch her! Stop her!" Mr. Donovan shouted. Ann and Rose lunged at Emily as she raced past them toward the *Rajah*'s stern. A piece of her skirt remained in Ann's hand—she stared at it, paralyzed, and let it fall to the deck.

Then Sarah ran. She flew after Emily, past Ann and Rose, and she was nearly, nearly upon her when Emily leaped onto some wooden crates stowed near the stern and turned to face her. Bertie was shouting, too, now as he tried to wriggle free. Emily had both arms around him, and was clutching him under the armpits, clasping him to her bosom like a shield.

"He's mine!" she screamed. "Go away, Sarah, he's mine! She wasn't a good mother, not like me. I'm a good mother. I'm the best—the best mother. I'm Freddie's mother! I'm the one who loves him. Me! Me! She didn't. Not really. Selfish, she was. I wanted to tell her. I was going to tell her how much I loved him. How he's Freddie when he's with me. He likes being Freddie."

"He's not yours, Emily," Sarah said, with more strength and calm in her voice than any of the others had heard before. "And he's Bertie. Freddie is someone else. You must give him to the captain. Let me have him, and you can come back and sit with us again."

"He's mine! I'm not giving him up! Never! If I can't have him, I'll drown both of us. I will! I'll throw him over the rail. Yes, and me after him."

Help was coming, but Sarah seemed not to notice anything around her. Did she see that sailors were approaching Emily from every direction? Shinning down the rigging to catch her by surprise, creeping up on her to approach her from behind if they had to, though there was little space between her body and the stern rail.

"Emily," Sarah said, "you can't have him. He's not yours. He's Hattie's son. You loved Hattie, remember? You didn't mean to do her any harm, did you?"

That made Emily pause. She stood quite still as if weighing something up. Then she said, "I did love Hattie, but she couldn't see. Couldn't see he's mine . . . my baby. I love him more. My Freddie. My angel. Ever since we came to the *Rajah*, I knew."

"But if you love him, how can you say you're going to let him drown? Give him to me, Emily, and then we can talk." Sarah's voice was higher now. There was terror in it. "Please. Show some kindness, if you really love him. Don't let him die, Emily. You'll never see him again if he dies, will you? Please, Emily, think of what you're doing."

"I know what I'm doing!" Emily shrieked. "I've always known! Freddie's *my* child—he has to be! I had to stop her! He's *mine* and

I'm keeping him. I'm not his pretend mother anymore. I'm his only mother . . . his proper mother."

Everything moved quickly then, and many things happened together. A wild light came to Emily's eyes as Sarah leaned forward and grabbed Bertie's waist, wrapping one arm around his body, while prying Emily's right hand from under his arm. Bertie helped. He wriggled and twisted with new vigor, then fell into Sarah's embrace and she pulled him off the boxes, both of them stumbling to keep their balance. Emily was making noises that no one near her had ever heard before, saying words from which all reason had departed. Sarah was rocking to and fro on the deck with Bertie, sobbing and trembling, in her arms. There was screaming and shouting. Emily's name was called. Shrieks of "No! No!" The other women were clustering around Sarah, and Miss Hayter was putting her arms around her as she was holding Bertie, saying, "Sarah, let him go. Let me take him. Come, Bertie."

Sarah released the child and Miss Hayter gathered him to her side. They began to move away. Mr. Donovan and Mr. Davies were at the stern with Isaac Margrove. A cry went up. The captain strode down the deck, bellowing, "She's overboard. Lower the boat. Now. Don't delay. She may be alive still."

"She flew! I saw her," said Beth. "I swear it. She flew!"

Susan leaned over to look at the water swirling below. "How could anyone . . ."

The women lined up along the ship's rail, watching the small boat that was being lowered, with four sailors. Then they were rowing as fast as any men ever did, but the sea was stronger. The wind in the *Rajah*'s sails was carrying her ever further away from where Emily had gone into the water.

"She's drowned, for certain," said Izzy.

"They may bring back her body," said Ruth.

Lottie cried, "No, they're turning back—look! They're coming back without her."

The boat was making its way toward the *Rajah*. Everyone watched as the sailors climbed aboard and the boat was raised to the deck. The waves raced along, lines of white crests chasing one another and disappearing behind the ship. No one uttered a word, and the women returned to where the coverlet had been left on the deck. Miss Hayter was nowhere to be seen.

"She's left it behind," said Phyllis. "She's thinking of Bertie now. But nothing must happen to the coverlet. Not now it's so near finished."

She stroked the fabric of the sheet, then took up one corner. Dora went to another and together, in a sad, silent procession, they walked across the deck, rolling the patchwork as they went. The others stood and looked on as the bundle was wrapped in its linen sheet. Then Phyllis asked Isaac to take charge of it and put it in Miss Hayter's cabin.

44
NOW

✦

16 July 1841
One hundred and two days at sea
KEZIA

They stood up as she came into the room: Charles, Mr. Donovan and Mr. Davies rising to greet her. Kezia said nothing but inclined her head in their direction. Instead of taking her seat alongside them, she went to the chair where the women suspects had sat during the inquiry.

"We've missed you, Miss Hayter," said Mr. Davies. "We know it's been a hard time for you, these last few days."

"I'm glad the voyage is coming to an end," said Kezia. "But there are things I need to explain.

"Everything has become clearer now that we know it was Emily who attacked poor Hattie. You were told of Sarah's crimes, but you missed—we missed Emily's madness. I ought to have noticed it long ago and I regret that I didn't. For she *was* mad, you know.

She'd lost a child of her own, from smallpox, and I fear she let Bertie take that child's place in her mind. And his name. I found out something shortly before she . . . before the end that might have convinced this inquiry she was the guilty one. If you'd known it, she'd have been facing the gallows. Death by drowning might be preferable to death by hanging."

Charles leaned forward in his seat. "Please tell us what you discovered."

"I was thinking of how Bertie came to the deck too late to see his mother, although Emily had been asked to fetch him quickly. So I spoke to Maud, who hadn't been on deck at the time but was in the convict quarters when the stabbing took place. She told me that when Emily came down to fetch Bertie, she didn't bring him to the deck at once, but first took him to the water barrel to wash his face. Maud would have thought nothing of it and, because we'd decided that only the women who'd been on deck could have been involved, had never thought to mention it."

"And now we know the truth of Emily's guilt," said Mr. Donovan, "we can see that Maud's account confirms that Emily had time to wash away any blood from her hands."

"Perhaps," said Kezia. "She must have reasoned that the longer she took to bring Bertie on deck, the more likely it was that Hattie would have died."

"Would she not fear that we'd find out? That she would lose Bertie if we did?" Mr. Donovan was frowning.

"By the time she stabbed Hattie, I fear she was so deluded that she never thought of consequences. She must indeed have been terrified at first, but then she perhaps felt she could deny, and with no proof, who'd suspect her? She, alone of the convict women, knew there'd been a threat against Hattie and what it was. She'd have thought *that* person would be suspected, and she was right. And everyone knew her as Hattie's greatest friend. We would never conclude that she wanted Bertie for herself. She seemed often to be irritated by his presence, though he was very attached to her."

Mr. Davies sighed. "But there's still the matter of Sarah Goodbourne. She's done great harm. Taking another woman's name, escaping her sentence of hanging . . . We must hand her over to the authorities in Hobart as soon as we arrive there."

"No," said Kezia, with more force than she intended. "What good will that do? Another woman will die. Has there not been enough death? Can we not be merciful? Isn't one of the benefits of transportation that the women might be given another chance? And does Sarah not deserve great credit for saving Bertie's life? If it were not for Sarah at the end, Emily would surely have taken him overboard with her. We must give her some reward for that, can't you see?"

"It's our duty to deliver justice," said Mr. Davies.

"Your duty is to be *Christian*, sir," she said, so sharply and so angrily that he stared at her as though he were seeing her for the first time. "You're not a judge. Neither are you master of this ship. Your *Christian* duty is to forgive. To be as merciful as our Lord would be. Sarah's a sinner, but she's done a good thing and we should acknowledge this."

"But what about her punishment? Would you not see her pay the price for the crimes she's committed? She's done nothing but lie to us ever since she stepped on this ship under a false name. She killed a man."

Kezia sprang to her feet, trembling. "He had *violated* her. He had killed her companion. She was acting out of terror. Why don't you understand?"

"I understand well," said Mr. Davies. "But whatever the provocation, she is responsible for a man's death. How can that go un-punished?"

"She's being transported, sir," said Kezia. "Is *that* not a punish-ment?"

Mr. Davies said nothing for some moments. Then: "It is a punishment but not, I think, a sufficient one. I would prefer Sarah to be put under guard and handed over when we disembark."

Kezia wondered if either of the others would say anything, but no one spoke. "Then there's nothing more to say," said Kezia. "Good afternoon, gentlemen. I will not be dining with you tonight."

She left the room as quickly as she could, hardly able to see for the fury that possessed her. A strong desire to kick over one of the leather-upholstered chairs had assailed her, but she had gone before she could yield to the impulse.

45

NOW

✤

17 July 1841
One hundred and three days at sea
CLARA

"Two of them," Tabitha says. "Fish food, both of 'em. They'll be nibbled to the bone."

"Shut your face, you hag." That's Ruth, snarling at Tabitha. "Heartless, that's what you are. How could you? Emily was one of us."

"Bloody stabber, she was. I don't hold with no stabbing." Lottie purses her lips. "I'm glad she's gone. Always did think she was too good to be true. Clinging to Hattie, and all the time only after her boy. Should've been saved from drowning and hanged, I say. Teaching the children and acting kind. Singing hymns with a face as nice as pie. You never know, that's what I say, never know what anyone's really like."

"What about you, then, Sarah Goodbourne? You're a dark horse and no mistake. I never would've reckoned you to be so fast on your feet." That was Izzy.

We've been talking about Emily's death for some time. The other women, those who weren't on deck, are listening to a small group of us, the lucky ones, those who saw the drama unfold. Everyone's looking at me. There's no escape. I won't say I knew Hattie before we both came aboard the *Rajah*. Miss Hayter will have told the captain and the others that the warning on Hattie's pillow was my doing, but among the women on the lower deck, only Hattie and Emily were aware of it. I'll be silent about the man I killed. But I decide I will tell them my real name and how I lost it.

"Well, there's a story like I've not heard before. You're a shady piece of work and no mistake. What about the real Sarah Good-bourne?" Dwyer says, when I've finished speaking. "What'll happen to her?"

"I don't know," I say. "I think of her often and feel remorse for what I did to her."

"Our captain'll surely give you a good character. Ask Miss Hayter to speak to him. He's so soft on her," Alice adds.

"They've fallen out," says Joan. "Isaac told me he'd seen them and they were quarreling."

"That's bad!" says Marion. "She should be happy. Deserves it."

"You're soppy," Rose mutters. "Soppy over the matron."

"She helped me." Marion sounds sad. "She helped all of us."

"She did," says Joan. "Some didn't see the point of what we were doing together. You, for instance, Rose, and you, Beth. I heard the grumbles and moans when it was time to work on the coverlet. Beth, you often took up your needle with a face like a lemon."

"I did not." Beth is pouting. "I liked the work."

"Could have shown it a bit more, then," says Tabitha.

I'm quiet, hoping the attention has moved away from me but

it hasn't. Selwood asks the question the others seem to have forgotten. "You, Sarah or Clara or whatever you call yourself, answer
me this."

I turn to her and she goes on. "What were you in Millbank for,
then? Must've done something to get there in the first place."

I must answer her. I cannot lie any longer. I have to tell them,
after all. And I tell the truth. They're all looking at me, their mouths
open. I speak for what seems to me a long time.

"They'd have had you swing for that. Murder. Even if you had
reason."

"They wanted to. Caught me and wanted me dead at the end of
a rope. Didn't matter that I was forced to do it. Didn't matter that
it might have been me lying dead if I hadn't . . . That's why I had to
get onto this ship. I might have done anything to get on the *Rajah*
and sometimes I'm glad it was only leaving poor Sarah Goodbourne
there in my place. I told them, when I came on board, that I was
guilty of stealing linen from a market."

They look at me, half stunned. Some mouths are gaping, and all
the eyes turned on me are wide with astonishment. Dwyer's wandering one comes to rest on my face.

"Dark horse, you are, Sarah, if ever I saw one," she says at last,
but I notice that even she, who pretends to have done and seen
everything, to be the most seasoned convict on the lower decks, is
shocked.

I smile. "I was being raped," I say again. "Do you not understand?"

Silence fills the space. Then Rose says, "I've kicked and screamed
against a man many times, but never killed him. Why didn't you
just lie there? Would have been over soon enough."

How to convey to them the white hatred that filled me? "He had
stabbed to death the one person I loved in the world. I was . . . I was

not myself." At this, they nodded. Revenge was acceptable, easier to understand than outrage at being treated as a whore.

Later that evening, I happen to glance at the other side of our quarters and see Becky and Lily sitting together on the bench, eating ship's biscuits. Lily takes one and dips it into the fatty liquid that passes for gravy, which is congealing in a bowl nearby. I don't see them speaking to one another, but Becky senses what's coming and opens her mouth, like a small bird knowing its mother's brought her a worm. Lily's looking after her. Becky is happy to be looked after. The sight of them makes me feel more hopeful.

Then I remember my own situation. I lie on my mattress, staring at the blackened wood above my head, and tremble at the thought of what they'll decide, Miss Hayter and the others. Tomorrow, at first light, I imagine men coming down the companionway ladder and placing me under guard. They'll hand me over in Hobart and I'll be hanged after all, far from home.

46
NOW

✤

17 July 1841
One hundred and three days at sea
KEZIA

Sewing by lantern light was hard, and harder when most of her attention was concentrated on remaining calm and governing the impulse to tear to shreds every piece of fabric she touched. Kezia couldn't remember a time when everything she looked at, thought of or remembered was more painful. She was half a world away from England, her brothers and sister, Cousin George, the Queen and the gray streets. Her beloved Mrs. Pryor might as well not have existed. Here, on the *Rajah*, everything had turned to sadness, regret and uncertainty. Every hope she had from the voyage, every dream, had vanished like smoke in a high wind.

Only this. Only the coverlet gave her any consolation She looked at it, spread out on the bunk. It was almost done. A central panel, surrounded by squares and triangles patterned with every imaginable design, and at the bottom her embroidered dedication to the Ladies' Committee. Kezia thought, The design has come together, but the true glory lies in the work. Every one of the women she'd chosen had stitched most diligently. The very act of coming together every single day, of sitting quietly sewing, one next to another, of knowing that what they were achieving was something of beauty: *that* had made them more than a gathering of individual souls; *that* was what had transformed them into a sisterhood. The women would be parted on landing. Some would thrive and others fail, but everyone would remember this spread of flowers and leaves, colors and stripes, dots, lozenges and her own *broderie perse* in the middle, with its bright birds and posies. They'd remember their contribution to its making. They'd recall their fellows with affection. They'd grown so used to stitching together, to exchanging words, laughter and outbursts of temper, they would miss the closeness when they were on dry land again.

I can't save her, she thought, and felt a lump of misery rising in her throat. Sarah, or Clara, would be handed over when they landed. Taken to another jail and hanged, maybe.

A knock came on her door, and Kezia jumped up, smoothed down her skirt and tried to pat her hair into a more suitable arrangement. She could feel that it was coming unpinned and hastened to put it up more neatly. At last she opened the door and there was Isaac Margrove, holding a piece of folded paper.

"Captain sends his greetings, Miss, and says, will you kindly read this letter?" He held it out to Kezia and she took it from him.

"Thank you, Isaac," she said. "Good night to you."

"And to you, Miss." Isaac smiled at her and left her holding the sheet of paper. She longed to know what it said and dreaded the words.

My dear Kezia,

    I have been speaking to Mr. Donovan and Mr. Davies for many hours. I am writing to inform you that I have persuaded them in the matter of Sarah Goodbourne and what should happen to her.

    They have come to see that saving Bertie's life goes a long way toward making up for her many crimes. Therefore, they have assured me they will not divulge her real name or mention her to the authorities in Van Diemen's Land, and she will be allowed to start again with a clean slate.

    I would very much like to speak to you privately. Tomorrow in the morning, before you settle to your work, I will be in my cabin and I pray that you will come and hear what I have to say.

    Yours,
    Charles

Kezia read the letter three times. She felt overcome by near dizziness. Her hands were shaking as she pulled on her nightgown and knelt beside her bunk. Where were her prayers? Where was everyone she wanted to remember? All her mind, it seemed, was taken up with Charles. What would he say to her? What do I want of him? Love. I love him. The distance from England, the isolation of the ship, the precarious nature of the voyage, even with all the good luck in the world there was still danger from the unforeseeable accidents of the weather . . . All these things have changed me. She finally realized what she wanted—wanted so fiercely that she had not allowed herself to put words to the thought until this moment.

---❖---

Chilled, wet sailing: the Rajah is soaked and sodden and her sails drip water onto decks that are already dark with it. The wind is keen and blows from the south, from the land of deep ice.

---❖---

47

NOW

✤

18 July 1841
One hundred and four days at sea
CLARA

"Where's she gone?" Dora wants to know.

It's true that Miss Hayter's generally here before the rest of us. She's the one who brings the coverlet and spreads it ready for us to work on. There's not much left to do. Only sewing in the ends and making sure the edges are neatly and firmly stitched. We've used so much fabric, so many different patterns and colors. When I've left this ship, the patterns will come to me in dreams.

"She'll be in the captain's cabin," says Izzy, and Rose nods in agreement. "She's not on the lower deck and she's not here, so stands to reason."

"They'll be talking about me," I say. "Deciding what to do with me. How long till we land?"

"Isaac told me three more days," says Joan. She's sitting in her

300

usual place, with Bertie beside her, playing a cat's cradle game she'd taught him with a length of twine. He never leaves her side. Since his mother's death, since Emily's death, he's a changed child, no longer running about the ship, but like a shadow clinging to Joan. He seems contented enough, but what of his heart? The world is freighted with much sorrow, but he seems too small a boy to carry very much of it.

"I'd rather not land," I say. "They'll take me off to a cell and get a gallows ready for me."

No one answers. They can't because what I'm saying is true. I won't dwell on it. I'm ready for it. In the end, a price has to be paid.

"But you saved Bertie," says Phyllis, "and you were one of us. One of Miss Hayter's company. What we've made, that's something to be proud of."

"It's very beautiful," I say. "I never thought of how it would be when we started. Just one piece of fabric coming after another. But here it is, and there's so many bits of cloth and they make something. I'm proud of that. Once I'm dead and gone, my work'll be in this coverlet. That's what lasts in the end, doesn't it? Us . . . we'll be dead soon enough."

That's what we, too, are like, us women. We're a patchwork. One person next to another, then her next to a third, and on and on, different people pushed together. Some neatly beside our neighbors, some out of shape and awkwardly sewn into a botched closeness. We've arranged ourselves into this shape: fair ones and dark ones, older, younger, thin, fat, ugly, pretty and everything in between, and near on two hundred of us on this ship and taken far away, existing side by side, sleeping together, eating together. Here are friends and enemies. We've turned ourselves into something. We're many small pieces, each of us different but now stitched together. A patchwork of souls.

48

NOW

18 July 1841
One hundred and four days at sea
KEZIA

Charles stood up as she came into the room. "Kezia," he said. "Please, sit down."

"Thank you for telling me the good news," she said, hoping her voice sounded braver than she felt. "I'm delighted that the men have finally reached a sensible conclusion and I'm grateful to you for persuading them." She wanted to ask, *How did you do it? What changed their minds?* but lately had become more uncertain of Charles's feelings toward her. As if reading her thoughts, Charles began: "It was an uphill battle. Mr. Donovan has a very kind heart, as you know, and, besides, he feels affectionately toward you." He gazed searchingly at Kezia, who met his eyes before quickly looking down. Charles continued. "Mr. Davies was harder work, but with James and myself pressing him on theological definitions of forgiveness and mercy, and summoning everything we remembered about erring sheep being welcomed into the fold, we moved him in the end. In my private opinion, the desire to have the whole matter over and done with, tidied up and settled, also weighed in the balance. Less fuss. He wouldn't have to give any evidence, appear at a hearing and so forth. I'm sure he's anxious to continue his life among his congregation, by whom he's much respected and admired. Or so I'm told."

Kezia said, "I'm most grateful to you for throwing your authority behind this. Thank you. Will you tell Sarah and the others, or should I?"

"I'll talk to all the women this evening. Tell everyone what conclusion we've come to. It won't take long. And Sarah must be told that she will have to remain as Sarah Goodbourne now. You know that they'll be looking for Clara Shaw in London. The authorities in Hobart, too, will be forced to send her back to hang if they discover who she really is. But most of the rest may pass in silence."

Charles picked up his brass paperweight and turned it over in his hands. The air in the cabin, Kezia thought, was growing chilly, and she wished she'd brought a warmer shawl. Charles, too, seemed uncomfortable and he rubbed his hands together.

"I must return to the deck." Kezia glanced at the floor, then raised her eyes to meet his gaze. "We're nearly at the end of our work."

"Please don't go . . . I want to say . . . May I say a few words to you?"

"Of course."

He walked round the table and leaned against it, close enough to Kezia to touch her. She saw him reach out, then draw back, as if unsure of what would happen if his hand met hers.

"I'm truly sorry. I shouldn't have dismissed your opinions and I hope you'll forgive me."

303

She was believed. She was considered an equal of the men. Kezia felt as though she'd been awarded a shining prize.

He kissed her then. A thousand thoughts ran through Kezia's mind. It wasn't suitable, respectable, appropriate . . . She wasn't ready, wasn't prepared, didn't know what to do, not really. Had never done such a thing before. And then the thoughts ceased and Kezia allowed herself to be overwhelmed by her feelings.

"I've something to tell you," said Kezia, still dazed, and still feeling a little light-headed from the unaccustomed sensations she was experiencing as she took her place in the circle of women stitching under the awning. She'd wondered whether she should single Sarah out and speak to her privately, but the others would be watching. They'd know at least part of what had happened from Sarah herself already.

"Good morning," she began again, and everyone joined in the greetings.

"Top of the morning, Miss," said Tabitha. "You look better, Miss. Than you've been lately, I mean."

"You're right," said Kezia. "I'm relieved to have this matter settled. That's what I want to talk to you about." She looked round the circle till her eye fell on Sarah. "I'm sure Sarah's spoken to you about . . . her predicament."

"She's told us her real name, if that's what you mean," said Rose. "Not sure what to call her now, if I'm telling the truth."

"She has to be Sarah Goodbourne," Kezia said.

"What if the real Sarah comes out to Hobart on the next transport? What if they found her at once, understood what happened and simply packed her off on the next ship?" That was Phyllis. "Best if I keep Sarah living with me till such a thing happens."

"And I shall tell you this." Kezia looked at Sarah searchingly. "Because you saved Bertie's life, at great risk to your own safety, the captain will say nothing to the Van Diemen's Land authorities about your case. He'll recount the circumstances of both deaths, and emphasize your part in rescuing Bertie. That's all. If you're taking Sarah Goodbourne's name, you will also take on her crime."

"Thank you, Miss," said Sarah. "I don't know what to say. I hadn't dared to hope. Thank you . . . Oh, forgive me for my weakness." She brushed away the tears that had begun to roll down her cheeks. "I'll work to be better in this new country. I'll never forget what you did for me. Not if I live to be a hundred. I'll become a different person."

"I'm sure you will. You've worked so hard and so well, all of you, and you should be proud of this coverlet. I'm proud of it for you."

She stood up, before she too was overcome with emotion, and began to walk slowly away, but Beth called after her. "Miss? Miss?"

Kezia turned. Beth was standing up. "Please, Miss, will you come back? There's something we'd like to ask."

Kezia went back and stood near the women, waiting for the question, but no one said anything. "Well?" she said. "What is it?"

"You ask her," said Izzy, pointing at Phyllis.

"No, you ask her, Joan. Go on. You're the oldest."

"What's that got to do with anything?" Joan was blushing. "You ask her, Rose. Or Izzy. Go on, ask."

"We want to know if you and the captain are finally courting," said Izzy at last.

Kezia smiled. "I suppose we are."

"That's good news, Miss," said Izzy, and Rose added, "You've been going about lately with a face like a dead fish."

Kezia was overwhelmed with affection for her women. They'd worked hard. They'd had their differences, but they'd also come together. They liked her and respected her and were glad for her happiness.

"Thank you . . . thank you very much indeed. I hope that you'll be happy in your new lives. I'm very grateful for your devotion to your work."

"*Your* devotion, Miss," said Tabitha, and the sight of her teeth indicated to Kezia and the others that she was making a joke. "We didn't choose to be here, did we? You picked us. It wouldn't have done to say no!" She cackled to show there was no malice in her remarks.

"Are you sorry, any of you, that you agreed to work on the patchwork?" Kezia asked. "I did say, didn't I, that none of you had to join the group?"

"Course you did, Miss. Course you did," Tabitha agreed. "I'm only needling you! Oh, hark at me! *Needling*, eh? D'you hear that?" She was laughing so much at her own jest that she was almost bent double. "I'm a wit!"

"We're honored, Miss," said Elsie, who didn't often speak. "Every one of us, and that's the truth. And the coverlet's pretty enough for a queen."

"That's thanks to you. You've worked hard and made something of great worth and beauty. The coverlet will be displayed to the governor and his wife, Sir John and Lady Franklin, when we land. You'll be presented to them and I'd be most obliged to you if you joined me in singing our hymn, 'Teach Me, My God and King,' while we're out on deck showing them the coverlet. Are you willing to do that?"

"Sing?" Susan looked panic-stricken. "On deck? All of us? In front of gentry? Oh, I daren't, Miss. I couldn't."

"Don't be such a ninny, Susan," said Beth. "You know it by heart and we'll be singing alongside you. And we're happy to be landing, so the noise will be grand."

"We'll sing, Miss," said Phyllis. "We'll sing our hearts out, don't fret!"

"And someone," said Kezia, "must put in the last stitch . . . We're so nearly done. Who should I choose? Every one of you is worthy."

"It must be you, Miss," said Joan. "You thought of it. You saw it in your head before we made it together. You must put in the last stitch. It's only right." She took a threaded needle and handed it to Kezia, who stared at it.

"Go on, Miss! It has to be you. You do it. That's the final touch." All the voices came together and soon the women were clapping.

Kezia pricked the needle into the fabric for the last time, and sewed a few stitches, then fastened off neatly.

"You need scissors, Miss," said Phyllis, "to cut that last thread."

Kezia wanted to thank them, wanted to say something, but the words would not come. She took the scissors, blinked away the tears and snipped the last thread.

49

NOW

✦

19 July 1841
One hundred and five days at sea

Fifteen weeks at sea. Everyone, from the most sea-weathered among the crew to the women who'd suffered most during the voyage, was longing for a glimpse of land. The last night on board was a strange one: joy for the end of imprisonment at sea, and longing for a night in a real bed, with clean clothes that weren't stiff from being rinsed in seawater. There'd be fresh food. There'd be steady land beneath their feet. There would be space to walk, wider and longer than the *Rajah*'s decks. Everything would be new. Some feared this, and worried that they wouldn't find their way.

"We've got used to the *Rajah* now," said Maud Ashton. "And they'll put us ashore and we'll have to fend for ourselves."

"Silly cow!" said another, but with some affection. "Going to find us work and lodging and give us food, and who's to say we won't some of us be together on dry land? Wherever we fetch up."

They fell to singing. Vowing undying devotion to their friends. Overcome with sadness, some of them, at the thought of parting from companions who'd grown more familiar than the families they'd left behind in England.

Everyone gathered on the rail at first light, waiting for the cry of the lad in the crow's nest: *Land ahoy!* When it came, all eyes peered at the horizon.

"Where is it?" said Joan. "Where's the land?"

"Put your spectacles on, you silly old woman," said Dwyer, though she said it with laughter in her voice. "I can see it. That line, over there. A dark line."

"I don't want a line. I want hills and houses and trees. Remember what trees are? I miss 'em. I do."

"Freezing out here," said Rose, pulling her shawl close around her.

"Wind off the ice," said Isaac, who'd come up to stand as close to Joan as possible. She'd picked Bertie up from the deck and was holding him close now, near her shoulder, for a better view. Isaac went on. "There's mountains and plains of ice just south of us, and the wind comes from there."

"Isn't it meant to be summer?" That was Marion.

"Opposite seasons on this side of the world," Isaac told her. "English summer's the winter down here."

Marion shivered and bit her lip, not quite certain in her head about the notion of opposite seasons. "Seems mad to me," she said at last. "Winter in July."

"There it is," shouted Izzy. "Van Diemen's Land. I can see it. I can see hills."

The *Rajah* had sailed toward the dark line of the horizon, and as she approached land, what could be seen from the deck grew and changed until the smallest details were visible. Hills rose above the harbor, and there was snow on the highest slopes.

"Snow!" Joan cried, pointing it out to Bertie. "There's snow!" She turned to her left where Isaac had been standing, but he was gone and she saw him striding along the deck, summoned by the first mate. As she watched him, a pain went through her heart at the thought of never seeing him again. I can't cry, she thought. I must be cheerful for Bertie.

"Look! There are people . . . They look like us," Marion said. "Just like people in London, I mean."

"Why should they be different?" Phyllis asked.

Beth said, "You didn't think they'd be upside down, did you?"

Marion said nothing but stood looking over the rail and frowning.

"She did!" Tabitha chortled and slapped her hands on the rail. "Marion thought everyone here'd be upside down! The other side of the world, eh?"

"Couldn't properly say why they aren't," Susan said. "But I'm heartily glad to see I'm still the right way up!"

Bertie stood next to Joan, staring at the shore. He liked her well enough, and the hand he was holding felt safe. But she's not my ma, he thought. She's not even my pretend ma.

"We'll be leaving the *Rajah* soon, Bertie," Joan said. "Won't it be nice to feel firm land under our feet? Look at the snow on the hills. Doesn't it look grand?"

"Snow!" Bertie agreed, and he smiled. The snow would be good. Rolling around in it. Maybe they'd make a snowman. He felt happier when he thought about that. I won't be so sad now, he told himself. But I still won't tell anyone. Emily said I mustn't, not ever, and I won't. I saw what Emily did with her knife, but I didn't tell. She stuck it in Ma's side and ran away. She was crying. I don't know why she did that. I ran away, too, I ran and ran away from the deck before anyone saw me. She loved my ma, I know she did. But she said I was her boy and she was my pretend ma, and we liked that game. So when Emily killed my real ma, I never said. I never told Miss Hayter or the captain. They'd have taken Emily away to a horrible prison, because she did such a bad thing, and then my pretend ma would be gone, too. I wouldn't have any ma then. I never told Emily I saw her do it. I never told her I'd watched, and she's dead now, and Joan's going to be my ma.

"You're very quiet, Bertie," Joan said. "What're you thinking about?"

Bertie didn't answer. He was thinking about after. After what he saw. How he'd run to his bunk and hidden under a blanket till Emily came looking for him, how she'd taken him to wash his hands and then up on deck to see his real ma, only she was gone and there was just blood where she'd been. He couldn't say that to Joan, so he said, "It's a nice place, Hobart. Isn't it?"

"It looks so to me. Lovely big buildings and trees. Can you see the trees?"

"Will we go up the mountain?" Bertie asked. "Will we make snowballs?"

"I don't know, dear," she answered. "We'll see. I've missed the trees."

Bertie's eyes were wide. He didn't answer but went on gazing at the harbor and the snowy hills above it and the trees growing near the buildings and the people walking about the dock.

50
NOW

19 July 1841
One hundred and five days at sea

Kezia had been up since dawn. She'd stood at the rail with the others as the *Rajah* approached the harbor at Hobart, but as soon as she could she returned to her cabin. She felt a mixture of excitement and nerves at the prospect of their visitors' judgment on the work they'd done during the voyage. The gown she'd put into her luggage in London was spread on her bunk. It had spent fifteen weeks neatly folded in the chest of drawers, and she was happy to see it again. She had kept it for this particular occasion: the presentation of the coverlet to Sir John and Lady Franklin.

The women on the lower deck, she knew, had also been getting ready. More washing than usual was being done, and tangles carefully teased out of hair. Anyone who'd brought a precious piece of clothing in their bundles searched for it and would wear it when they landed.

The Franklins were expected in the early afternoon. The coverlet was wrapped in its sheet, ready to be spread on deck. When a knock came at the door, Kezia went to open it.

"Ah, Isaac, thank you. Here it is. Shall I carry one end?"

"I'll manage, Miss, thank you kindly. I can carry it like this." He put the bundle over his shoulder and looked back at Kezia. "Just like a carpet seller, in one of them bazaars in the east."

"Have you been to the east, Isaac?"

"Oh, yes, Miss. I've been all over. China, North Africa. Patagonia. All over. But England's best."

"Indeed, it is," said Kezia. "But I've heard good things of Hobart."

"A fine place. A good place for these women, to be sure."

They'd reached a clear space on deck where the wood had been swept ready.

"Where d'you want it, Miss?" he asked.

Kezia had spent the last few days thinking about how best to show off the work. "Over there, please. Perhaps you'd help me to lay it out."

"My pleasure," said Isaac.

Kezia unwrapped the coverlet and they spread its colors over the deck.

"Never thought it would be as fine as this, Miss. Not while you were making it. It's a splendid piece of stuff, I reckon. A beauty."

"Thank you, Isaac. I'm pleased with it, too. Everyone has worked very hard to make it."

The women filed into the space Kezia had left for them. She noticed that Susan and Tabitha had found bits of lace to pin to their hair. Sarah had taken off her headscarf, plaited her long dark hair and

313

twisted it into a complicated braid fixed at the nape of her neck. Every hand was clean. From the beginning, they'd not been allowed to work on the patchwork before washing thoroughly in a bucket of fresh seawater, and today was no exception.

"Allow me to introduce you to the women who made the coverlet," Kezia said to Lady Franklin, who was standing next to her husband. Sir John's uniform was bright with gold frogging. Lady Franklin wore a fine hat, and as she looked out from under the brim she smiled in a general way at the needlewomen. Kezia felt suddenly protective of them. She knew they were poorly dressed, but all were clean and they had done their best to make themselves presentable. Even Lady Franklin would struggle to maintain her fine appearance in conditions like those in the convict quarters of the *Rajah*. Suddenly, though, Lady Franklin left her husband's side and went up to the nearest person in the line. Kezia was pleased at her interest, and said, "This is Rose Manners."

"Delighted, I'm sure," said Lady Franklin, and they passed from one woman to the next, Lady Franklin shaking each hand as Kezia introduced them. Everyone gave their version of a curtsy, and if some were no more than a bob, others were quite elaborate: a proper bending of the knee and a solemn lowering of the chin. When she came to the end of the line, Lady Franklin turned to them all and said, "You're to be congratulated on your efforts with the coverlet. Excellent work, to be sure. Thank you for what you have done."

Kezia returned to her place, unsure of how she was feeling. Relieved and overwhelmed by the sight of the coverlet spread out for all to admire. Pride in the women and a kind of happy relief filled her heart. She said, "We'll now sing you the hymn that has guided and sustained us through the voyage."

Remembering her own singing lessons, she turned her back on the Franklins, the captain, Mr. Donovan and Mr. Davies, and smiled at the women, noticing how terrified they seemed, as if they were being led toward some dreadful punishment. She raised her hand, gave the signal to begin and started to sing. The others joined in after a word or two, until the music grew to a respectable level. Hattie, Kezia thought, as the verses unrolled their perfect harmony of music and fine words. How I miss Hattie. And Emily's voice was beautiful, in spite of her madness and her crime. Sarah was singing with more vigor. Joan, too . . . Kezia's voice rose with the rest.

When the hymn came to an end, everyone applauded and Kezia smiled with pleasure. How well the ceremony had gone! How perfectly the women had behaved! They filed away to the lower deck, good wishes following them, with cheers, too, from the sailors who'd heard them singing.

"You're to be congratulated, Miss Hayter," said Lady Franklin. "You've done your work well. Those women are a credit to you, and I'm quite sure they'll find a better life here in Hobart."

"Thank you," said Kezia. "I've grown fond of them and I'll miss them. But the work of their hands abides."

She thought of everything that had happened, everything that was not in the coverlet. Every feeling and emotion, the laughter and tears. The patches remained as silent witness to so much that could be recalled only in the thoughts of the women who had made it. Others will have to guess at such things, Kezia thought, but I will remember every day of this voyage when I look at it. Every day and all that has happened.

The Franklins had gone ashore, and Charles and Kezia were alone in his cabin. "I am delighted that Lady Franklin so admired the coverlet," she said. "I was proud of the women."

"Quite rightly. And, yes, the Franklins were pleased with the work." He was gazing out of the window and spoke over his shoulder to Kezia, but then turned to her. "Kezia, will you sit for a moment? I must ask you something."

"Of course." Kezia went to sit in one of the chairs that had been arranged for the guests. Charles took another and sat facing her, though he stared hard at the floor.

"This voyage," he began, then paused and started again. "I've never known a voyage like this, Kezia. Not in all my time at sea."

"I have—" Kezia stopped. She'd been on the point of saying she'd enjoyed it, but was that true? Were there not many times when she was despairing, angry, sad and desperately homesick? After a long moment, she said, "I've learned a great deal on the *Rajah*, and much of it was hard for me, but I don't regret any of it. I'll always be proud of what the women have made." She couldn't say that Charles's presence on the ship had transformed the journey from a penance to a daily pleasure. And the kisses they had exchanged . . . about those, she could also say nothing, though they were in her mind. "Our walks on deck together . . . I enjoyed those very much," she said at last.

Charles leaned forward, took one of her hands and held it between both of his. Kezia was aware of his warmth spreading into her fingers and she felt herself blushing. He looked directly at her for some time and Kezia was the first to turn away her eyes. From their first meeting, his gaze had been both kind and honest. "Kezia, dearest Kezia. The thought of sailing back to England on this ship without you, not long after we dock in Hobart, leaving you behind here while I move to the other side of the world, well, it pains me more than I can say. I can't imagine not seeing you every day."

This so expressed what Kezia was feeling that she stared back at him, unable to answer.

"I've tried to convey my feelings to you and perhaps you may have guessed at my intentions but I never . . . I should have spoken sooner. Will you be my wife? Will you marry me, Kezia? It would make me very happy."

Kezia closed her eyes, suddenly dizzy. All her expectations, all her feelings had been thrown into tumult by his words and she found she could not speak.

He's asked me to marry him, she thought. He's asked me to be his wife. Kezia Ferguson.

51

NOW

"An unlined . . . coverlet of plain and printed cottons, it features a central panel of white cotton appliquéd with sprigs of flowers and smaller birds, encircled by four large printed cotton birds. The panel is contained within several printed borders of dress cottons pieced in geometric designs . . . The outermost border has a design of appliquéd cottons and an inscription finely worked in silk yarn."

19 July 1841
One hundred and five days at sea
CLARA

The living quarters, normally scattered with clothing, belongings, bits of dropped food and half-finished pieces of knitting, are cleaner and tidier than they've ever been. No longer a place of imprisonment, the space is like a dockside warehouse, piled with bundles, everyone ready to be called up to the deck to disembark. We're anxious and hiding our fear of what we'll find on land. Some are solemn, sad to leave friends. No one, I think, likes to part from those they know.

Becky and Lily are sitting together, with two very small bundles beside them. Becky's head is bowed, as usual, and she looks pale. Lily does her best. She's not talkative or very cheerful, but she's earnestly whispering in Becky's ear and Becky, for once, is listening.

Something like a smile comes to her lips and then it's gone. Perhaps I imagined it.

"Becky," I say, "I hope you're looking forward to your new life here."

She nods unenthusiastically. I want, suddenly, to make her think of the future as full of possibilities. "You can be anything you like now," I go on. "And, Lily, will you . . ." I don't know how to say, *Are you going to look after her? Are the two of you comfortable enough with one another to stay together if you can?*

"Yes," says Lily. "We'll try to keep together, won't we, Becky?"

"That's good," I say. "We must take care of one another. Look up, Becky. Promise me you won't look down."

Lily and Becky both start laughing. "That's proper daft, Sarah," Lily says. "What if there's steps? Or mud puddles to keep our feet out of? A person's got to look down sometimes."

"Puddles and steps," I say. "But look up for most things. Or at least straight ahead. Don't turn your eyes to the ground, Becky. Promise me."

Becky stands up and looks straight at me. "I will, Sarah," she says. And before I know what's happening, she's embracing me. "I won't forget what you did for me, Sarah. God go with you."

"And with you, dear Becky," I say, and go to find my own bundle of possessions. When I find them, there's so little that I wonder for a moment if I ought to leave them on the ship. Nothing I value is in that bundle, except my scissors, which will remind me of so much.

When I told Mr. Donovan I was a milliner, that first day aboard the *Rajah*, I was lying. But I may make it true. I have a fanciful dream of setting up in a small shop, and the fine ladies of Hobart and even Lady Franklin coming to me and letting me provide them with beautiful bonnets. The words we sang so often come back to me: *Who sweeps a room as for thy laws, makes that and th' action fine.* I'll try to make my actions fine, according to man's laws, whatever I do in Van Diemen's Land.

Miss Hayter is standing next to the gangplank, saying good-bye to each of us as we leave the ship.

"Sarah," she begins, and can't say another word. She comes very close to me and puts a hand on each of my arms. We're both trembling. "Thank you," she says.

"Thank you, Miss Hayter," I say, for the last time, and then I walk down the gangplank to the shore. I turn to look at the *Rajah* as I walk away.

There's Isaac and William, and I can see Jack and many others, folding the sails, fastening them to the masts. Mr. Donovan's there, waving at us as we're led away. Mr. Davies has his cabin trunk at his side, and a crowd from his congregation has come aboard to welcome him home. Truth is, there's only two people I'll miss and think of in this new land. The first is, and always will be, Edmund. The second is Miss Hayter. I owe her my life. I've no time for prayers, but if I did, I'd pray to see her again in a different circumstance. She's standing close to the captain, leaning toward him, and they're smiling. I think they will spend the rest of their lives together and they'll be happy.

I look up at the *Rajah*. She's carried us halfway across the globe and her tall, slender masts are graceful against the blue of the sky. Birds have settled in the rigging. She's brought me to a new life here, and on this welcoming shore, I'll be a new person. I will be Sarah Goodbourne.

HISTORICAL NOTE

In April 1817, the social reformer Elizabeth Fry headed a committee of twelve ladies whose aim was to improve the conditions for women prisoners, first in Newgate and then in other prisons. A year later their work was extended to include women convicts being transported to Australia. A chance encounter with Captain, later Admiral, Young gave Fry the idea that patchwork was useful both as a means of employment during the sea voyages and a way of teaching the art of sewing. From that time each convict was given a bag containing a Bible, two aprons, a cap, two pounds weight of patchwork pieces and various sewing notions.

The barque *Rajah* sailed from London in April 1841 with one hundred and eighty female convicts on board. They had all been convicted of crimes that merited transportation and were being sent to Van Diemen's Land, present-day Tasmania. Also on board were ten children; a Royal Navy surgeon, James Donovan, MD; and a small number of passengers including a returning clergyman, the Reverend Roland Davies; and twenty-three-year-old Kezia Hayter, who was described as *"a female of superior attainments"* in the Annual Report of the Ladies' Society for 1842. Kezia was given free passage on the understanding that she should devote her voyage to the care and improvement of the prisoners. Between April and July 1841 she oversaw the making of a large patchwork coverlet, known as the Rajah Quilt, which is now in the collection of the National Gallery of Australia in Canberra. Kezia Hayter was first cousin to John and George Hayter and niece of Charles Hayter, who were all painters at the royal court, and it is likely that the coverlet's frame design was hers.

This is a very well-documented voyage. We have the Surgeon's log and the Captain's log. We have the convicts' names and a record of the crimes for which they were being transported. Prior to the *Rajah*'s voyage Kezia Hayter had been at Millbank Penitentiary for ten months and had worked with Elizabeth Fry and others on the Ladies' Committee to improve prisoners' lives. Documentary evidence shows that Captain Charles Ferguson, master of the *Rajah*, and Kezia Hayter fell in love during the voyage and were engaged to be married before the ship reached Hobart.

This novel is a fictional account of the voyage and I hope that I have used the historical background respectfully. It has been suggested that upward of twenty convicts worked on the coverlet but I have chosen to name only eighteen. We also know that one woman died before the *Rajah* arrived in Hobart, but the events in my story are entirely a product of my imagination and in no way related to this death. In addition, I have given my convict characters invented names because descendants of the real women who made the Rajah Quilt still live in Australia and more especially in Tasmania.

BIBLIOGRAPHY

Bell, Robert, *The Rajah Quilt*, The National Gallery of Australia, 2015

Cowley, Trudy and Snowden, Diane, *Patchwork Prisoners: The Rajah Quilt and the women who made it*, Research Tasmania, 2013

Ferguson, Carolyn, "A Female of Superior Attainments," *Textile Perspectives* 43, Summer 2007

——"A Study of Quakers, Convicts and Quilts," *Quilt Studies* 8, 2007

——"Rule of Thumb or Rule of Eye," *Textile Perspectives* 46, Winter 2008

——"As wise as Serpents and as Harmless as Doves," *Blanket Statements*, AQSG, Spring 2010

Fry, K. and Cresswell, R. E., *A Memoir of the Life of Elizabeth Fry Edited by Two of Her Daughters*, vol. 1, 1847

Gero, Annette, "Quilts and Their Makers in Nineteenth Century Australia," *The Quilt Digest* 58, 1987

Pitman, Emma R., *Elizabeth Fry*, 1884

Prichard, Sue (ed.), *Quilts 1700–2010: Hidden Histories, Untold Stories*, V&A Publishing, 2010

Rolphe, Margaret, "The Convict Ship," *Down Under Quilts*, June 1990

INTERNET SOURCES

https://www.femaleconvicts.org.au/docs/ships/Rajah1841_SJ.pdf

https://discovery.nationalarchives.gov.uk/details/record?catid=5038909&catln=6

https://www.femaleconvicts.org.au

http://freepages.rootsweb.com/~dferguson/genealogy/Capt.Ferguson/CKFerguson.htm

ACKNOWLEDGMENTS

I first saw the Rajah Quilt at the Victoria and Albert Museum in London in 2009. I've wanted to write about it ever since. For most of that time, Sophie Hannah has been encouraging me, discussing the book, helping me with plot quandaries, reading numerous versions and bits of versions and I owe her an enormous debt of gratitude. Jenny Geras has constantly supported and encouraged me, too, and has given me much good advice, both practical and editorial.

Very special thanks to my friend Carolyn Ferguson, who knows everything about nineteenth-century textiles and the Rajah Quilt in particular. I've been very reliant on her tireless research and eagle eye for detail.

Thank you to Lizelle de Jager and Jeremy Michell, MA, of the Royal Museums, Greenwich, who were helpful about nautical matters.

I am grateful to the Conservation Department of the National Gallery of Australia for the sight of photographs of the many rics from the quilt.

ACKNOWLEDGMENTS

I feel extremely fortunate to have Nelle Andrew of Rachel Mills Literary as my agent and Jillian Taylor of Michael Joseph as my editor in the UK. They and my USA editor, Amanda Bergeron of Berkley, have worked tremendously hard on my behalf, and I'm very grateful to them all. Thanks, also, to copy editor extraordinaire Hazel Orme.

My early readers Laura Cecil, Ann Pilling, Sally Prue and Linda Sargent have been stalwart supporters for years, and it's been a comfort to have their friendship along the way, as well as their comments and advice. And thanks, too, to Francesca Hornak, and the "Gladstone Girls": Linda Newbery, Celia Rees, Helena Pielichaty, Julia Jarman, Yvonne Coppard, Cindy Jeffries and Penny Dolan, who have been constantly encouraging.

Last, but not at all least, thank you to Helen Craig and Judith Lennox, who have listened to me talking about this novel for several years.